CONTENTMENT

Part 2

The Chronicles of the Light Princess

Kristen Dovnik

Books by Kristen Dovnik

Conflictus

This book is for
My amazing mother in law

Alexandra Dovnik

You helped me bring my dreams to life.

Chapter 1

Shock and pain overwhelm me as I look down at the fire sword sticking out of my chest. *No!* I scream inwardly and before I have time to react, Willow reaches forward. With chained hands, she grabs my sword and lifts it up, plunging it deep into Damon's heart. The blade squelches as it's driven deep into his flesh. The hairs on my arms stand on edge as I watch the light leave his eyes and notice a Crawler's soul leaving his body instead of his own. *You've got to be kidding me! He was possessed?!*

A great boom echoes throughout the small room as Damon's body hits the floor at the same time I fall down next to Willow. My body is weak and my lifeforce is fading. *This cannot be. I need Duncan.*

I feel my body calling for him, searching for him to take the pain away. Hopefully, he'll be here soon, I fear I'm about to pass out.

"Kyra sweetie you need to stay awake." Willow urges beside me as I force myself to keep my eyes open. "We will get you some help, just as soon as I break out of these chains." Willow holds my sword next to the locks on her bindings and the buckles immediately begin to melt away, setting her free. "Will you be able to walk? We need to get you out of here." I shake my head softly as Willow moves to stand up beside me. Glancing around the room she looks for anything she can use to help get us out of here. *I can barely move, let alone stand and might I add, I still have a sword sticking out of my chest! Come on Duncan, where are you?*

From somewhere outside the room Duncan shouts my name and with the little strength left in me, I call out to him. The pain in my chest is unfathomable however, I need to hold on. Within seconds he comes barrelling through the open door heading straight for me. Willow takes a step forward as if to protect me although after seeing the determination in his eyes, she decides against it. With an outstretched hand he reaches for me as I do him, craving that touch that will heal us, making us whole. The moment our hands connect the pain on my face instantly switches to pleasure and a moan escapes my lips. Willow watches on in astonishment as she observes the blade exiting my sternum by some magical force, then hitting the ground with a mighty clang.

Electricity spreads throughout my body, whizzing over every injury like wildfire. Power builds within the centre of my chest as it starts to heal the gaping wound left by Duncan's blade. After what feels like an eternity, Duncan and I sigh in relief as we relax against each other on the floor.

"Are you ok?" Duncan whispers as his eyes roam all over me, frantically examining to make sure our gift did exactly what it's designed to do.

"I am now, thanks to you," I murmur while giving him a weary smile. He raises his hand to my face and strokes his thumb along my cheekbone. Leaning forward he moves his mouth closer to mine before stopping himself a short distance away. With a cocky grin, he waits there patiently for me to come to him and as I move my lips closer, Willow pipes in from above.

"I'm guessing this is your boy then?" Willow asks looming over us. Standing a few feet away, she crosses her arms over her chest and gazes down upon us like small children who just got busted about to make out. *Wow, could this be any more embarrassing?*

"Yes sorry, Willow this is Duncan, Duncan meet Willow, my Elder," I say gently while getting to my feet and walking over to her. *After all this time I can't believe we actually found her.* Stopping directly in front of her, I fold my arms around her shoulders, enveloping her in a big hug. I feel her grunt within my grasp, yet she doesn't stop me.

"You know you didn't have to come and get me. I was doing just fine on my own." Willow utters as I drop my arms back to my sides and step away.

"Are you sure? You didn't look fine to me. You were in chains after all." I state while glancing around the room and notice it's completely empty. *What did she use when she needed to go to the bathroom?* A putrid stench fills my nostrils and I have to stop myself from gagging. *Sorry, I asked.*

"Did it ever occur to you that I could have gotten out of this if I wanted to? I was biding my time until the Dark Prince showed up. I believe he was the one who orchestrated all of this. Unfortunately though, as you can see, he was not. The man behind you was." Turning around I look at the two men behind me, one deceased and the other, my mate. "Damon had us all fooled. The creature told me how they managed to kill so many troops in Gage those many years ago. The Crawlers figured out that Damon was the team leader and cast a spell, bringing back the soul of their master and placed him the body behind you.

"I'm still baffled as to how they managed to pull it off because that sort of magic isn't supposed to work around here anymore..." Willow declares as she gazes down upon Damon's lifeless body on the concrete. For many years we were fooled by the demon, working side by side on missions and tactical trainings. We even spent time creating strategic plans on how to take nests down together.

"Damn..." I whisper as an unsettling feeling washes over my being, "How did he manage to infiltrate our command post without us sensing anything off about him? Zagoria! We told him everything. I bet the Dark Prince knows all of that now too. I can't believe this monster was able to trick us all for so long and get away with it!" I state angrily as I glance down at the dead body at my feet.

Damon was practically a nobody before the Gage incident. He came back a legend, not only for being able to survive such an attack but for also killing so many Crawlers single-handedly. I bet all those beasts sacrificed themselves to grant them the intel they needed to help their dark master. "...So many soldiers looked up to him as their leader. There are going to be a lot of devastated people when they find out what's happened." I state grimly, stepping away from the lifeless body and closer to the woman whom we came here to retrieve.

"It's all a part of the war I'm afraid.... Now enough of this, let's get out of here, I'm in desperate need of sunlight. It's been a long few weeks down here." She says while linking her arm through mine and starts leading us towards the exit.

"Um... Are you just going to leave him here?" Duncan inquires just as we reach the door. I too was beginning to wonder the same thing.

"You can carry him out if you like or I can send someone else to do it. Up to you." Willow utters without a care in the world while we continue on our path through the doorway and back into the corridor. *Why is she not helping, it's very uncharacteristic of her to not want to help out.* Usually, she would be the one willing to carry the dead soldier out all by herself, making sure that no one is left behind. Maybe it's because the soldier whose body it actually is, died many years ago and now this is the lifeless body of a monster? Either way, she would never leave it here to rot. No matter the circumstances, he still requires a proper burial. *He was a soldier of the light after all.*

After a few minutes, Willow and I make it topside and see Elder Kit running in our direction. He stops a short distance away to regain his breath before opening his mouth to speak, "Willow you're ok. Oh, thank Zagoria." He says while giving her a once over. "Elder Fox and his team are on their way to assist the wounded. I would advise that you meet with them and get yourself checked out too."

"Do you now? Well, I will tell you the same as I'll tell them. I'm fine and I am going home." Willow states as she goes to step around him however, he moves to the left blocking her path. She raises her eyes to Kit's and gives him one hell of a death stare before remembering where we are and recovers her composure. A sweet innocent smile plays out on her lips before she begins to speak again, "Come now Kit, don't start to protest as you know it won't work. I will make a note to come by the compound later to debrief the order but right now, I need my rest and her Highness has graciously offered to escort me home." She says whilst gripping my arm a little tighter. *Obviously, I'm not allowed to say no.*

"Yes, ah... I am, however, I also advise that you get a medical examination Willow, just to be sure I mean," I murmur as I gaze between the two Elders standing beside me. *Why do I suddenly feel like a little girl again?*

"Fine, I'll think about it ok?" She states while manoeuvering us around the groups of people standing in our way and begins leading us towards the trucks parked at the end of the street.

"Oh Elder Kit?" I call out over my shoulder, "Can you please tell Duncan when he comes up, that I'm taking Willow home and that I'll meet him back at my place later?"

"Sure thing Your Highness." He confirms as Willow and I move further away.

About a short while later we reach the line of trucks at the end of the street. Willow rushes towards the first one we see and jumps into the passenger's seat, slamming the door shut behind her. Startled by her odd behaviour, I run around to the driver's side and climb on in. *Seriously, what's gotten into her? Why the sudden rush?*

"What's going on? You're acting stranger than a fairy on jiggle juice."

"I'm just eager to get out of here, that's all." She states irritably while buckling up her seat belt. Shaking it off, I flip down the visor and the keys fall into my lap. Putting them into the ignition, I pause as Damon's lifeless body pops into my head and I glance at the woman sitting beside me. *I need to be sure.* "Why aren't we moving?" She asks while flicking her eyes towards me and then back at the road.

"During my training, how many times did I pin you on the mat?" I ask commandingly. *Only the real Willow will know the answer to that.* She always told me to tell people that my number was higher because she didn't want anyone knowing she is stronger than she looks. It has always been our little secret.

"Why are you asking me this? Can't we just leave?" She asks impatiently while tapping her fingers against the armrest.

"Just answer the question Willow." I snap almost angrily. Slowly I begin to draw in a little power, fueling the fire deep within me just in case I need to use it.

Willow whips her head in my direction in utter disbelief. I've never been so direct with her before and maybe I should have calmed my temper prior to speaking but I need to know. If it turns out that she too is a soul of a Crawler, I would like to take care of this now rather than later.

Willow takes a deep breath in before sighing her reply, "Once… you pinned me once." I physically relax and let go of the power I'd built up. *Good! Now we can leave.* As I turn the key, the engine roars to life and I ease the truck out onto the open road.

Chapter 2

It's a long drive back to Willow's house from the station and it felt even longer because she slept the whole way. I didn't mind though. She may be in dire need of a bath and a good scrubbing but otherwise, she is ok and that's the main thing.

"Nothing beats being home." Willow sighs as we make our way up to her front door. Laying her hand upon the wooden frame, she whispers something under her breath and the door unlocks, swinging wide open. Inside is dark and extremely quiet. The only noise I can hear is the hum of electricity coming from the appliances scattered throughout her home. As she crosses the threshold, every light within the property comes to life. She takes a few small steps and stops a short distance away before turning around.

"Not to be harsh my dear but I believe you should add some more protein into your diet. You've lost a lot of weight since I saw you last." She states while looking at me and rakes her eyes up and down before turning and heading towards the kitchen. Glancing down at myself I notice she's right, I have lost quite a bit of weight in the last few weeks. My armour still fits but I acknowledge it is pretty loose in some areas. While we were on the hunt for Willow, I abused Duncan's ability to heal me instead of eating when I felt hungry to re-nourish me. So, it was inevitable that there would be some changes. *His arms around me definitely made me feel so much better.*

Shaking my head, I follow her into the kitchen as something she said earlier crosses my mind. Willow stands at the sink washing her grimy fingers as I come to a stop behind her.

"Hey, after I found you, you said that you could have gotten out if you wanted to. What did you mean by that?" She glances over her shoulder before turning off the tap. Reaching to the side, she grabs a towel to dry off and spins around to face me.

"What I meant by that was…I was only there because I chose to be. I knew they were coming, I saw it." She states tapping a finger against her temple. *Of course, she did.* "I made the decision to destroy my own wards to let them in. I was curious to find out what they wanted with me. I thought it would be beneficial for everyone if we were able to grab some intel on them instead of the other way around for a change. I believe the Prince has eluded us for way too long. *Zagoria*! It's been over three hundred years since the rebirth and we still don't even know what the monster looks like.

Unfortunately though, it seems the Prince didn't orchestrate that attack. So I endured all of that for nothing." She states heatedly, while throwing her arms into the air before stepping away and into the pantry. Willow grabs a few things off the shelf and then places them on the kitchen bench beside her. After a few quick manoeuvres, she has everything prepped and ready to go before placing the contents on the stove to heat up. She rewashes her hands and then turns around, crossing her arms over her chest before leaning back against the bench.

"It wasn't all for nothing. You found out that Damon was misleading us this whole time. That he was in fact, a demon in disguise and if you ask me, that was pretty vital intel. Now we have to assume that the Dark Prince knows all of our plans. The Crawlers wouldn't have been stupid enough to withhold that information from him." I utter mirroring her stance. Willow gazes at the floor in front of her for a moment before raising her eyes back to mine. She has a weird expression on her face and for the life of me, I can't pinpoint the cause of it.

"If you put it that way, I guess you're right." She utters as she turns around. *What no rebuttal?* Willow grabs a spoon from its holder next to the stove and begins to stir the pot. "Anyway, enough of that, I want to hear about your party. I bet it was grand." She says over her shoulder with her back to me. Placing the spoon next to the stove, she hikes up on her tippy toes and grabs two bowls from the cupboard above her head.

"Um... What party?" I asked confused as I pull out a chair at the table in the middle of the room. As my butt hits the cold wood, it finally dawns on me. *Crap! I missed my own birthday.* "Oh, that... umm..." I utter sheepishly knowing full well that I'm about to cop an ear full for this. "We didn't get a chance to celebrate it this year. We were all too concerned looking for you to even remember it was my birthday." I avert my gaze the moment I see her irritated eyes turn towards me. *Oh, here we go...*

"What do you mean you didn't celebrate it? How could you miss such an important occasion?" Willow half yells at me while throwing her hands into the air again. "Seriously Kyra, have I taught you nothing these past few years? Your birthday is never to be overlooked. It's the only day of truce we have here in Zagoria. The one day of the year where the Prince can come out of hiding and you just simply forgot. In saying that though, I do understand dear why you may have forgotten but the Elders... doubtful." She pauses her outburst to get lost in her own thoughts. I scratch my head trying to think about what we were doing that day, but nothing comes to mind. I bet we were in the hanger pondering over some statistics or maps on where the Crawlers may have been hiding. That's practically what we were doing every day until we found her.

"You know what," Willow says from across the room. "I bet the other Elders feigned forgetting about it too, just so they could get out of hosting the party themselves. They never want to do it, the lazy buggers." She pauses to raise her eyes to mine.

"Oh well, what's done is done and we can't change it now. The day of truce may be well and truly gone but that

~ **12** ~

doesn't mean I still can't throw you a party myself. It was your three hundred and forty-eighth birthday after all." She states while spinning around and I almost missed the smile on her face before she begins to stir the pot once more. *Cheeky bugger!* She knows exactly how much I hate the festivities. *All that attention on me, Ergghh...*

Besides, I would much rather our time and resources be spent elsewhere. There are hundreds of other things we could be doing instead of dancing and singing the day away. However, Willow is right. My birthday is the one day of the year where the Prince can show his face and no one is allowed to touch him. *Although now that I think of it, if I was in his shoes and had been hiding for as long as he has, there is no way in Zagoria that I would want to show my face. Even if it was a day of truce.*

"Come on Willow, trust me it's fine, I don't need or want a party. Besides, I have way too much on my plate at the moment anyway. For instance, did you know that monsters are coming back from the dead? Creatures that we vanquished millennia ago are walking around freely and we have no idea how they are doing it.

You may have recently faked your own kidnapping, which in return did expose Damon, so that wasn't so bad. But it did take us way longer than necessary to find you, which is a huge problem when it comes to the Order's tracking abilities. On top of all of that, I'm still trying to wrap my head around this whole Duncan being my soulmate thing." I stop myself for a second as a conversation I had with Duncan weeks ago pops into my head. "Oh, which reminds me, I wanted to talk to you about that too. Did you not know that soulmates can heal each other? That a single touch can bring forth unfathomable power?" Willow glances briefly over her shoulder before slightly shaking her head and returns to prepare our food.

"If Duncan didn't show up when he did the other week after the Cerberus attack, Zagoria knows what may have happened. I realize now how much I should have let you stay that night and I'm really sorry for that. It probably wouldn't have done any good anyway, especially as I discovered later that Duncan is the only one who has the power to save me." Willow turns around and gapes at me dumbfounded for a moment. Sorrow fills the air as she takes a deep breath before opening her mouth to speak.

"I must apologise to you my dear, I did hear the rumours about that sort of thing however, I didn't want to mention them to you in case they turned out to be untrue. Many millennia ago, I heard that when two souls connect they become one, and forever intertwined. The stories mentioned that if one of you is injured the other can feel it, if one needs power the other can grant it and if one of you dies the other will too. However, these were just rumours to me because like I said, I had never encountered mates with the bond before." Willow reveals as she pours the now ready stew into the two-awaiting bowls on the benchtop beside her. After grabbing some spoons from the drawer, she walks over and places a steaming bowl of goodness on the table in front of me. *It smells and looks amazing.*

Without saying a word, I begin to eat before Willow even has the chance to sit down. I didn't realise how hungry I was until I devoured almost all of my stew in a matter of seconds. Willow gazes at me with amazement before pointing back to the stove as if to say there is more over there. I smile at her appreciatively as I get up from my seat and help myself to another bowl of stew. *It's so good to have her back and not just because of the food.*

We make small talk while finishing our meal and I help Willow wash up, making sure everything is in order before going home.

"Do you really have to go? You know you can always stay here any time you want. I really don't want you walking out there by yourself anymore. Especially because if they have the guts to come for me here, then they will come for you and your boy too. They will stop at nothing to get to you, you know that right?" She states worriedly as we walk through the kitchen and into the parlour, stopping directly in front of the main door. I lean forward to give her a kiss on the forehead as I wrap my arms around her shoulders. *My little worrywart.*

"I'll be fine Willow, trust me. I'm ready for them, always have been and always will be. Besides, I told Duncan that I would meet him back at my place earlier and I don't want to keep him waiting. I'll make sure to drop by the compound tomorrow to check on you, alright?

And please for my sake, and also yours, get yourself checked out." I instruct her while giving her one final squeeze. *She feels so small in my embrace.* She may not like my intrusion into her personal life, but she knows I'm right. It was disgusting down there.

I let my arms drop back down to my sides and turn around, open the door and step out into the beautiful cool evening.

Chapter 3

As I step closer to the little house in my garden, I'm immediately greeted by my three little angels. They all sweep into a low curtsey as I take a seat on the ground in front of them. "Hello ladies, how are you this evening?"

"We are well Your Highness, it's always so pleasurable to see you. Do you bring great tidings?" they all ask collectively. Their little dresses sway to the left in the warm summer breeze and their beautiful curls follow suit. It feels like forever since I saw them last, even though it's only been a couple of hours.

"I most certainly do. We managed to track down Willow earlier today and the Crawlers that took her. The Order of the Light and I managed to vanquish all the beasts and were able to bring Willow home safely. Also, I do however have some distressing news to add. We discovered the soldier known as Damon Steel had been possessed by the soul of a Crawler some time ago and although the demon was put down during our fight to get Willow back, it won't make up for all the information they probably obtained. So we must remain vigilant." It continues to baffle me just how he managed to elude us for so long.

He was a creature of the dark living in the body of a light. Surely we should have been able to feel his presence. *Unless Damon's body was blocking it somehow? I should really talk to Duncan about this. There could be a story about it in these so-called books of old of his.* Shaking my head, I drop the subject and return my focus to the three little women in front of me.

"Oh no miss, we are terribly sorry to hear about the loss of such a fantastic soldier. We will make sure to re-fortify and strengthen the wards immediately however, it may take us some time..." They pause to gaze upon each other with great concern then return their attention to me. "Will that be all Your Highness?" They inquire eagerly, fidgeting from foot to foot as they wait for my reply.

"Yes, thank you ladies that will be all. Please let me know when you have completed your task. I'm pretty sure I'll be here all night."

"Very well Your Highness." They quickly curtsey again before rushing inside and slamming the door shut behind them. I smile and shake my head again while getting to my feet. As I make my way up to my front door, I notice that all the lights are off and presume Duncan hasn't arrived yet.

Now that I am able to physically relax, exhaustion begins to weigh heavily on my body as I walk through my living room. *Maybe I should have a nap while I wait for him.* As I ascend the stairs, I glance down at myself and see black ooze clinging to my boots. *Eeww, yuk! Maybe I should have a shower too.*

Passing through my bedroom and into the bathroom, I catch a glimpse of myself in the mirror and halt as shock fills my senses. *Are you kidding me?*

I look absolutely horrid, I'm covered in so much muck I can barely recognize myself. Lifting my arm to my face, I take an unnecessarily large whiff and almost gag. *Omg, that's gross!* Burnt rubber mixed with body odour, seriously it's not a good mix.

Stripping off my armour, I drop it to the floor before jumping into the shower. The water is lusciously warm as it cascades down my body. This is exactly what I needed after a day like today.

Grabbing a washcloth, I scrub all the day's awfulness off of me. I don't ever want to go into a nest like that one ever again. There were hundreds of beings and nowhere near enough soldiers. If for whatever reason I was unable to make it, the order would most definitely cease to be. We were lucky to even come home with as many warriors as we did.

Once I've triple checked that I'm squeaky clean, I switch off the water and begin drying myself off with a towel. I exit the shower and decide to leave my dirty armour where it's laying on the floor and seek out a clean set from my closet. As I enter my bedroom I'm once again met with silence and begin to wonder what's keeping

Duncan. *I hope he's alright, although I'm pretty sure I would feel it if he wasn't.*

Whilst hunched over in my closet doing up the last buckle on my boots, I glance over at my bed and realise I haven't slept up here in weeks. I've either spent time on the couch downstairs or in the bunks at the compound. Suddenly it feels as if the mattress is calling my name and I'm more than willing to answer it. My eyelids begin to feel heavy as I make my way over and pull back the blanket. Climbing on up, I rest my head against the pillow and before I know it, my mind is taking me on a marvellous adventure.

It feels like hours have passed when I'm suddenly awoken by a loud bang reverberating from the bottom level of my home. *Seriously why does he always bang the door?* Groggily I throw off my blanket and jump down off the bed. While cracking my neck to the side, I walk out into the hallway. A tingling feeling stirs in the pit of my stomach and I can't figure out if it's due to days old hunger pains, or a creature lingering somewhere nearby. Going by the fact that I ate my first meal in three days only hours ago, I bet it has something to do with that. My stomach can be a little temperamental at times.

I hear another bang and a hushed grunt as something gets knocked to the floor downstairs, and I begin to pick up my pace towards the stairwell. *What in the world is he doing? And why hasn't he turned on any lights?* I reach the stairs in record time and I'm about a quarter of the way down when I freeze. *Oh, Zagoria!*

Bile rises in the back of my throat when I see multiple pairs of gloomy eyes staring back at me from within the darkness. As quick as lightning I conjure up my immortal flame and light up the entire room. The whole first level of my home is filled to the rim with Cerberus's, Bubak's, Crawlers, Spiders, Bats you name it, they are all here. *Oh, this is not going to be fun.* At the foot of the stairs is a Crawler who freakishly tilts his head to the side as he stares up at me.

"Any last words...*Princess*?" It spits my title back at me like a snake.

"I would tell you to go to hell but I'm pretty sure you've already been there!" I seethe whilst gripping my sword tightly with two hands. As the last word leaves my mouth, the whole room erupts into a flurry of movement. The swarm of beasts is like a wave as it heads towards me. The Crawler at the base of the stairs is the first to launch forward and I hold out my blade hitting it right in the neck. With a quick twist of my sword, I take its head clean off and allow it to bounce back down the stairs to the awaiting monsters below. Its body falls back seconds later, blocking the path of many but it won't be long until I'm overrun. The creatures try as hard as they can to claw their way through the throngs around them to get to me, and I'm beginning to realise that the stairs are literally the worst place for me to be right now. Taking a deep breath, I leap over the railing and land square in the middle of the mass of beings waiting below.

Even as I swing my blade all around and manage to take down all of those closest to me, it still doesn't feel like enough. There are so many of them here and only one of me. My power alone should be sufficient to take them down, but I feel I could use Duncan's help to end it all. If only I could use the full power of the sun but I don't think I'll have enough time to will it to me. There is a high possibility that I may die here and there is nothing I can do to stop it. *However, if I am going down, I'm taking as many as I can with me.*

Blood and ooze is flicked all around my living room every time I swing my sword. Bodies jump at me from all around trying to grab me even though it's fruitful, I am so slick with sweat that they can't grasp a decent hold.

Sharp teeth manage to latch onto my swinging blade and I kick the Crawler back slicing through its cheeks as it disappears into the masses surrounding us.

Exhaustion begins to weigh heavily on me, yet I know I can't stop. I move faster than the speed of sound ending one life after another, completely covering my walls with the green blood of the dead. My screams and shouts would be heard from miles away and I understand that I require back up but I need to battle this one alone. *No one else needs to die for me.*

I'm starting to gain some ground when razor-sharp claws sink into the flesh on my back. Instinctively I let out a blood-curdling scream and accidentally drop my blade. *Oh no!* Ignoring the pain, I quickly dash forward to pick it up but I'm already too late. A Bubak to my right grasps my weapon within its long wooden fingers and dangles it in front of me while it breaks out in a vicious smile. All the beasts begin to roar with victory as they believe they have won this battle. They now hold in their possession the one weapon that has the power to kill me. *SHIT! How am I going to get it back?*

Closing the gaps, they circle me like vultures ready to strike. The Bubak comes closer as I quickly bring forth a little fire, willing it directly into my palm. It won't be enough to do much damage however, it will buy me some time. Moving fast I throw the burning sphere, hitting my target square in the face. The scrawny scarecrow is thrown back roughly a meter or two, giving me just enough time to form a ring of fire around the both of us.

Wielding almost all my remaining strength, I leap forward and grab ahold of the floating monster. Using my elbow, I raise my arm and smash it in the face multiple times causing its head to fall back. It lets out an unearthly screech and I almost lose my grip as it flails around my living room like a balloon letting out air. When the beast finally comes to a stop, I jump down and grab hold of its arm snapping it away from its body, ultimately reclaiming my sword. I hear grunts coming from numerous beasts that surround me as I hold my blade high in the air for all to see while willing more power into me.

"You're all going to burn bitches!" I announce while releasing my ability. A firestorm shoots from my being and travels throughout my entire house. Screams of anguish ricochet off the walls making them seem like they go on forever.

While I swing my sword around in a clean circle, I slice through every creature within my reach. Charred bodies fall to the floor and within seconds, they all begin to evaporate into a puff of green smoke, giving off the illusion as if they were never here.

The body count seems to be endless. For every monster I kill, I swear two more enter my property. *Did He really send every dark minion here to kill me instead of coming here himself? Is he seriously such a coward?*

Seconds turn into minutes and minutes into hours. I have absolutely no idea how much time has passed when I'm momentarily distracted by the commotion at the front door. I look over to see another fire blade waving high in the distance and I'm instantly filled with dread. *No!*

"KYRA?!" Duncan screams over the horde of beings blocking his path and I call out hoping he can hear me. Duncan swings his blade hacking off the head of the Crawler directly in front of him and the instant the monster's head lulls to the side, our eyes connect. A wave of calmness washes over me from seeing him alive and well however, I fear it will only last a moment.

"What are you doing here? You need to leave! You have to get out!" I yell hoping he will see reason. I cannot hold them back and try to protect him too, even if it is pointless.

"Fuck that! I'm not leaving you!" He shouts while fighting his way over to me. I thrust my knife into the chest of the Cerberus to my right, while dodging a spider that leaps towards me from my left. Turning around, I chop off four of the spider's legs making it tumble over onto its back. Twirling my blade around I try to kill anything I can, before plunging my blade deep down into the spider's abdomen. It flails a bit as it slowly dies and eventually dissolves into nothingness.

I see the back of Duncan's head about six feet away and extend my arm out to grab him. Monsters claw at my outstretched limb yet I try to ignore the pain, I just need to touch him. Duncan turns to face me and immediately lifts his arm and extends his hand out towards mine. *Just a little bit more.* I jump forward trying to close the gap between us but just as our finger's touch, we are ripped away from each other and thrown back into the masses surrounding us.

"DUNCAN!!" I scream as the beasts force me back towards the staircase moving me further away from my mate. My back hits the wall at the same time the beasts high above me begin to jump over the railing to get me. A Cerberus lands on my shoulders forcing me to the ground as its weight becomes too heavy for my legs to handle. *Shit! They're trying to smother me to death!* More and more monsters pile on top at the same time I decide to dissolve my blade. I'm not giving them another opportunity to have that power over me again.

"KYRA!!" I hear Duncan yell through the chaos but it's muffled and sounds very far away. Blood-curdling screams uncontrollably leave my mouth as the beasts above me start ripping into my flesh. I feel the warmth of my blood as it runs down my back and over my arms. I'm being pulled in every direction as each monster takes its turn tearing out a chunk of my flesh. I continue to scream until my lungs feel as if they have nothing left. I can hear Duncan calling out my name over and over again, encouraging me to hold on but I'm struggling. I think I'm losing consciousness.

Death seems inevitable and dread starts washing over me. Totally exhausted, I begin to cry, knowing what my death will mean. Eleven years of the Dark Prince reigning over everyone and everything within both realms, while my successor learns about her fate and role within this war. So much for her to learn and so much she'll have to face in order to get to where I am now. This whole horrible cycle starting again.

And for some reason, I begin to plead with the creators that she too will one day be able to find her mate, just like I did. I may not have spent as much time as I would have liked with him, but I will always treasure the few moments we got to share together.

As the dark creatures continue to rip the life away from my body, I imagine the three little words that I will never get to say to Duncan. *I love....*

"ENOUGH!" Booms from somewhere within my home and I instantly lose my train of thought as I recoil at the noise. The new voice is filled with so much malice and hatred that all creatures stop their assault the moment they hear it. *Oh, Zagoria! He's here!* "I remember telling you, you stupid morons that the Princess is *mine*! So, who wants to explain to me, what you're all doing here!?" He rages at the creatures within my home and I begin to feel their anxiety rise. *Oh my god, they are terrified of him.*

I feel blood sliding down the side of my face and I want to swipe it away, although I don't dare move. I need to stay hidden for as long as possible. *If only I could reach Duncan, then maybe we have a chance of getting out of this alive.*

I hear heavy footsteps travelling throughout my home and objects hitting the ground as the creatures move out of the way for their master. The beasts above me have gone as still as statues and the only noise they are making is the sound of their breathing.

"Where is she?!" The Prince spits at his disciples, causing a shiver to run down my spine. I know I have waited my whole life to meet this man, yet at this very moment, I wish I was anywhere else but here.

Without saying a word, the creatures on top of me all start to move. *Bugger!* One at a time they take their turn to climb down from on top of me. Little gaps open up within the remaining bodies and I begin to see my living room. The entire ground level of my house is completely engulfed in black and green smoke, it's so thick that I can barely see one metre away. This must be a trait of his Highness because it's something I've never encountered before.

"Come out, come out, wherever you are." He taunts, as he gets closer with every step. Three beasts remain on top of me and I honestly don't want them to move. I'm not ready to be seen yet. Slowly with my right palm flat against the floorboards, I draw in some of the power from beneath my feet. I'm trying to be as inconspicuous as I can so those around me won't notice. With my left arm tucked tightly into my chest, I conjure up a sun dagger. It may not be enough to kill him however, my immortal blade would be too noticeable right now.

The final Cerberus rises off me and I use my remaining strength to stand up. I feel my blood sliding down my back and onto the floor. Cool fresh air hits my flesh and a different sort of pain ignites. Gritting my teeth, I force myself to take a deep breath. *I will not allow him to see me in pain.*

A dark figure begins to take shape within the smoke and I inhale as he comes into focus. A man standing six foot six with slicked-back hair and a rounded nose with a square-cut jaw. A face many women would swoon over. The whites of his eyes are blackened out, yet the irises are a beautiful shade of blue. He's wearing black armoured pants with a long sleeve black shirt that has intricate swirls in the centre of it. The swirls are very much like my own.

I raise my eyes to his face just as he opens his mouth to speak. "Well don't you look like the perfect damsel?" He smirks seductively while cocking his head to the side. I'm overwhelmed by shock as I realise I'm not looking into the eyes of a stranger, but into the eyes of a man I've seen many times before. *You have got to be kidding me!*

Chapter 4

"Are you completely lost for words or are you just shocked by my pure awesomeness?" Duncan gloats while spreading his arms open wide for everyone to see. *How in Zagoria did I let yet another dark creature get so close to me and I didn't notice a thing?*

My mouth all but hangs open as I stare at the man before me. Not in my wildest dreams did I ever imagine this could happen. My mate turning out to be the Dark Prince, but then again, he looks almost unrecognisable in this form. *It's his eyes that give him away.* I'm so curious as to how he managed to pull it off. How was he able to shield himself not only from me but from the Elders too? It has to be a form of trickery that even the Elders aren't aware of. *Oh, I think I'm going to throw up.*

Glancing around the room I notice that all the beasts seem to be on edge as they continue to stare at their master. Some of them even appear as if they don't know whether to flee or fight. Duncan on the other hand is parading himself around like he owns the damn place. *Well, I am sorry to tell you this buddy, but this is my house.*

"You're a real bastard, you know that!" I'm completely overcome with disgust for the man that stands before me. *He played me like a fool.* He didn't need Damon to give him the information because he was getting it all by himself. He assisted us on scouting missions and helped us decide the perfect locations to send our troops. I bet he even stationed more of his vile monsters there to potentially wipe out our brigades before the final battle.

"Me... A bastard?" He asks while placing a hand over his chest and takes a step back in feign horror. "Sweetie, I think you have me mistaken for someone else." *Oh, I don't think so.* Duncan gives me a panty-dropping grin which makes me want to vomit. *Oh Zagoria, what have I done?* Wasn't it just the other day that I almost made love to him on my kitchen floor? Bile begins to rise in the back of my throat and I have to physically swallow it to keep it down.

I completely understand that old human saying now, keep your friends close, but your enemies closer. This is one enemy that I will never let close again. *Even if it kills me.*

Changing my stance, I ready myself for an attack. He has made a mockery out of me and I won't let this go on any longer. He deceived me into loving a monster and these assholes have found a way to shield themselves from us and I am sick of it. *This ends now.*

Hiding my dagger against my wrist, I ignore the pain coming from my back and charge forward. Duncan swings to the right trying to dodge my attack but I anticipate it.

Moving to the left, I catch his right arm with my blade, slicing deep enough that I can feel its effects coming down the bond. I'm so blinded by my rage that I no longer care if I injure myself too. I just want to hurt him.

He whirls around to face me again at the same moment I rush forward but, this time he's faster. He grabs me around the neck and I'm momentarily delirious as a rush of healing energy ignites from his touch. Using my euphoria against me, Duncan lifts me off the ground, ramming his head against mine before dropping me back to the floor. He lets out a hideous laugh as the creatures circling us begin to swarm in, wanting their own piece of the action. Some of them even get close enough that I can feel their warm breath on my cheek as I blink away the stars dancing in my vision.

"DON'T TOUCH HER!!" Duncan roars and every creature within the vicinity shrinks away from the noise. They move so far back that they now line the walls of my home. He gives them all one hell of a death stare as he declares "She's mine!" before lowering his eyes to mine.

As I stare up into his now blacken eyes, I wonder how he managed to fool me so easily. He takes a deep breath before whispering, "She's mine," again but this time for only me to hear. Moving my body ever so slightly, I prepare to kick him in the shins. As I bring my leg forth, Duncan quickly drops into a squat, grabbing it just before impact. He glares at me while giving me an impatient look that sets my soul aflame. *How dare he...*

"Why don't you just kill me already, we both know you want to. Oh, wait!..." I pause my speech to smack the side of my head with my palm. "You can't now, can you?" I gloat as it's now my turn to glare at him. His monsters are obviously unaware that we are bonded otherwise, they wouldn't be here. *I think it's about time they found out what would happen if they killed me.* "If you..."

"Now, now my precious. Don't be so petty." Duncan begins cutting me off. I scream internally at his arrogance and watch as a smirk breaks out across his lips. He knows exactly what he's doing. *Asshole!* "Why do you think I want to get rid of you? I want to have control over you, not kill you. We have always been perceived as enemies, though that doesn't give me a reason to want to hurt you." He tilts his head to the side, giving me a little wink. *What's he up to?*

"Come on Princess, you should have learnt by now that my main desire is not to kill you, but to rule over both our realms and I cannot possibly do that without you. Even if you and your little order are standing in my way, I will always get what I want in the end. You see, I have learnt a few things while working with you these past few weeks. Like how to eliminate them all in one clean sweep but I'll get to that later...

Weeks ago when I first laid my eyes on you, I knew you and I were destined to be mates. I could feel it deep within my bones, also because I couldn't stop staring at the superhot blondie heading towards Flick and I that day. Oh, that reminds me, poor little Flick, she was so utterly heartbroken when I told her it was over. You're such a bad friend for what you did to her. Didn't you know she had been longing for me since the day I began working there? Anyway..." he says with another smirk on his face. "Enough of that, where was I... Oh yes, me wanting to rule.

So Sweetie, it's going to go down like this. You're going to do everything I tell you to do without question, or I will slaughter every single person that you hold most dear. Including the little brunette." Duncan utters casually before eerily tilting his head to the side just like the Crawler did, hours ago at the foot of the stairs. *Why do they do that? It's so creepy.*

I consider what he said for a minute and get the feeling he's trying to tell me something, however I can't figure out what. *It doesn't matter though really because he doesn't honestly believe he can hold me, does he? I'm the Princess for crying out loud.*

Duncan gives me this look that makes me want to punch him in the face and I begin to think I was wrong about the whole thing. Anxiety and anticipation roll deep within the pit of my stomach from his threat and I know exactly what I must do. I have to fight. I will not allow him to get away with any of this.

"Duncan, I believe you must've hit your head pretty hard if you think that I won't fight you on this. Because it's like I've told you many times before, I was born to fight. Or have you just simply forgotten that?" I pause to glare at him. "Heed my warning when I say that I will stop you and for whatever reason that if I can't, I will just turn the blade on myself. Since, as you know my *love,* if I die, you do too."

I smile as I watch his smirk turn into something a little darker. *Good! Now I've got your attention. He will not win this battle no matter how hard he tries. I won't let him.*

I hear snickers coming from those around us, as they now know the repercussions for killing me. Maybe they should have been made aware of that factor before he sent them here. *Why did he send them here?*

As I prepare myself to stand up, Duncan places his hand upon my shoulder holding me down. *Oh, I don't think so, buddy.*

As quickly as I can, I draw in enough power to create a small fireball within the palm of my hand. Raising it up, I flick it towards Duncan hitting him square in the chest, knocking him back into the minions that line my walls. He instantly gets to his feet and franticly begins patting his chest, trying to put out the flames. After a few moments, he raises his head and looks towards me with hatred.

"You're going to pay for that." He seethes conjuring up his sword, a weapon very much like my own. The hilt is almost identical however the blade is made of lightning and green smoke. I'm rooted to the spot while I gaze upon its magnificence. Never in my lifetime have I ever seen another immortal blade. *I would say it's beautiful if it didn't contain the power to kill me.*

"Let's play," I announce as I conjure up my own weapon after getting to my feet. Holding it to the side, I ready myself for the attack. *Bring it on!*

"You asked for it," Duncan says calmly. An evil smile spreads out across his lips as he launches himself forward. His sword is aimed high and ready to strike. When our blades connect, a bolt of lightning three inches thick bursts out hitting the Crawler closest to our left, killing it instantly. Duncan whips his head to the side just in time to see his minion explode into a puff of green smoke. Quickly he turns his gaze out to the rest of them and screams, "GET OUT!".

All of a sudden the creatures begin rushing towards the exit, not wanting to defy their master. *Probably also not wanting to be hit by another lightning bolt either.* "I am going to make you wish that didn't just happen." Duncan thrusts his arm between our conjoined blades catching me off guard and grabs me around the neck. He pulls me forward and gives me a chaste kiss upon my lips before letting me go again.

"HOW DARE YOU!" I scream refraining myself from nearly spitting in his face at his audacity.

"Come on babe, I know you wanted that too. Don't deny it. You wanted to taste me at least one more time before our final demise." The last of his minions exiting the door whirl around to face us. Their hatred fills the room, though they don't dare move. I feel their desperation to fight but also their conflict over not wanting to defy their master. Duncan senses their eyes and moves his head to face them, "LEAVE! Before I turn my blade on you instead!" He commands and all of them run for the open door. Within seconds we are completely alone. A memory from earlier on today surfaces and I'm instantly filled with rage.

"Down in the station it wasn't Damon they were talking about now was it? It was YOU! They all thought you were there to save them, not kill them. They could see your true form even when we couldn't..." I push hard against our conjoined blades forcing him to take a step back. I saw what he was like down there, he didn't care about them. He showed no mercy and killed them as if they were his enemies, not his disciples. "How can you live with yourself? You killed so many of your own people just to keep your secret intact!"

I swing my blade, aiming for his ribs but he anticipates my move and catches it. My veins feel like molten hot lava underneath my skin as I try to rein in my temper. *Yet, I want to rip his head off.* Wielding his blade high, Duncan and I move into a rhythmic dance of knives as we jump back and forth as we move throughout my living room.

"You're wrong, they *were* talking about Damon. He was their leader, not I, but I still did what I had to do." He states with sorrow lingering in his voice. Even if he believes what he did was right, it still doesn't make up for how many he killed. *There is no way in Zagoria I would kill my own, no matter what they did.*

"You disgust me." I seethe while dropping my hand to my side and quickly conjuring up another fireball. Swiftly, I bring my arm up and aim it at his head before releasing my power. Duncan quickly drops into a squat, causing the burning sphere to whiz past him, missing him by a hair. *Damn!* Spinning around he gazes upon the scorch mark left on the wall behind him. Using this distraction to my advantage, I run for the open door. I make it just over the threshold when a wave of green smoke rips me back inside, causing me to trip over the rug in the foyer. I land flat on my back as Duncan comes to stand by my head. *Ouch! That hurt.*

"Not so fast missy, I'm not done with you yet." Duncan jokes while I gaze up at him from below. Moving fast, I swing my leg up and kick him in the stomach, forcing him to the ground beside me. With him now out of the way, I put my hands on either side of my head and lift my legs high. Jumping up, I land flat on my feet and quickly turn around, preparing myself for the next attack but he's gone. Shit!

As slow as a tortoise I creep around my living room, checking behind all the furniture. I begin to feel a little anxious when I don't find him and head towards the kitchen. *Where could he be?*

"BOO!" Duncan yells in my face, appearing out of thin air. He raises his leg high in the air and front-kicks me in the stomach. Forcing me to fly backwards, landing on the couch in the middle of the living room. Winding me upon impact. *What the hell? Oh, he's going to get it now.* While drawing air into my lungs, I conjure up a huge fireball and fling it at him, not caring where it lands. It hits him hard in the shoulder, forcing him to turn around. Duncan quickly begins patting away the flames with his right hand as he conducts some swirly manoeuvres with his left. *Uh, that can't be good.*

Before I have a chance to react, a tornado takes over my living room and I'm being smothered by a revolving green mass. It sucks all the oxygen out of its centre, leaving me completely without air. It's choking me from the inside out. I try to call out to Duncan but it's of no use, nothing leaves my mouth. The smoke continues to circle as it begins to lift me off the couch and spin me all around the living room, smashing into everything.

I continue to gasp for air, trying to do anything I can to get rid of the enchantment but it doesn't work. My power evaporates as quickly as it comes. Duncan is my one true match in this world and right now, I believe he is proving that.

Breathlessly I try calling out his name again, demanding him to drop the spell. I even try calling down the bond for him but it feels as if he can't hear me. *More like he doesn't want to hear me.* Dark spots begin to line my vision and I know that soon I'll be powerless against the growing darkness. My lungs begin to burn with a need that I've never felt before and I know I'm running out of time.

Flinging my arms out wide, I feel around for anything I can hold. Within seconds something that resembles wood skims my palms and I grab it. I hold on for dear life. I'm afraid if I let go the smoke will rip me away again. *Hopefully, now I might be able to get myself out of this madness.* Before I have time to do anything the enchantment changes direction. My palms scrape along the wooden surface as I'm forced down towards the ground. *Ouch!* I momentarily lose my grip as the smoke flips and I begin hurling back up towards the ceiling. I smash into the framework hard as the smoke disperses around me and I immediately begin falling to the floor.

The moment I hit the ground I take a huge gulp of air, choking back my sobs as oxygen starts to fill my lungs once more. *Finally!* Whipping my head around I see Duncan leaning against a wall to the far side of the room. The cocky bastard even has the nerve to smile at me. *Asshole!*

"What the hell are you playing at?" My voice sounds hoarse from the lack of oxygen. "I thought you said you're not trying to kill me!" I yell weakly, ending my outburst in a cough.

"I'm not, I just thought I'd have a little fun while I'm at it." He moves away from the wall and comes to stand by my side.

"You really are an asshole," I utter while pushing myself up onto all fours and to my surprise, Duncan leans forward and grabs my elbow helping me up. I quickly rip my arm out of his grasp and watch as his hand falls back to his side. "Don't touch me," I order while getting to my feet and taking a step back. I hate that feeling of longing that ignites between us when he touches me. The notion that reminds me that we are connected in more ways than one, makes me want to cry. *Why him? Out of all the people in Zagoria, why did it have to be him?*

Averting my attention away from Duncan, I glance at my now destroyed living room. All my potted plants are knocked over and my walls are covered in so much blood that you can't even see the gorgeous wallpaper beneath it. Sighing heavily I turn my head back and notice Duncan is staring at me. His eyes are filled with so much love yet his persona gives off a different vibe. Hatred like I've never felt before radiates off him causing my stomach to do somersaults. *It's all so confusing.*

Duncan dissolves his blade and I too am no longer in the mood to fight. I don't agree with what he did, but I can't go back and change it even if I tried.

"Duncan, what are we doing?" I breathe another sigh as I shake my head and dissolve my own blade. "We can't kill each other, so what's the point of all this fighting?"

"I don't know about you but I kind of find it fun, also if I remember correctly, you rushed me first." He smiles as he crosses his arms over his chest. *Is everything a game to him?*

"True..." I answer with a nod, I did attack first. "And normally I'd apologise, but before I say anything else, I need you to clarify something for me. If you knew that killing me would kill you in return, why on *Earth* did you send your minions here? That's just suicide." I state while spreading my arms open wide, my temper begins to flare once more. *How could he be so stupid?*

"You need to reign in your temper and listen!" *Excuse me? Did he really just say that to me?* My eyes go wide as I anticipate another fight. "I didn't send them, ok? They came here of their own accord and trust me when I say this, they will be severely punished for it." He growls before turning towards the open door and gazes out into the darkness. His beautiful smile is gone and I believe he's fuming over the actions of his minions.

"They rebelled?" I ask while taking a deep breath to calm my raging temper as Duncan nods his head. I would be angry too if I was in his shoes, how dare they go behind his back like that. "When I saw them here in my living room, it brought up a memory of a story my elder once told me about. The one how the last Princess died. How she was severely outnumbered and it led to her death. Maybe it happened just like this. Perhaps a horde of beings broke into her home and killed her the same way they wanted to kill me... I honestly thought I was a goner." A shiver runs down my spine as I think about that day. *I have no doubt she went down swinging.*

"Hmm?... Well I can tell you one thing, she wasn't killed by my people." He states as he glances over his shoulder at me.

"What?..." I ask dumbfoundedly "Of course she was! Because if it wasn't them, who was it then?" *Does he seriously think I'm that stupid*?

"Yours." He declares as a matter of fact while turning his whole body to face me. My mouth drops open from pure shock at his remark. *What did he just say?*

"Bullshit!" I exclaim propping my hands on my hips. Fire hotter than the sun burns within my veins. *He's lying, there's no way!*

"No shit." He states mirroring my stance.

"I don't believe you! It was the only time Willow ever gave me any information about my past self, so there is no way she would have lied to me about this." I feel my blood boiling underneath my skin. *How dare he blame my disciples? Who in Zagoria does he think he is?*

"Well maybe she didn't exactly lie to you, she just didn't give you the full truth."

"Not a chance," I utter before realisation hits me. *He could be on to something here.* A sensation like cold water floods my senses as I think back to what she said that day. Willow told me that the last Princess was outnumbered, however she never stated by who or what eventually took her life.

"It doesn't matter what she said because what I'm telling you is the truth. You just need to believe me." He speaks solemnly. *Even if Willow didn't tell me the whole story, I still don't believe him. How can I?*

"And how am I supposed to do that Duncan when you have lied to me about so much already." I go to walk around him heading towards the door but he steps to the side, blocking my path.

"Because I'm telling you the truth damn it! I read it in the Book of Old. Every time one of us dies it gets documented within its pages. It records all the dates and times on how we came to be." He gives me this look that makes me want to believe him, but I just can't.

"That may be true but you've lied to me already, so how am I supposed to believe anything you say? You hid who you really were this whole time and you never said a word. You even killed your own to hide your true self. So, I'm sorry but that makes anything you say at this point irrelevant." I'm having a hard enough time deciphering what's been real or fake between us. *If any of it was real in the first place...*

"And I get that but humour me, Kyra. Would you have trusted me if I told you who I was from the very beginning?... Think about it.... You were told your whole life to hate the opposite of what you are. To not trust us, to kill and never think twice about it and why is that? Why do we have to be like this?... Do you really want to know why I killed those Crawlers?" He asks with his arms spread wide open, daring me to say something. "I killed them because they too went behind my back. They kidnapped a damn Elder for Zagoria's sake."

"They listened to the stupid ramblings from Damon, their leader, because he believed he was doing what was needed to assist the crown." Duncan finishes off by pointing at himself. "I knew something was off about him. I just couldn't figure out what and by the time I did, it was too late." I suddenly realise he's losing his hold over his minions and it looks like there is nothing he can do to stop them.

Although, what he said about us killing each other, that does make me think. During my upbringing, the Elders always warned me to never trust the darkness, that it was an unnecessary evil that we had to rid from the world. Because, if we didn't, they in return would destroy us all and rule Earth. The Elders told me that the Prince, well Duncan, would stop at nothing until I am dead. He had the chance to do it before we even met and he didn't, so I'm beginning to believe that he would never truly hurt me.

"You're right you know, I wouldn't have trusted you. I would have tried to kill you because it's like you said, I have been trained my whole life to go in for the kill. To never leave any monster alive and going by recent events, it was for good reason." Uncontrollably my temper begins to flair and I feel ten feet tall. It's about time he got a piece of my mind. "If I was not taking down your minions left right and centre, there would be so many of them out there rebelling against you that we wouldn't be able to catch up. Because Zagoria forbid that you're actually able to pull them back in line yourself." I state glaring up at him. My anger over the earlier incident resurfaces and I'm ready for a fight. Duncan stands a little straighter as his eyes also flare in anger.

"Don't be a bitch, it doesn't suit you." He seethes looking down his nose at me.

"And how do you know what suits me?" I huff back in response while taking a menacing step forward.

"Because I know you... better than you think." He stands his ground while my stomach drops at his declaration. *What's that supposed to mean?* I feel my body cooling from his words and hate the fact that he makes me second guess myself.

"Well it sucks that I cannot say the same about you now isn't it." He gives me this look as if I've struck a nerve and I watch as his body physically relaxes before me.

"Kyra..." He sighs. "Look, what I said back there... in front of my minions... It wasn't true, it was all for show. I didn't mean any of it... I had to demonstrate to them that I can be the big bad guy that they perceive me to be. My plan was to scare them enough so they'd fall back in line. I'm so sick of all this rebellion, it's making everything so much harder.

Earlier when I was passing a street over, I felt your anguish pulsing down through the bond. It frightened the absolute shit out of me and when I got here and saw so many of them, I just knew I had to do whatever I could to get them away from you. I don't even want to think about what may have happened if I didn't show up when I did."

He gazes at the destruction surrounding us before his sorrow filled eyes conncct with mine.

"I'm sorry for what they did to your beautiful home. I'll pay for it all, to get fixed I mean or if you need help rebuilding, I can do that too." Duncan reaches forward and takes my hand, this time I don't stop him. The instant our fingers touch it's like a bucket of cold water gets dumped on my head and I have to stop myself from jumping into his arms.

"There is no need for any of that but thank you," I say pleasantly while looking up at him. My girls in the garden probably already alerted the clean-up crew, they will come by later and see to the repairs.

"Kyra," Duncan utters my name as he tugs on my hand and lays it upon his chest. "I need you to believe me when I say that I don't want to hurt you. I never have and never will. What I said earlier about wanting to rule, again it was all just for show. I've never wanted that either, no matter what I led them to believe. I just want you and only you, exactly the way you are... because I... uh..." He begins rubbing the back of his neck with his free hand and diverts his gaze.

He looks like a child about to confess his deepest, darkest secret. "To hell with it." He whispers to himself before flicking his big black eyes back up. "I adore you Kyra. I have since the moment I saw you. It may have only been a couple of weeks but my feelings for you are stronger than I ever could have imagined.

I will admit though that I let myself get carried away earlier and I'm really sorry for that. I let my temper get the better of me and I know that doesn't excuse my actions. However, you need to understand that you called my hand in front of them and I had to demonstrate that I was in this for them, not for us. They need to have confidence in me that I can lead them, even if I hate doing it... I know I may be asking a lot from you but would you be able to find it within yourself to forgive me?" He looks down at me with these big puppy dog eyes. *Does he seriously believe that one quick apology and a sweet declaration will work? I thought he knew me better than that.*

"Forgive you?" I ask withdrawing my hand from his and taking a step back, "Duncan you cut off my air, I couldn't breathe. I was begging for you to let me go but you didn't. Your minions were long gone by then yet, you still held your power over me. You wanted to prove your dominance on a grand scale, so if you don't mind," I push past him and this time, he doesn't stop me. I'm no longer in the mood to talk and there is something else important I must do.

As I cross over the threshold, I feel his eyes on my back as he follows me out.

"And I am really sorry about that too, truly." He says behind me but I keep walking.

"Duncan, just drop it, ok? It doesn't matter now anyway. It's in the past and there's nothing you can do to change it, so we may as well move forward. It doesn't mean I forgive you though." I whirl around to face him and poke my finger into the chest. He raises his arms in surrender as he nods his head in agreement. He gazes down upon me saddened and I have to make myself look away.

I will not allow him to get to me right now, especially when I'm trying to prove my own dominance. "I have to check on my girls," I declare without turning my eyes back to him, hopefully he will hear my command and stay put. *I need to be alone for a moment.* Turning around, I walk down my front steps and into my garden. Thankfully he doesn't follow.

Chapter 5

The night air feels crisp against my skin and its coolness helps alleviate some of the bad energy I built up during our fight. Running my hands up and down my arms, I try to regain some of the strength I lost as I cross a small patch of grass to the little house within my garden. The moment I approach the wooden structure, I notice that all the lights are off and immediately fear the worst. The creatures once again managed to break through the barrier and not just any creatures, Bubaks did.

I fall to my knees and quickly knock on the tree trunk beside their house. I wait for what feels like an eternity before I see a light turn on through the open window. Sighing a breath of relief, I wait patiently for them to come outside. Lucy slowly opens the door and sticks her head out to make sure that the coast is clear before they all rush out to greet me.

"Good evening Your Highness, we apologise for taking so long, we didn't expect you to come by at this hour", they utter as they all sweep into a low curtsey.

"No need for the apology ladies, it is I who should apologise to you. I should have waited until morning, but I wouldn't have been able to sleep without knowing if you were alright. Now that I can see that you are, I need to know if you had any trouble? And also, how's the barrier now? Have you had time to repair it since the break-in?"

"It is alright Your Highness, we understand. The monsters didn't come our way thankfully and yes, the barrier is fully restored. We repaired it the moment we saw the last of them leave earlier. With that being said, is everything alright now miss?"

"I'm not quite sure, but I believe so." I glance over my shoulder at Duncan who is standing at the foot of the stairs in all of his dark glory. The memory of the first time I saw him pops into my head. He appeared so godlike even back then and I wonder how in the world I missed it. Green smoke surrounds his handsome figure and I have to fight the urge to run to him. His presence brings out so many different emotions in me and I cannot begin to fathom what will happen if I succumb to them. I want to embrace him and have him wrap his arms around me like he has for the past few weeks. Yet, on the other hand, I also want to punch him in the face just for being who he is.

Duncan senses my stare and turns his head towards me. Before our eyes meet, I quickly return my attention to my girls.

"Ladies, I have a question for you, do you sense an anomaly on the property at all? Like something isn't quite right?"

"What do you mean Your Highness?" They all take turns looking at each other concerned.

"Not to be alarmed, but we let someone through the barrier who managed to deceive us into believing they were someone else. I want you to find out how they managed to do it if that's possible?" I ask politely.

"Oh no..." A frightened expression crosses their sweet faces and they all instinctively begin backing up towards their front door.

"No it's ok, trust me. You're safe. But please find out how they managed to do it ok?"

"Yes, yes of course your Highness. We will get on that right away." They all turn and begin to run back towards the entrance to their home. However, they stop a few feet shy of their front door and as one, they all turn to look at me.

I giggle at their behaviour. "It's ok ladies, you may go."

"Thank you Your Highness but that's not why we stopped..." They glance at one another again and this time it makes me nervous. *What's wrong?* "Your Highness, we believe there is a human on the property." I inhale sharply as I whip my head to the side and gaze upon my front gate, it's wide open. *Shit!* There are only a handful of humans who are allowed on the property and all of them I have no desire to see right now. *What are they even doing here so late?*

"Thank you ladies, that will be all." Before they have a chance to reply I get up and run back towards Duncan. "I have to go Earthside. There is a human here and they cannot just see me appear out of thin air." I utter as I run past him and back into the house, I move through the lounge room and into the kitchen. I didn't have time to sense where they were, so they could be right outside my front door for all I know. Fading out takes almost all the energy I have left and I curse myself for not grabbing Duncan on my way in. *Too late for that now.*

My doorbell chimes at the same time I become whole and I begin to make my way towards the door. As I step into my living room and see the chaos, I realise I should probably check myself out first. Dashing into the downstairs bathroom, I give myself a once over in the mirror and thank Zagoria I did. My blonde hair is a complete mess and I have green blood splattered all over my face. I quickly wash it off and run my fingers through my unruly hair, trying to make it look like I just got up from a nap instead of a supernatural fight with my boyfriend. I pause for a second as I just realised I referred to Duncan as my boyfriend. A small smile spreads out across my lips at the thought. *That's a term I've never used before.*

I almost have my hair under control when I hear the bell chime again. Not wanting to keep my guest waiting, I dash out of the bathroom and head towards the door. My living room is in complete disarray so I will have to keep my guest outside. Turning the knob, I open the door and standing before me is the one person I *really* don't want to see right now.

"Oh ah...Hey Flick." I utter with uncertainty as she raises her eyes to mine and my stomach drops instantly. Her bright nature is gone and her face is swollen from many hours of crying.

"Omg! You're still alive! I have been so worried about you. It's been weeks since I last saw you. I have been trying to call you almost every day but you never seem to answer your phone." Flick goes to take a step forward but, I'm quicker. I step out over the threshold and shut the door behind me. She looks confused for a second before shaking it off and takes a step back. *She's probably wondering why I won't let her in.*

"I'm so sorry, I didn't think that me taking some leave would affect you so much," I say guilt-stricken while sliding my hands into my back pockets. *Could this be any more awkward?*

"Oh, it hasn't, well not really. I just... I've needed someone to talk to and you always seem to know the right thing to say..." Now she is the one giving me a guilty look. "It feels like ever since I went on that stupid date with Duncan everyone's been avoiding me. You don't come to work anymore, Connor is always too busy for me and don't get me started on Duncan. I think I may have seen him once or twice in the last three weeks and when I have, he walks straight past me acting like I don't even exist. It's so embarrassing Kyra." She starts sobbing right in front of me and I begin to contemplate what I should do. *Do I try to comfort her knowing I'm the reason for her pain, or should I just make it go away entirely?* Willow always warned me not to mess with human emotions, it usually gets ugly.

"I'm sorry Flick, I didn't mean to cause you any pain. I have been dealing with some things to lately and I often didn't want my phone with me. You should know me by now, that I don't always take it with me and to be honest, I'm not even sure where it is right now." She smiles at my comment, knowing full well that I'm telling the truth. "How about we sit out here in my garden and talk. It's such a beautiful night." She nods in agreement and turns around. We make it to the bottom of the stairs when the front door swings open behind us. *You have got to be kidding me!*

I glance over my shoulder while my stomach drops with unease. Duncan saunters through the doorway with a mischievous smirk on his face. *Oh, what are you up to now?* Flick peeks back to view the newcomer and stops mid-step as her mouth falls open. Her face expresses pure shock as she slowly turns around and starts flicking her eyes between the two of us before settling them on me. *Oh no!* I try to conjure up the right thing to say but as of right now, I have nothing. It wouldn't matter anyway because she closes her mouth, lifts her hand and slaps me hard across the face. *Ouch!*

Chapter 6

"You *BITCH*!" She turns away from me with tears in her eyes and runs down the stairs to the pathway leading out towards the road. I chase after her, grabbing her by the arm and pull her back to face me.

"Flick wait, please it isn't what it looks like," I say with sorrow lingering in my voice. *How am I ever going to explain this to her without causing her pain?*

"It's not? Then what is it Kyra?" She asks angrily as she looks at me sceptically.

"Uh..." *Shit, I don't know what to say because it is clearly what it looks like.*

"See you can't even tell me..." She stares deep into my eyes allowing me to witness all the pain I have caused. I can feel my soul fading away knowing full well I'm the reason for so much sadness. "How could you? You knew how much he meant to me and still, you went behind my back and did this?" She begins bawling her eyes out and there is nothing I can do to stop it. "Fuck you!... Fuck you both." Flick spits angrily towards us before lifting her hand and gives me a vulgar gesture. She extends her arm out a little to the left and gives one to Duncan too. The jackass leaning against the pillar behind me even has the nerve to chuckle, which makes Flick's features deflate further.

I turn around at his response and give him the finger too which only makes him laugh louder. Shaking my head, I circle back and try to think up a way I can defuse this situation, "Flick please, I swear I didn't mean for any of this to happen, it's just..." *Fate, but how can I tell her that.* She wouldn't believe me even if I tried, especially as I haven't seen her since the day I met him. She's probably thinking that I didn't come to work because I was trying to avoid her, which is entirely untrue.

"Save it Kyra, I don't want to hear any more bullshit coming out of your mouth." She turns to leave and even though I don't want her to go, I don't stop her. She is the closest thing I have ever had to a sister and now it feels like I've lost her for good. I take a step forward wanting to forcefully make her see reason but just before my fingers touch her skin, I drop my hand. I can't do that to her and it's probably for the best anyway. I should never have let myself get so attached. It's not good for me and it's definitely not good for her either. Tears begin to roll down my cheeks as I watch my only real friend walk out of my front gate and probably out of my life forever.

"You shouldn't be so hard on yourself. You knew this was coming sooner or later." I turn to him as my anger flares. *I want to beat the crap out of him for what he just did. This never would have happened if he had just stayed inside.* I storm up to him and make sure I get right in his face. Duncan crosses his arms over his chest and tilts his head down so we are eye to eye. The asshole even dares to smile at me.

"You're a real prick you know that! She was just fine and I was thinking of a way to bring you up, but then you *had* to go and show your ugly mug and ruin EVERYTHING!" I shout as I poke him hard in the chest. *How dare he! He...* I stop and think about it for a second... *oh that does it!* "You did that on purpose, didn't you?" I rage and his answering grin is the only response I need. Bringing my arm up, I slap him as hard as I can across the face. His head swivels to the right as a tremendous smack lingers in the air around us. My fingers tingle a new sort of pain as I watch him blink a few times before shaking his head and returning his eyes to mine. He has an even bigger grin now than the one before and I realise that he is actually enjoying this.

"You know, you're really hot when you're mad. I think I should make you angry more often." he voices seductively and I move my arm back, ready to strike a second time. *Oh, you're going to get it now.* As I swing my arm forward, Duncan grabs a hold of my forearm, stopping my hand mere millimetres away from his face. "However, if you slap me again, I'll break your arm." He threatens while glaring down his nose at me.

"You wouldn't dare." I spit at him.

"Try me and see where it gets you." His words are smooth as they leave his mouth and my anger all but disappears as he brings my hand to his lips. Duncan nips the inside of my palm with his teeth before kissing the spot immediately after. Electricity is flowing between us and I feel the pull that binds us together, it calls to me, it wants to be set free. We are standing so close to each other that I can feel his breath upon my cheek and a new sensation ignites.

Instinctively I move closer, pressing my body up against his. Duncan's smile falters as he drops his eyes to my mouth and before we have time to comprehend what is happening, we are wrapped up in each other. Our arms are moving at a frantic pace and our lips seem to just not be moving fast enough. I press myself as hard as I can against him, wanting to feel anything other than this internal volcano waiting to erupt. Lowering my hands to the hem of his shirt I slowly raise it over his abdomen when a blinding pain ignites in the back of my head and everything goes black.

I notice something hard pressed against my back as I begin to blink away the darkness lining my vision. The surface is hard and cool beneath me however there is also something warm around my head. I see and feel almost nothing, it's like my senses have disappeared. Far in the distance, I can hear someone mumbling my name but who is it? The voice sounds so familiar but, I can't grasp where I know it from. I think something is hovering above me too, yet I'm unsure as I can only make out a faint silhouette. The shadow turns away from me and points to something on my left. Turning my head I blink as hard as I can as another silhouette begins to take shape in the distance. The voice above me gets louder and louder but it's no longer calling my name, it is growling at the shadow in the distance.

I feel something wrap itself tightly around my bicep and I begin to feel our power flow. *Duncan.* I gaze up at my mate yet I still see nothing. *What's going on?* Quickly I bat my eyelids as I try to regain some of my vision as the healing powers from our connection take hold. After a minute or two, I am able to hear the far-away voice as Duncan's handsome face comes into focus above me. I hear sobs coming from my left and I turn my head again towards the noise. Flick stands far off in the distance trembling from the onslaught Duncan is throwing her way. "Are you really that stupid, you almost killed HER! What the fuck are you doing here anyway, I thought you left?" The words are still partly muffled but the anger in his voice is undeniable. As I look across the yard to my friend, I notice a tree branch lying at her feet. *Did she hit me with that? Is that why I blacked out?*

"I'm so sorry! I came back to apologise and I saw you two kissing and I just got so angry. I didn't mean to hurt her." Flick splutters out through her tears and as my vision begins to clear, I notice she is staring directly at me. She gives me an apologetic look and slowly I nod in understanding. *I get it now.* Blinking away the last of the fuzziness that lines my vision, I turn to Duncan.

Anger intensifying the longer he stares at Flick and I cannot let this continue. Feeling the need to do something, I lift my hand and place it upon his chest. As soon as my palm connects with his skin, he turns his beautiful blue eyes to me. His anger completely disappears and is instantly replaced with concern. I mouth the words 'I'll be alright,' yet I don't miss the scepticism in his eyes.

There is movement on my left and Duncan's anger instantly returns as he lifts his head. "DON'T FUCKING MOVE!" he growls as he points towards Flick and she stops dead in her tracks. I remove my hand from his chest and place it on the side of his cheek, turning his face to mine. I plead with my eyes and beg him to let her go. I don't know the full story but whatever she did, I already forgive her. She would have done it out of hurt and anger and that is not something I can hold against her. Duncan shakes his head as if to say no but this is not his decision, it's mine.

"Let her go," I whisper while he stares at my face trying to see if I mean it. It feels like an eternity before he finally closes his eyes and nods his head, huffing out a sigh of defeat. I turn to face Flick, her eyes focused on Duncan. She gazes at him in shock. Feeling my eyes on her she glances down towards me. She goes to take a step forward but halts mid-step as Duncan growls again. He sounds like a lion protecting his pride.

"OK, ok." She says as she hangs her head and takes a step back. Lifting her eyes to mine once more, she takes a deep breath before she opens her mouth to speak, "Kyra, I'm so sorry I didn't mean to hurt you like that. I saw you two kissing and all of a sudden I got so mad and I just wanted to get you away from him. I really didn't mean to hurt you, I'm... oh god... I'm so sorry..." Her tears begin to fall like rain as her sobs rack her entire body. It kills me to see her like this. I open my mouth to say something but Duncan cuts me off.

"Save your grovelling, she almost died because of your fucking stupidity and now what, you want forgiveness or something? You're a real piece of work, you know that? I can't believe I ever went out with you!" I snap my head back to look at Duncan as I feel the need to tell him off. No matter what she just did to me, he should never say that to her.

Feeling the movement below him, he lowers his eyes. "What?" He asks impatiently and if I had more strength I would slap him again.

"You know what! Drop it and let her go, can't you see that she has been suffering?" Flick's slim frame appears to be even smaller since the last time I saw her. She obviously hasn't been taking care of herself lately.

"HER?" He shouts at me while pointing towards Flick. "Suffered? Are you fucking kidding me, Kyra? She beat you on the back of the head with a fucking branch and you're telling me she's suffered." His nostrils flare as he speaks reminding me of cartoons I used to watch as a youngling. The thought makes me chuckle.

Duncan stares at me confused while I feel his pull coming down the bond, pleading with me to reconsider. He wants me to fight Flick for what she did but I can't. I know what she did was wrong but I have to let her go. For no matter how much he wants me to fight, if the roles were reversed and I saw her making out with him, Zagoria may not have been able to save her.

As slowly as I can, I sit up and rub the back of my head. My fingers get caught in this sticky wetness and I see blood on my hand when I pull it away. Taking a deep breath I force my eyes away from the deep red and lift them back up to my mate.

"Yes." I breathe then turn to face Flick. "I understand why you were angry; trust me I do. I have wanted to tell you for weeks but honestly, I didn't know how to put it into words. I didn't want to hurt you and in every scenario that I came up with, you hated me in the end, and I really didn't want that. It was selfish of me to keep us a secret from you.

Not even in my wildest dreams did I ever plan for you to find out this way but you did, and I am sorry for that." Witnessing her cry, a sickening feeling rises within me, knowing full well that I am the one who caused those tears. "I hope that one day you will be able to forgive me and for us to be friends again, but I will respect your wishes if you decide against it." I almost whisper the last part as tears begin to flow down my own cheeks while I gaze upon the one person I love like a sister.

Flick closes her eyes and nods her head while I watch helplessly as her tears flow steadily down her cheeks. Without opening her eyes she turns around and walks down the pathway towards the road. It feels like a small crater forms in the centre of my chest the moment she leaves my property. A hole I don't think will ever be filled.

Without warning, Duncan scoops me up into his strong arms and takes me back into the house.

"I believe we both need a shower after that ordeal." He whispers into my ear while ascending the stairs two at a time. With my head resting against his shoulder, I nod as words feel too difficult to summon at this point. Uncertainty clouds my vision and I feel like I could sleep for days.

Duncan kicks off his shoes outside my bedroom door before sauntering over into the en-suite bathroom. He places my butt down on the benchtop and goes over to the shower, turning on the water before spinning back around. "Do you need help getting undressed or can you do it yourself?" He asks semi-seductively and without saying a word, I lift my arms permitting him to come and remove them. Desire ignites in his eyes as he returns to his spot directly in front of me. As gently as he can, he lifts me off the benchtop and places my feet back on the floor. Reaching down he grabs the hem of my shirt and slowly lifts it until it clears the top of my head. With hooded eyes, he stares down at my semi-naked torso while I slowly bite the corner of my bottom lip. A tingling feeling begins to wash over me from his heated gaze.

"You're so beautiful," he whispers as he gives me a chaste kiss on the neck as he drops to his knees in front of me. With careful fingers he begins to unbutton my shorts, moving ever so slowly from one button to the next. At a leisurely pace, he begins to slide my pants down my legs until they make a pool of fabric on the floor. Deeming the job complete, Duncan prepares himself to stand, however I hold him down with a hand upon his shoulder. He looks up at me with heavy eyes and I place a finger over the lacework on my underwear. "You want me to remove those too?" He breathes inches away from me and I nod. *Oh yes please.* He produces a luscious smirk before placing his hands on both sides of my thighs. His fingers feel like feathers as he moves them along my legs until he reaches the hem of my undergarments. Hooking his fingers underneath them, he slowly begins to pull them down as nervousness rises within me from being this bare. This is the first time that I have let a man see me like this and it is waking every fibre within me.

Duncan sits there for a few moments breathing heavily before getting to his feet. By the time he reaches his full height, I've turned to face the mirror and I'm sweeping the hair away from my back. His fingers feel heavenly against my skin as he begins to unclasp my bra. "You seriously are the most amazing creature I've ever seen." He whispers as he places another kiss in the crook of my neck before stepping away. I witness him removing his shirt behind me and avert my gaze. *Oh my gosh, we're going to be naked with each other. Well, how else do you expect him to get clean dummy?* Butterflies swirl deep within my stomach and I smile at the thought of him undressing. I'm about to turn around when he comes to a stop by my side.

Duncan must feel my nerves pulsing down the bond because he whispers, "It will be alright," as he slides one arm under mine and the other under my legs, picking me up once more. I rest my right arm across his shoulders as he carries me over to the shower. Without dropping me he manages to open the door and steps us into the running water. It feels absolutely wonderful as it sprinkles down upon us, so warm and inviting. Duncan places my feet on the floor and makes sure I'm steady before letting go. He gives me a delectable smile as he begins to massage my scalp under the running water. "Let me know if this stings, ok?" I nod as he moves me to the side and grabs some soap off the shelf. He squirts it on top of my head and then massages the fragrant liquid into my hair. Leaving it to rest for a moment, he steps away to quickly wash himself.

I can't help but stare as the water cascades over his perfectly sculpted body, watching every drop as they roll over his pecks to his abs. *Oh, this man is yummy...* I think as he turns to me with soapy fingers. His hands roam all over me and I get little zaps of electricity as he washes me from head to toe. Duncan moves me back under the water and finishes what he started. It feels like pleasurable torture, but I'm enjoying every second of it.

After a few minutes, he switches off the water and grabs the first towel off the rack as he steps out of the shower. He quickly wraps it around himself then reaches back and grabs another one for me. He places it over my shoulders as he steps forward to help me dry off however, I shake my head. *I think I can take it from here.* With a sexy smirk, he nods his understanding and backs away. I walk over to the sink and stand there staring at myself for a moment. *I think it's time to have some fun.*

With a smile, I remove the towel from around my shoulders and gradually slide it down my arms and my torso. Lifting my leg, I place my foot on the benchtop and start to dry my toes. I feel his eyes on me the entire time so as slowly as I can, I work my way up my right thigh and make sure I stop just before my apex. I hear his breathing become heavier the longer I persist, so next time I decide not to stop. I switch to the other leg and continue my slow ascent as we lock eyes in the mirror.

In a flash, Duncan moves directly behind me as I finish drying off and stand up straight. I have no idea why but I hold my towel in front of me like it's a shield. *As if it's going to protect me from him.* I quiver as Duncan slowly skims his finger up and down my arm as he moves his lips towards my ear. "Did you have fun torturing me like that?" He asks before lowering his mouth even more and places a kiss on the side of my neck. "You're such a tease."

Instinctively I back up a step so I'm flush against his abdomen and I feel his growth hitting my lower back. I physically gulp at its size. *It's huge.* Fire ignites within from his heated stare and my body begins to tremble with excitement. No other man has ever made me feel the way that he does.

Duncan reaches around, grabbing the towel from my grasp and drops it to the floor. "You won't be needing this anymore." He purrs as he moves his lips back up to my ear, "Tell me what you want, Kyra." He whispers before sucking my earlobe into his mouth and bites it hard. *Oh…*

I begin to rub my ass against him letting him know exactly what I want. "Ah… You want this?" He asks while pushing his hips forward, forcing his length into my back even more. I almost melt against him as sensation builds deep within me. Lifting my right arm, I wrap it around his head and force his lips back down to my skin. *I need him to kiss me.* I catch his panty dropping grin in the mirror as he lowers his mouth into the crook of my neck. *I feel like I'm on fire.*

Duncan's slow assault has my knees going weak. He wraps his arms around my waist to hold me steady, whilst pulling me closer against him. I feel my power deep within me, the eternal fire that wants to be free and I start clawing at his arms demanding more. Duncan senses my need and begins to kiss me more deeply. He removes one of his arms from around my waist and sweeps it low along my abdomen until he reaches the top of one of my thighs.

Using his fingertips, Duncan creates slow-moving circles along my skin as he makes his way over to the apex between my legs. My body is so overcome with ecstasy that I throw my head back and rest it upon his shoulder. *I think I'm going to burst.* I feel his hot breath upon my skin as he moves his lips along my neck towards my ear. He whispers the words, "Let go," and it's like a switch is flipped within me. Light explodes from within my being, creating tiny yellow stars that dance all around my bathroom.

If Duncan wasn't holding on to me the moment I exploded, I would have fallen to the floor. Breathing heavily, I try to regain some of my equilibrium as I lift my head from his shoulder and notice he is staring at our reflection in the mirror. "Thank you," I whisper as a blush creeps over me.

"No need to thank me. If I knew your pleasure would be so exhilarating, I would have made you do it sooner." He presses a kiss beneath my ear and lingers there for a moment longer than expected before slightly pulling away. "Can you stand by yourself?" he asks as he clears his throat and loosens his hold from around my waist. I quickly test my footing and nod as Duncan lets go. He moves about three feet away to where his clothes are piled up on the floor and leans over to pick them up.

"You know if you're going to continue to have showers here, you might as well bring some clothes over. That way you don't have to keep putting your stinky ones back on." I giggle as a cheeky smile breaks out across his face. He holds up his blood-splattered clothing in front of him and grimaces. *I wouldn't want to put those back on either.*

"Are you asking me to move in already?" He asks as he hoists up his pants and fastens the button. Sliding his hands into his pockets, he pushes the waistband down just over his hips. I can't help but stare at the little patch of hair underneath his belly button knowing full well what lies beneath it. I can't help but bite my lip at the thought.

"No, no, no, just your clothes." I quickly avert my gaze and look at myself in the mirror. *I think I can do this!* Deciding I want to be brave, I forgo my towel and head towards him on my way to the closet. Duncan gives me a curious look and licks his lips as I approach him. Trying to be cute, I give him a little wink as I brush past and I'm almost to the door when Duncan quickly turns around and slaps me hard on the butt. *OUCH!* I let out a little yelp as I scurry faster into my room. His laughter behind me has me blushing for a whole new reason.

"So, you're saying my clothes can move in, but I can't? Don't you think that's a little bit unfair?" Duncan feigns outrage yet I can still hear the laughter in his voice.

"Oh I don't think so, your clothes are much nicer than you are after all." Duncan breaks out laughing and I can't help but join in. *I'm not kidding though, the boy has fine taste.* Once I've decided what I'm going to wear, I grab the jeans off the second shelf and hold them out in front of me. I hear Duncan clear his throat from within the bathroom and turn my senses toward the noise.

"Hey, I'm curious. Why didn't you just use your mind control ability on Flick instead of letting her go? It would've been a hell of a lot easier on you both if you had." I'm stunned by his bluntness. *How does he even know about that? I'm pretty sure I haven't disclosed all of my abilities to him. Well, not yet anyway.*

"What are you talking about?" I ask, defecting its existence.

Duncan comes into the bedroom drying his hair while I begin to put on my pants. I try not to make eye contact as I quickly pull them up and fasten the button. Reaching high, I grab the first shirt off the top shelf and throw it on.

"Don't kid yourself, Kyra. I know all the powers you possess. I read it in the Book of Old." I turn to him in utter disbelief. *Is that how he knows so much about me?*

"It really says that in there?" I glance at him as he just nods his head. *Wow, I wonder what else this book contains.* Needing to do something with my hair, I walk back past Duncan who's lingering in the doorway and into the bathroom. I eye my brush on the bench and go over to pick it up. I feel Duncan's eyes on me the entire time and begin to wonder what else he knows.

"You need to tell me what else this book contains," I utter as he leans against the doorframe while eyeing me from head to toe. He watches as I grab my towel off the floor and roughly dry my hair before combing it out again.

"I'll do one better, I'll show you." My mouth falls open as I whip my head in his direction and almost drop my brush from the shock. Duncan gives me a smile so infections that I can't help but smile back. "I think it's about time I take you to the library of the ancients."

"Really?" I ask excitedly. *I can't believe it.*

"Yeah, as a matter of fact, as soon as you're ready, we'll leave." Overcome with so many emotions, my body reacts before my brain and I barrel over to him. Gripping his face within my palms, I pull his lips down to mine and give him a big smooch. He chuckles against my mouth as he grips my hips and I wrap my arms around his neck. I let out a little moan as Duncan's tongue starts massaging mine and I move my body closer to his. He slowly lowers his hands until he's touching my ass and in one swift movement, I'm hoisted off the floor.

A huff escapes me the moment Duncan presses my back up against the adjacent doorframe and I wrap my legs around his waist. Duncan moves his fingers further down my ass until he skims over the sweet spot between my thighs. My mouth uncontrollably whispers, "I want you," against his lips and Duncan lets out a growl as he begins to kiss me more ferociously.

Breathing in deep, I kiss him as if my life depends on it. Fuelling that fire that needs to be free. White lights begin to dance behind my eyelids just as Duncan pulls away. I watch his chest rise and fall with every breath he takes as he lays his forehead against mine. "Why did you stop?" I ask almost sobbing. *I thought he wanted this as much as I did.*

"Because I had to... Don't get me wrong Kyra, I want you, I really do. But this isn't the right time to be doing this."

"Why not?" *Why should we wait if we are both ready for it?* Uncontrollably my body begins to tease him with a simple movement of my hips. I feel my blood begging to ignite when a tiny moan escapes my lips.

Duncan stares deep into my eyes as he groans inwardly before mouthing the word stop. I see his inner turmoil yet my body doesn't listen, it wants that sweet release that I know is bound to come. Biting his lower lip, Duncan closes his eyes and with strong hands, he grips my hips halting my movements. I whimper at his denial.

"Kyra..." He whispers my name. "I want you so badly it hurts but we can't, not now... You have to understand. There are things you just don't know and I want you to be one hundred percent sure before you make this choice." I feel him sigh heavily beneath me. "Do you realise that we almost died today? I have no idea how Flick managed to do it, but I felt the pull on my life force the moment she hit you... You have received multiple blows from my creatures since the moment we met and I've never felt that sensation before. It scared the absolute shit out of me. I thought only a special kind of weapon or being could kill us, not a measly human with a stick." He looks at me concerned as I recall a memory from the Crawler nest. *Maybe he would know?*

"Back in the station, Damon's men had arrows forged of the immortal flame. Did you give them to them?" He gazes upon me wide-eyed as he quickly shakes his head. A sickening sensation washes over me and I begin to wonder. *If Duncan didn't make them, who did?*

"I've never known that sort of thing ever existed but I'll be sure to bring it up with Elder Snow later." Duncan slightly releases his hold on my legs and I slide back down to the floor. He gives me a chaste kiss on the forehead before turning around and exiting the bathroom, leaving me completely alone.

Roughly half an hour later, I'm making my way downstairs when I hear cupboards banging in the kitchen. The noise makes me cringe and I decide to investigate. *What in Zagoria is he doing?* Duncan is standing at the bench rifling through the top cupboard. "You got anything to put on bread?" He asks over his shoulder without taking his eyes off the contents within the cupboard.

"Where did you find bread? Are you sure it's not off?" I ask while stepping into the kitchen.

He glances at me before pointing to the opposite side of the room. "I found it in the freezer. Firstly, I thought it was a strange place to keep it but now I'm really glad you did. I've taken a few slices out to defrost and hopefully I'll be able to find something to put on them because other than this, there is seriously nothing else edible in this house." He winks while smiling before turning back around to rummage through the cupboard. I shake my head and walk into the pantry. Eyeing the peanut butter on the shelf, I grab it and walk over to stand by Duncan's side.

"Here," I say handing him the spread. "Willow must have put the bread in the freezer the last time she was here. That woman is always thinking one step ahead."

"Well, she is a seer, isn't she?" He flicks his eyes towards me while grabbing a knife from the drawer.

"Yeah, but that doesn't change the fact that she's always taking care of me, even long after I moved out." I smile at the thought but it falters as I watch Duncan grimace beside me. "What?" I ask concerned.

"Nothing." He says shaking his head and spreads out the peanut butter on a slice in front of him. I contemplate what may have caused Duncan to pull that face before I decide to drop it. I should really help him prepare our food if I want to eat too. *I'm so hungry I could eat a dragon…*

Chapter 7

I'm sitting on the bench with my legs crossed licking the crumbs off my fingers while Duncan is over at the sink doing the dishes. My home is completely destroyed. Debris lies everywhere around us and I am surprised my benchtops are still in usable order. It pains me to think that even if I do renovate, this place will never resemble its former self.

Duncan dries off his hands and comes to stand by me. "You ready to go?" he asks while holding his hand out. I nod eagerly as I grasp his fingers and hop down from the bench before heading towards the front door.

"Did your crew have to destroy almost every piece of furniture I own? Thankfully they never made it upstairs." I joke as I throw my left arm out, pointing towards the upper level of my home while we make our way through the living room. So much history was demolished within just a few short minutes. Wood chips and glass lie all over the floor and my furniture is either all knocked over or broken. *It's definitely going to take my people some time to fix this place.*

As we near the door I see a tiny scrap of colour lying on the floor and my blanket comes to mind. Slowing my pace, I stare at the tiny piece of wool and remember all the beautiful colours and the swirl of our two worlds combined. Duncan notices my gaze and slows his pace too.

"What is it?" he asks, glancing between me and the purple remains.

I shake my head, dropping the subject and continue walking through the front door. That blanket meant the world to me and there is nothing I can do or say that will bring it back.

The night air is crisp against my skin as we step out onto the porch. *Maybe I should have worn warmer clothes,* I think as I glance back at the door I just exited. Feeling warmth to my right, I look over and see Duncan standing there in all of his god-like glory. Fire instantly ignites in the pit of my stomach and I force myself to look away. *I don't think I'll be needing that jumper after all.*

A beautiful fragrance travels up from my garden and I close my eyes and inhale. *Mmmm...* All the flowers are in bloom and create such a sweet aroma, it's invigorating.

"Hey! So now that we are on our way, are you going to tell me where this mysterious library is or is it another big secret that I'm not allowed to know?" I nudge him in the ribs as we walk down the stairs toward the front gate.

"Well now that you've asked, it IS actually a big secret and even though you are allowed to know I'm still not going to tell you because it's like I said before, you never know who may be listening." He looks around at that statement, as we continue walking along the path to the boundary of my property.

"That's fair enough, I can't argue with that." We reach the gate and he fades into our realm. Closing my eyes, I do the same. Earth's hum is something I have grown so accustomed to that I miss it when I go home. It's eerie quiet here in Zagoria, no joke, you would be able to hear a pin drop from a mile away. Opening my eyes, I turn around and immediately jump back in fright. *What in the world is that!?* Right in front of me is a ginormous bat-like creature, a being so big it could swallow me whole.

Startled by my sudden movement it hisses in my direction. Its huge fangs prod out of its massive mouth close enough to cut me. The creature has an upturned nose and huge pointed ears. I notice it's been fitted with a saddle; the leather's wide enough for two people to sit on it comfortably. The thing has beady looking eyes and these mighty wings, wings that could rival the length of football fields. *I would definitely not like to be caught alone with this creature, that's for sure.*

"Did the mean old lady scare you?" Duncan coos to his beast as he walks beside its head and begins patting its fur. "It's ok baby, I know she looks scary, but she won't harm you, trust me." He says while stroking the beast's face. Moving to its side, he grabs ahold of the reins and jumps up onto the saddle.

"Well, that's good to know," I utter while walking over to the beast and allowing Duncan to help me up.

"I wasn't talking to you." He whispers to me before wolf-whistling and with one mighty flap of its wings, we're catapulted into the skies as I let out a terrible shriek. I knew this is where we would go but I honestly didn't expect us to take off so fast.

The wind's roar is deafening against my ears as we head high up into the stratosphere. We are moving at rapid speed and I have to blink away the tears that form. *I should have worn goggles or something for this!*

The beast reaches its desired altitude and levels out, hopefully it's all smooth sailing from here. I'm finally able to see clearly and decide to risk a glance over the edge. *Wow, we are high up!* The streetlights below look like tiny stars and I'm beginning to forget which way is up. I'm hit hard by a wave of vertigo and have to force myself to look away. Leaning forward I rest my head against Duncan's back and tighten my grip around his waist. I feel him chuckle beneath my grasp and I curse my dizzy head. *Asshole!*

In an attempt to be supportive, he starts running his fingers up and down my arm, leaving little warm circles in his wake. After a few deep calming breaths, I'm finally able to speak.

"So, is this your usual mode of transport while here in Zagoria?" I ask over his shoulder while trying to distract myself by looking out at the distance and not below. We are so high up and it's scaring the shit out of me. I may have travelled by plane many times before on Earth, but that was behind closed doors, and I was always strapped in. As for right now, we would have to be at least fifty thousand feet off the ground and did I add, we have no seat belts! My body begins to shake uncontrollably from all the nerves and have to rest my forehead again against Duncan's back. *Why am I like this?*

"Usually yeah, Fang here helps me escape the monotonous duties of being the ruler of the underworld," Duncan says lovingly while patting the beasts hide.

A short time later I begin to get used to the altitude and my body stops shaking. Raising my head I look around and see all the wonders the universe has to offer. The stars above us look so vibrant against the blackened sky. I can clearly see the milky way, the southern cross and even Orion's belt. From the ground you can never see so many all at once, it's absolutely phenomenal.

Tightening my grip around Duncan's waist once more, I pull myself even closer as the air around us becomes colder with every passing second. His warmth seeps into my skin through the fabric of his shirt and I feel the fire deep within me glow a little brighter. Gazing far out in the distance, I see smoke rising from the ground as another memory surfaces. "Hey, how did Damon manage to get ahold of your sword?" I blurt out as Duncan's fingers still along my skin. *I suddenly realise he didn't give it to him!* Duncan sits there for a moment in complete silence and I begin to wonder if he's ever going to answer.

"When you left to find Willow, I was helping some of the wounded when the biggest Crawler I've ever seen jumped out of a trap door beneath my feet. The order and I tried to fight it off but, I was thrown back into a wall and accidentally dropped my blade. When I finally got back on my feet minutes later, the blade was gone. I'd just begun searching for it when you pulled on the tether that binds us together. Immediately, I forget about the blade to come find you as I had an overwhelming feeling of helplessness wash over me. You may not have given me an immortal blade, but it definitely did some damage."

"You knew it wasn't an immortal blade?"

"Of course I did. I'm your equal remember? Also, I feel your flame running through yours whenever I'm close to it. The sword you gave me was empty, hollow even. In saying that though, Damon was obviously unaware of that factor. He probably didn't know that we can only conjure one immortal blade, the rest are just replicas. I think that's why he tried to kill you with it." As the last words leave Duncan's mouth a chill runs through my chest. It may be fully healed but I will never forget the pain I felt when the blade entered my body. *Not many Zagorian's know that my sword has the power to kill me too, so I wonder how he found out.*

Duncan and I are pondering over our own thoughts when suddenly the air around us becomes completely freezing. I watch with amazement as steam begins to rise from Duncan's skin. *What is going on?* Curiosity getting the better of me, I glance over the edge and see snow-covered mountains below us. *Huh? How is that possible?*

"Did we just travel through time or something? How can there be snow in the middle of summer?" I ask dumbfounded. Looking around, I notice that I've seen this mountain range before, it's the Blue Mountains. Though I have never seen them here in Zagoria, I know for sure at this time of year they are definitely not covered in snow.

"No, we did not just travel through time and yes it is summer. I thought it was common knowledge that this mountain range is always covered in snow here in our realm. No matter the season." He peers over his shoulder and gives me a sly smile before returning his eyes to the wide-open air before us.

"Please tell me this is not where we are stopping," I say as I peer down at my attire. I am practically wearing nothing. *Bugger! I knew I should have brought a jumper.*

"Thankfully no," He states happily. "The library is just over the next ridge and I swear it will be much warmer there." *Oh, thank Zagoria.*

Chapter 8

We land sometime later in the middle of a dense forest and I owe Fang an apology. I didn't believe she would make it through here without hurting us or herself. We had a few close calls, but she manoeuvred around every tree like she's done it a thousand times before. Duncan wasn't kidding either when he said it would be warmer down here. The weather is so humid that I begin sweating almost immediately.

"How do all of the books in this great library not get ruined by all this humidity?" I ask hopping down from the saddle. The ground is soft and spongy beneath my feet and I am thankful for my thick boots. Everything around us is so lush and green and I begin to wonder how often it rains here. Rays of sunshine peek through the gaps within the trees and the wind adds a beautiful rustling of the leaves, creating its own sweet melody.

A thud sounds from behind me and I turn around to see Duncan standing beside Fang. His hand is on her hide as he moves slowly along towards her face. He rests his forehead against her nose and begins to take a few deep breaths as he looks deep into her eyes. He whispers something I cannot hear, closes his eyes and takes one final deep breath. Moving away from the ginormous beast, Duncan nods his head and Fang spreads her mighty wings and takes off into the skies.

"I really hope you're ready for this," Duncan utters as he walks past me. He stops about ten metres away and I see him whispering something as he swirls his fingers around like he's casting a spell. A green glowing doorframe begins to take shape out of nowhere and I'm awestruck by the sight of it. *Magic!? He knows how to cast spells! I thought that was something that faded out millennia ago.*

"...Fate." Is the only word I hear as the double stone doors in front of us swing wide open. Stepping aside, he puts one arm behind his back and the other he sweeps into the doorway. "After you, Your Highness." He mocks playfully and ushers for me to cross the threshold.

I'm momentarily rooted in my spot as I gaze at the beauty in front of me. A semi-long corridor that leads down into what appears to be an overly large room. No stonework is to be seen in the passageway as creeper vines cover the walls.

Cautiously, I take a step forward and make sure to watch my step. The smell of old paper and ink hits my nostrils and it reminds me of the good old days, back when everything was printed by hand and not machines. I reach the end of the corridor and lying before me is a staircase leading down into what used to be a grand library. I increase my glow and almost light up the entire space. There are shelves upon shelves of leather-bound books as far as the eye can see. *I have never seen so many books in my life.* And yet the place appears to be in ruins.

Stacks have fallen over and crumbled as mother nature has taken over and everywhere I look there seems to be some sort of greenery. The more I gaze around, the more I begin to notice that this isn't just any room. It's a beautiful old conservatory and moonlight filters down through the windows high above. In the centre of the room is a magnificent three-tier water fountain that has long been out of use. The top half of the walls that surround the stacks are lined with statues of women, warriors in every pose imaginable. Monuments of men mark the bottom half of the walls and I turn my gaze to the closest male sculpture. *I can't believe it.*

A warrior in a grand pose stands before me, however it's not just anyway warrior, it's Duncan. I whip my head around to gaze upon the closest female statue on the other side of the staircase and my hand flies to my mouth. *It's me!* I walk over and run my hand along my arm made of stone. The likeness is uncanny.

"I used to stare at that statue a lot when we came of age. I think I was partially in love with you before we even met." Duncan voices from behind me and I jump at the sudden noise in the quiet room.

"Far out Duncan, you scared the shit out of me," I exclaim moving away from the sculpture of myself while putting a hand over my erratically beating heart. "How long have you known about this place?" I ask as I glance at him and then back at the grand room. Duncan is leaning against the wall of the passageway we just entered through, but I don't give him much notice, the room before me is just too beautiful to tear my eyes away from. *There is so much knowledge here and I never knew about it until now.*

"I grew up here, this is where Snow brought me to train in the ways of old." I whip my head in his direction completely dumbfounded. *He grew up here!*

"Really! How come I was never told about this place. It's a little unfair that you got to learn so much about me, but I never knew anything about you." I walk down the stairs and pick up the first book within reach. *Maps.* The book contains all the maps from our past, it shows how the world has changed over time and all the geographical wonders to be discovered. *This is amazing.* I put the book down and pick up the next one as Duncan comes to stand by my side. He peers over my shoulder and together we read the scribes about how the world used to be.

"I believe your last question is one that only I can answer I am afraid." Startled by the sudden intrusion, I turn to face the newcomer. My mouth almost hits the floor as I gaze upon the last person I expected to see here. "Hello, Kyra," Connor announces as he descends the stairs and heads straight for us.

Chapter 9

My boss walks over, taking the book from within my grasp and places it back on the shelf. "It's ok love. I think you can close your mouth now." He says with a chuckle as he lifts his hand to close it for me but I jump back.

"How?" I ask as I stare at him in disbelief. He looks slightly different but it's definitely Connor, except now he has the radiance of an Elder. "How are you guys able to do this? You're both able to elude my senses and hide your true forms. For Zagorians sake..." I raise my voice as I gesture towards the handsome man standing beside me. "...You're the damn Dark Prince." I flick my eyes in his direction and watch as a smile plays on his lips. *Oh, I bet he's enjoying this...* "... And you... You're an Elder? What in the world is going on? I should be able to feel your power but I feel nothing." I say as I begin to rub my chest. I should be overcome with this intense tingling feeling standing this close to him, and yet I feel hollow.

"It's a trick I learnt many millennia ago Your Highness. I can explain more on that matter later if you like." Connor sweeps himself into a low bow as Duncan chuckles beside me. Connor lifts his head and moves his arm forward to give Duncan a vulgar gesture. *I guess formalities are not a normal thing between them.* "I must apologize for my rudeness, Your Highness."

"No it's ok, trust me. Honestly, it's a breath of fresh air. I'm not a fan of the whole formality thing anyway, I've tried getting the others to drop it for years, but they wouldn't." I say waving off his apology.

He nods, "Well then, you will get no more bowing from me." Connor crosses his arms and stares at me as a small smile appears on his lips. He opens and closes his mouth a few times as if he is going to say something but at the last second, he changes his mind. He looks towards Duncan and shakes his head as if he knows what is going on. I stare at them both as they seem to be having their own telepathic conversation. There is a lot of weird facial expressions going on and unintentionally I get angrier with every passing minute.

"Bloody hell Connor speak, or should I call you Elder Snow?" I spit as I cross my arms mirroring his stance. *Well, that might take me a while to get my head around.* Connor whips his head in my direction as he gives me a definitive nod and grips his biceps nervously. *What is he so afraid to tell me?*

"Yeah, sorry, Snow is fine. There's just..." He pauses and flicks his eyes towards Duncan. "... there is so much I need to tell you and I'm just a little afraid of how you might take it. It's not going to be easy and a lot of it you won't understand straight away however, I beg that you try. And also, going by the look on your face, I am guessing there is a lot you want to ask me too. The only question now is, who goes first?" As the last word leaves his mouth he flicks his eyes back towards Duncan, who out of my peripheral vision nods his head in some sort of approval. *What is going on?*

"I think I want to hear your story first. It might, in the end, end up answering a lot of my questions anyway." I say as I look at both of them in turn, feeling a tad vulnerable.

"I'm guessing I don't need to be around to hear this. I am pretty sure I've heard it all before anyway." Duncan says as he shrugs his shoulders and begins backing up towards the stairs. "You know how to call me when you need me." He says without waiting for a reply and dashes up the stairs, moving out of sight. I stare in his wake for what feels like an eternity before I turn and gaze upon the man I thought I knew. He wears a grey three-piece suit with the gloves to match and I must admit, he does look pretty dashing. He is clean-shaven, which was rare for the Connor I once knew, and his hair looks like he actually brushed it. If only Flick could see the man before me now, I bet she would be begging at his feet for him to take her. Her tear-stained face enters my mind and I have to shake it away.

"Forgive me, Kyra, it was never my intention to deceive you. I wanted to keep you safe and being your boss was the best option I could come up with. I needed you to trust me enough so when the time came to show you the truth, you would actually believe me. I'm Duncan's elder, your supposed enemy but that doesn't mean I didn't want to protect you.

You have been lied to for a very long time and now I need to set the story straight. It may be a little hard for you to take at first, but I believe once you have all the information you seek, what needs to be done will be as clear as day. So, if you don't mind, follow me and we'll head into my office. It's just up here and I promise I'll show you everything." He begins moving to the left holding his arm out for me to take but I don't. *What does he mean by lied to? By whom? Duncan?*

Intrigued but also a little frightened, I keep my arms crossed and motion with my head as I say, "After you." Snow nods and takes off towards a bare wall. *Where is he going?* He places his hand flat against the brickwork and whispers something under his breath while a glowing green doorframe starts to take shape in front of him. It looks just like the one Duncan conjured earlier. Snow stands there as huge double doors swing wide open and waits a few seconds before entering the vast space.

Ceiling to floor windows line each wall and I notice that it is a gigantic sunroom, well it would be if it was actually sunny outside. There is a solid mahogany desk sitting in the centre of the room with a chair fit for a king on the other side. Snow's office almost smells as good as my garden back home, potted plants are scattered throughout the room giving off a relaxing vibe. To the right, near one of the grand windows lies a daybed, well more like one of those couches you would see when you visited a therapist. The cushions are a vibrant red and it's so inviting that I go over and rub my hand along its smooth texture.

"You can lie down here if you like, it would definitely make it easier for me if you are." Snow comes to stop beside his desk and I whip my head in his direction.

"What do you mean?" I ask confused.

"Oh, please forgive me, where are my manors. I'm a telepath. I have the ability to speak into your mind by using the electoral waves in the air. I also have the power to show you images and memories with skin-to-skin contact." He takes off his gloves and sets them on his desk beside him. "The story I have to share with you is better if you see rather than me telling it. For instance, my memories are more powerful than my words." He says as he raises his eyebrows and looks at the floor.

"Alright, I think I understand," I say cautiously while crossing my arms over my chest again as I begin to feel a little uneasy.

Snow gestures towards the couch and I sit down on the edge before lifting my legs and sliding back into a comfortable position. "This may feel a little funny at first but it won't hurt, I promise." He says while moving to the head of the couch. Kneeling down he places his fingers on both of my temples before whispering softly, "Let us begin, please close your eyes." I oblige and at first, all I see is blackness. Fuzziness begins to appear like the static you would see when you can't get the tv station to work. Then out of nowhere an image begins to appear before my eyes. It's Earth in prehistory, a time before man.

"For you to be able to understand what I'm about to tell you, I must start at the very beginning. Creation, the beginning of our time. Many millennia ago, Zagoria was formed out of the atoms of a dying world. When the planet exploded it split into two halves, the light and the dark, creating its own separate souls." I see a planet from far away, red flames are peering down upon it as green smoke rises up to meet it. It's creating the perfect world, a perfect life. Then all of a sudden, there is a gigantic boom and the planet splits horizontally. The two halves swirl around for a moment as they morph themselves into two little stars. One a fiery red and the other dark green.

"You see Kyra, you and Duncan are not actually soulmates, you are the two halves of the same soul. You are the atoms that exploded out of the dying star." The image changes again and I watch as the two little stars race off, circling around each other until they collide with Earth. Their combined forces resulting in an explosion that creates a new dimensional layer around the Earth. The purplish realm that is my home, my Zagoria.

"None of us know how we were created or why for that matter, only that we are here to help guide you back towards each other. The Elders and I have always assisted in your quest however, we have never achieved completion. Something always happens and we have to start a new. In the beginning, we believed that once you were whole every realm within the galaxy would be at peace, there was to be no more conflict, no disorder." The image changes to one of two people, a woman standing in armour very much like my own, her hair of fire blowing in the wind and her green eyes shining brightly in the sunlight. A man dressed in all black surrounded by green smoke holds her hand as they gaze upon each other. The Elders formed a ring around them and are bursting with joy. Within the crowd, I can see Snow, Willow, Fox and even Kit. They all seem so happy.

"When the first halves were found and before they were fully reunited, Willow came upon a book within this very library, the Book of Old. No one knows how it came to be. Scribes would appear within its pages overnight without a person writing them. Divinations that have never been known to us. The prophecy it revealed about the two souls uniting threatened our very existence. So, some of the Elders sought to destroy the book and the two halves of the soul." The image morphs into one of Darkness, the faces of some of the elders grow angry, especially Willows. She looks upon the lovers with hatred. "They tried to wipe it from history and hunted down and killed the Royals. They wanted to start anew, change and control our future. Afraid of what the new Royals would discover when reborn, they attacked the library. They wanted to make sure that the information contained within these walls was never found. With the book gone, you would only believe what they told you and never know the real truth about Zagoria. However, myself and some of the other elders didn't agree with them or completely believe what the book was revealing.

I played along with their deceit only to find out what they were planning and when I knew, I acted. In the middle of all the chaos and destruction, I used my abilities and led them to believe that they had destroyed the library. I wasn't able to prevent all the damage, however I managed to prevent total destruction and save our valuable history. Only Duncan and myself know that it still stands. And now you. This knowledge is vital to our survival and I'll be damned if I let them destroy it." Snippets of history flash before my eyes, the mates running for their lives. Elders killing them with blades I have never seen before. An old leather-bound book with scribbles and images flashing on the pages as someone flips through it. All the dates and documents from life itself. I watch as Willow leads the attack that destroys half the library, using a Princess's fire sword to burn the pages of books.

"Three hundred and forty-eight years ago, many of us rebelled against the other Elders. The council believed that the two Royals were getting too close and they wanted to put a stop to it before it was too late. We heard whispers of how and when they were going to do it, so a few of us rushed over to the Princess' house. We were at the end of the street when we saw Elder Kit kill Prince Kearney with his own blade and by the time we got to Princess Dawn, it was too late.

Snow shows an image of a dead man lying on the ground before he evaporates into a puff of green smoke. Then of him standing out the front of a little house, light creatures surrounding the property with their heads bowed in sorrow. Snow runs up the stairs and sees Willow standing over the body of a lifeless woman. *Dawn*. 'What have you done?' Snow exclaims as Willow turns to face him. 'I did what all of you were too afraid to do, I ended it before they ended us.'

We all knew that you would rise again at Willows' so I rushed over there with the intention of saving you both. I thought that once you were fully grown you could bond and finally end it all, just like we believe you're pre-destined too." The image morphs again to the parlour at Willows'. There are two cribs within the small room, Snow dashes to the closest one and takes the baby boy into his arms. He moves to the second crib as someone appears in the doorway. 'What are you doing Snow?' Willow cocks her head to the side.

'I'm getting them away from you, even if it kills me.' He leans over to grab the second baby as Willow takes a step forward.

'If you wanted to die, all you had to do was ask.' She withdraws a blade from her side, aims it at his neck and charges forward. Snow jumps to the right dodging her attack and yet gets close enough to place a light touch upon her forehead rendering her unconscious for only a few short seconds. He turns back to grab the other baby but hears yelling down the hall and realises he's out of time. If he wants to get out of this alive, he has to leave now and leave the Princess behind. Snow gives the sleeping baby one last glance before dashing out of the house forever.

"Over the years the prophecies revealed by the book have changed. It originally stated that you both had to bond and when you consummated the link, the great divine would come and Zagoria would cease. That has now changed drastically. The creatures of the dark didn't realise that by casting the ancient spell to possess Damon's body they commenced the beginning of the end. The prophecy now states,

'For a war that is centuries old,

There are two who must be bold,

For when the pool of the dead becomes unstable,

There are only two who are able,

To save the realms from a terrible fate,

Those two must mate,

And to protect us from it all,

They must sacrifice themselves and take the fall.'

So you see, there are those that believe your relationship means the downfall of us all. Your bond makes you strong, but it also puts an even bigger target on your back and now that you have bonded, the others will stop at nothing to make sure you do not fulfil the prophecy that they believe as true. There is an uprising happening and whether we like it or not, it's coming." Images of the book, the prophecy, all of it flashes before my eyes. The images move so quickly that I barely have a chance to really look at them before they change again.

Snow removes his hands from my head and steps back. "You may open your eyes now if you wish. I bet you still have lots of questions."

I sit up and begin to rub my temples as a small headache starts to form. As I open my eyes slowly, I try to blink away the fuzziness that is still present from Snow's gifts. Turning to face him I see that he is resting against his desk again with his arms crossed over his chest as he gazes at the floor. *Can I honestly believe all that he just showed me? Was it really real or just another trick? I think I'm going to have to give him the benefit of the doubt.*

"Willow really killed my predecessor?" I ask in disbelief, out of all the things I saw that is still the most unbelievable. I have known Willow my entire life and I cannot imagine her lifting a finger against anyone like that.

"Unfortunately yes, she was the one who refused to let you both live out your destiny's. She led the rebellion and everyone decided to follow her. She raised you to believe that you were all high and mighty, that you ruled over Zagoria but in truth, she does. Willow believes that if she keeps you both separated forever, it will stop the end from ever coming to pass, but she is terribly mistaken, they all are. Keeping you both apart may have stopped one end, but the future is always changing, it's never certain.

When Willow came all those years ago to destroy the library, she stole a book of ancient spells. The spells contained within the book are so powerful that if they are not executed properly, they tend to have grave consequences.

Roughly one hundred years ago, Willow gave the book to the Crawlers to gain information on Duncan's whereabouts however, she was tricked. They had no knowledge of where the Prince was. The Crawlers used the book to bring back their leader who was killed many years prior. The spell was supposed to calmly slide the soul out of the river and place it within their chosen host. Instead, it ripped it out, causing damage to the pool of the dead and slammed it into Damon's body. If you were to look at the torso of the body the soul possessed, you would have seen all the tear marks where the spirit entered.

So, in Willow's endless pursuit to find Duncan she practically doomed us all. Creatures are escaping out of the pool daily and they are always more vicious than the last. There are only so many that Duncan can control and the worst are still to come." He raises his eyes to mine and sorrow is written all over his face. I almost can't believe this is happening and I wouldn't if I hadn't seen it with my own eyes. I saw the Cerberus's and the Bubak's and it scares me to think what else might be out there lurking in the dark. There are definitely worse beings out there than them and if the pool is broken, Earth's residents are in for a world of pain. The Book of Old crosses my mind and the prophecy Snow showed me. *Are we really the only ones who can stop what's coming?*

I take a deep calming breath before I speak, "I want to see the book." I declare as I stand up and head towards the door without waiting for a reply. I glance over my shoulder at Snow and with a nod, he moves away from his desk and follows me out of the room. I stop just shy of the first stack, realising I have no idea where I'm going. Snow brushes past me and I follow suit.

We walk for about five minutes through the labyrinth that is the ground floor of this gigantic library to a small room hidden in the back. He produces a small key on a chain from around his neck, walks up to the door and unlocks it. He stands there in front of the closed door for a moment before turning around.

"Everything within this room is very old and highly breakable. The book is in the centre of the room at the back. I'll leave you to read it on your own and you can come find me when you're done." Without saying another word he begins walking back the way we came. I stare in his wake, feeling a little nervous about what I am about to encounter and take a deep breath. *I can do this*. Once I feel a little bit more stable, I walk up to the door and tentatively take the doorknob in my grasp. The metal is cool as I twist the handle and push the door wide open.

Huge statues of armed soldiers line the walls of a narrow walkway. Right at the very end of the room is a white lectern with the ancient leather-bound book from Snow's visions. As I make my way over to it, the smell of old leather and ink hits my nostrils and I inhale. *Oh, it smells amazing... I love this scent.* When I reach the book, I look down at the pages before me. The first one has two lovers, wrapped in a loving embrace before a glowing pit of green, the second page is the prophecy Snow told me about earlier.

Tentatively I reach for the book and decide I want to start from the very beginning. There is no wording on the cover nor on the spine however, there is the same swirl from the blanket Willow made me all those years ago and I run my fingers along it. Moving to the corner of the cover I flip the book open and in large letters it says, 'Book of Old' and below it 'Zagorian's History'. *Interesting.* I flip the first page over and I'm startled to see a photo of myself dressed in my armour. I'm posing for a photo that I can't ever recall being taken. My eyes look radiant on the page as they stare back up at me. 'Kyra Reynolds, Light Princess' is in cursive writing below my picture.

Shaking my head, I flip to the next page and sure enough there he is, my strikingly handsome mate, again posing in the same position I was in. His blacked-out suit looks pristine, and his hair is slicked back. His eyes also seem to glow against the darkness of the picture. Even in a photograph, he is devilishly handsome. 'Duncan Memphis, Dark Prince' lies beneath his photo and I have to turn the page again to stop myself from staring. I feel the tug towards him even now and I force myself to ignore it. *I need to find out why Willow wanted this book destroyed so badly.*

Chapter 10

I emerge from the little room with so much knowledge swirling around in my brain that I can barely comprehend it all. The book has everything, absolutely everything there is to ever know about Duncan and me. It has our addresses, our phone numbers and even our work details. It contains all the information about where our predecessor's lived, how they died and also who killed them. That was the most shocking information of all, as the previous Princesses were all killed by the same person, Willow.

This book contains all the vital information Willow needs to destroy us. *If she were to discover who Duncan really is then we would be... Wait, she would know that Duncan is the Dark Prince as my soul could not have joined with another.*

With that in mind, I sprint towards Snow's office and forgo a knock as I barge right in. He's sitting at his desk pondering over a map spread out before him when I basically yell at him. "Why hasn't she killed me yet?" Snow snaps his head up startled by my sudden intrusion.

"I don't really know, and it's been beginning to baffle me too. She never usually waits this long. As soon as you have both bonded she usually comes for you straight away, sometimes even before." He says as he begins to rub his chin like he's deep in thought.

"She already tried, multiple times actually." Duncan pipes in from the couch on the side of the room. As I turn my head to look at him, exhaustion hits me like a brick. He's lying down with his eyes closed and his arms folded across his chest. Desperately craving his touch, I make my way over and without saying a word, he makes room for me to sit down next to him. I'm almost in a comfortable position when Duncan raises his arm and wraps it around my shoulders pulling me closer. Electricity surges between us and we physically relax against each other as we let out a sigh.

Duncan moves his head to the side and gives me a kiss on my forehead before I tilt my face up to meet his. He opens his eyes and shoots a glance towards Snow while a cocky grin spreads out across his face. He leans forward and presses his lips down upon mine. As soon as our skin connects we are lost in the taste of each other. Duncan removes his arm from my shoulders and slides it behind my back pulling me closer. His other hand makes its way into my hair, and I am lost, tumbling deeper and deeper into the pull of him.

I lift my knee so it's resting across his legs and in one swift pull, I'm now straddling him. He tugs my face down to meet his and my hands cup his cheeks. Duncan yanks my head back with a rough tug of my hair and starts trailing kisses down the side of my neck. A little moan escapes my lips and Duncan returns his lips to mine as his fingers travel up my body to the clasp on the back of my armour. He begins to untie the buckle when I hear a little cough to my left. Ripping my mouth away from Duncan's I turn towards the noise. Snow is still sitting in his chair pondering over the map.

"If you both want to continue, I would highly recommend that you do it somewhere else." Duncan chuckles underneath me while I blush. I was so lost in my own euphoria that I totally forgot that he was still in here. Feeling a little embarrassed I move to stand but Duncan stops me with a hard grip on my waist.

I glance down and see all of his longing staring back at me. I see years of torment, weeks of wanting but always denying himself. I feel the silent question coming through the bond and I nod my head. *I am so ready for this.*

With me still sitting across him Duncan turns us and lets his legs flop to the floor. In one swift movement, he stands and I wrap my legs around his waist and my arms wrap around his shoulders as he tightens his grip on my ass. Duncan carries us towards the door and I lift my head just in time to see the smile on Snow's face as we make our way around the corner.

"Where are we going?" I breathe. I move my lips to his neck and kiss each and every one of his little freckles.

"You'll see." He utters as he begins to pick up the pace. We round a few corners and I feel him groan beneath me when all of sudden my back is pressed up hard against a cold stone wall. One of Duncan's hands moves away from my ass to raise my arms above my head. "Did you know that your kisses are absolutely torturous? They make me want to do so many naughty things to you, but I've been longing to have you on my bed, not the wall. So tell me, Kyra, how am I going to get us there if you continue?" Duncan breathes mere millimetres away from my lips and presses his body hard against me. He grabs my face with his broad hand and lowers his mouth down upon mine. His kisses are harsh and desperate as he forces my mouth open with his tongue. *Oh my...* My flame immediately ignites and I melt against him, needing to feel more.

Once Duncan has had his fill of my lips, he rests his forehead against mine. "Now, will you behave long enough for me to get us to my room?" He says just loud enough for me to hear and I nod. I don't think I'd be able to form words right now even if I tried. "Good girl." He places a chaste kiss upon my lips before moving us away from the wall and continues walking down the long passageway. Duncan takes a few twists and turns until he stops directly in front of what I can only presume is his bedroom door.

"Did you want to walk in, or would you like me to carry you?" He whispers sexually into my ear as a shiver runs down my spine.

"I want to see," I mutter under my breath and Duncan begins to lower my legs to the floor. My body slides against his making me feel alive and then he turns me around to face the massive double doors before us. He pulls me back so I am flush against him and places his hand upon the doorframe. I feel his lips moving next to my ear and yet I hear nothing. Green smoke begins to appear underneath his fingertips and from within the room, I hear the distinct click of the door being unlocked. The second he removes his hand the doors swing wide open.

At first glance, the room was not at all what I was expecting. Books piled almost to the ceiling, cover the whole wall to the left of the room and in the centre lies a large four-poster bed with luxurious black sheets. *Does he not take the books back once he has finished with them?* On the right-hand side stands a desk that is stacked to the brim with papers and to the far side of the room, there are these magnificent double glass doors that lead out to the forest beyond the library.

"It's not much but I call it home." He lowers his head and slowly starts placing sweet little pecks along my shoulder. With one arm wrapped around my waist, he pulls me even closer and with his free hand, he moves my hair out of the way giving him better access. I moan inwardly as he licks a ticklish spot at the base of my neck, and I feel him chuckle behind me. "I could get used to that sound." He breathes and I quickly spin around to face him, grabbing his face between my hands and pull him down to meet me. The taste of mint and fresh coffee hit my tongue and I almost turn into a puddle on the floor as I melt against him. Duncan pulls me closer, lifting my feet just off the ground and begins backing us up towards the bed. My legs hit the mattress and I fall back with Duncan collapsing on top of me.

Giggling like an idiot I manage to roll us over so I am once again sitting astride him. Leaning down, I take his face in my palms once again and kiss him with all the love and desire that's been building up in me. He rests the palms of his hands on my thighs and I almost combust from the sensation. Wanting to catch my breath, I move my face away from his and see his own desire staring back at me. Feeling a little nervous under his gaze, I decide I need to look anywhere else but at the man beneath me and turn my head towards the huge stack of books to my left. Duncan senses my anxiety and sits up, cupping my chin he forces me to return my eyes to his. "It's ok babe. I understand that this is your first time and I'm more than willing to take this slow." He sweeps a lock of hair over my shoulder and trails little kisses in its wake. I look down at him and begin to run my fingers through his unruly hair. I feel our celestial connection more now than ever and begin to believe all that I've learnt over the past twenty-four hours. Duncan lifts his head away from my shoulder and we peer into each other's eyes and I see the very same emotions that are tumbling through me.

"Ok," I whisper and yet I fear the fire within me doesn't want to go slow. Feeling a little brave, I climb off of Duncan and proceed to slide off the bed. I stand at the end, gazing at my mate as I begin to unclasp my armour. He looks at me with amazement as I then undo each clasp in turn and allow my corset to fall to the floor, exposing my perky breast to the chilli night air. He stares at me for a moment before moving himself to the edge of the bed. He lets his legs fall to the floor and then grabs my hips, pulling me closer. I feel his heated breath hitting my exposed skin and I cannot help the shiver that runs through me. I gaze down at him and bite my lower lip as he yanks me forward so I am once again astride him. He slides me forward so my apex is resting against his growth and inhale at the thought of what's coming.

"You're so beautiful. You truly are a great wonder of this world. Although I'll have you know, this isn't what I had in mind when I said we would take it slow." He stares at my bare chest with passion and longing as his fingers create small circles on the back of my hips. *Obviously, there is something else he wants to be doing with his hands.*

"I know." I breathe as I put a hand on the back of his head and move his face closer to me. *I want to feel him...* Understanding my need, Duncan removes one of his hands from my hips and cups my breast before taking my nipple into his mouth. I throw my head back in ecstasy as the feeling completely overwhelms me. He sucks and licks the tender nub which is doing wonderous things to my libido. Without thinking I begin to rock my hips back and forth, trying to gain friction through the heavy material between my legs. *Oh, why do I still have the rest of my armour on?*

"You really don't know what slow means do you?" He chuckles in between licks while his other hand helps me move against him. Fire builds in the pit of my stomach and I feel my body shaking.

Duncan blows a cool breeze onto my hot flesh and then takes my nipple into his mouth once more when I finally hit my peak. A loud moan escapes my lips as I tumble endlessly through an overwhelming sensation that racks my entire body. Duncan continues his sweet assault on my nub until I am completely overcome and relax my body against his. "I honestly feel honoured that I get to witness you doing that. You really are a goddess." He kisses me on the forehead before letting me lie down next to him.

"Thank you," I whisper nervously as I stare up at the ceiling and Duncan chuckles beside me. He jumps off the bed and stands at my feet removing my boots before kicking off his own. He stares at me for a moment before placing his hands upon my shins and spreads my legs apart. I can't help but giggle as he climbs up between them and gazes down at me with a wicked grin on his face.

"Oh, don't thank me yet babe, the best part is yet to come." He says playfully as he points down at himself and then reaches back to remove his shirt. As quick as lightning the material is gone and he lies down on top of me.

"You're such a tease you know that." I smile while shaking my head. Lifting my weak arms, I wrap them around his shoulders and bring his face mere inches away from mine.

"Yeah I know, but I have to make you smile somehow don't I?" He declares grinning like the Cheshire cat.

"Just shut up and kiss me," I demand pulling him towards me.

"Oh, I plan to." He leans down and takes my mouth in a feverish kiss. We are lost in the bond that binds us. The soul that has been searching a lifetime to find its other half. I feel like I'm flying on a cloud and will never come back down.

I move my hand down to the buckle on his pants and begin to slide the leather through the strap. Duncan removes his mouth from mine to look down between us and after a few awkward manoeuvres, I manage to get his pants undone just enough to push them down, springing him free. We both stare at him for a moment and I bite my lip again as Duncan raises his eyes.

"I don't think I want to go slow anymore," I whisper close to his mouth and move my fingers into his hair. *It's so silky...*

"Were we ever going slow?" He jokes as he moves his lips to trail kisses along my cheek.

"I don't think so." I lift a leg and wrap it around his back and realise I still have my armour on. *Bugger!*

"Me either." He stops and takes a deep breath as he pushes back to glance down between us again. "Are you really sure about this? Don't get me wrong, making love to you is all I can think about lately, but you've read the book. You know there is no going back once we begin."

"I'm aware." Is all I say as I pull his face down to meet mine and we finally let ourselves be free. After what feels like forever, Duncan reaches down and begins to slide the bottom half off my armour down my legs. He pushes back to slide them over my feet and I sit up with him, not wanting to break the kiss. The second the fabric is off he's lying back on top of me and I wrap my legs around his back. We draw each other closer as we tumble and turn fighting for top position. My shins hit the mattress when I come to stop on top of him and Duncan's hands make their way into my hair. He yanks my head back and starts trailing kisses down the side of my neck. A loud moan escapes my lips as lights begin to flash behind my eyes. It feels like I'm in my body but somehow not. Like I'm a balloon above the surface watching the action unfold below. Everything is happening so fast and yet I don't want it to stop.

Duncan growls beneath me as he wraps an arm around my back and lifts me off him just enough to position himself beneath me. In one swift move, he enters my body and I throw my head back in agony as pain shoots through my entire abdomen. Duncan stills and places a sweet kiss upon my left shoulder while he waits for me to adjust. When the pain begins to subside, I lift my body ever so slightly off of him and then gently back down again. I set myself into a rhythm while Duncan moves his hands to grab a hold of my hips. "That's it baby. You're doing it." He breathes as he watches himself slide in and out of me.

His sweet words set me on fire and I feel my core temperature rising. I start to rock my hips even faster as his breaths become heavier. Duncan's grip on my hips tightens as he helps me keep time. He falls back against the mattress as the sensation intensifies. *OMG, I'm coming...*

My body begins to shake, and it feels like I'm about to explode but I can also sense Duncan moving me faster as his own climax builds.

Sweat lines my brow and I let out a cry of ecstasy as my orgasm racks my body. Duncan roars and stills beneath me while light shoots from my being illuminating the entire room. I fall forward and rest my head against Duncan's chest. All our built-up passion and conflicting emotions about who and what we truly are is over. We are now able to do exactly what we were created to do as our soul has finally become whole once more.

Chapter 11

Hours later I'm sitting on the edge of Duncan's bed, wrapped in nothing but his beautiful black silk sheets. I'm staring at the gigantic wall of books, contemplating how much knowledge I missed out on. How many stories, worlds that I'll never get the chance to explore, histories that will end up being forgotten. *It's sad really, if only we had more time.*

We spent hours making love to each other until we both physically couldn't do it anymore. Duncan left a while ago to fetch us some food and I have just been sitting here ever since. There are so many questions I need answered, so many more truths that need to come to light and my head is just a jumbled mess right now.

"Refreshments for my lady." Duncan declares while he saunters into the room. He's wearing nothing but his briefs as he carries a huge plate of food in one hand and a bottle of water in the other. He's grinning from ear to ear as he walks closer to me and I only glance in his direction before turning my head back to the wall. *How am I going to ask this question without it sounding rude?*

"What's wrong?" He asks as he places the tray of food on the bed beside me and hands me the bottle of water.

"Thanks," I say as I accept the bottle and take a much-needed sip. The water is pure gold as it slides down my throat and I let out a tiny ah when I finish off the last drop. A small droplet spills from the side of my mouth and I wipe it away with the side of my finger.

"If I had known you were that thirsty, I would have grabbed two bottles. Do you need more? I can go grab another one?" He asks but I shake my head. Turning my gaze towards him I look down between us and see a tray of fruits laid out before me. Reaching forward I grab a handful of grapes and pop one into my mouth. I raise my eyes to his and summon all my courage to ask him the one question that's been pissing me off since the moment I learnt the truth.

"Why did you go out with Flick if you knew who I was this whole time?" I stare at him as my anger slightly spikes. *After everything I have recently discovered this one thing still baffles me.* He told me that he used to stare at my statue a lot while growing up, so he knew exactly what I looked like before we even met. *And yet he still dated her.*

"Ah, I wondered when that was going to come up." He rakes his hands through his hair and then rubs his palms hard against his face. I see him take a deep breath before he comes around to the end of the bed and takes a seat beside me. "You have to know that I never wanted to ruin your friendship. I wanted to connect with you long before everything happened with Flick but Snow wanted me to wait. He believed that if I was to rush you before you were ready it could have caused unfathomable issues within both our realms. You knew nothing of the truth, only the lies that Willow spun and that made you dangerous. So, I did what I was told, I waited and watched you from afar.

I could feel you as soon as you entered the site every day, I was drawn to you long before we even bonded. I knew the prophecy and of our future together but I promised to stay away. It nearly killed me every time I saw you and I had to physically restrain myself from you.

Although, a couple of weeks ago you came to work in this beautiful gold dress, and you looked absolutely radiant. Your blonde hair was shining in the sunlight and you looked so happy as you spoke to Brice in the yard. I couldn't help but stop and stare. My beautiful Princess was shining like the sun for all to see. You are the most magnificent being I have ever seen and I was about to say screw it and walk over when Flick approached.

Mentally, I thanked her for saving me from Snow's wrath but hated the fact that I was standing there talking to her instead of you. She went on for ages talking about her interests and about this little Italian restaurant she had been dying to go to. The whole time though I couldn't take my eyes away from you. I vaguely remember her asking me out and I stupidly said yes. I remember staring at you over her shoulder and saying that I had been meaning to ask her out for some time now too, I just didn't know how.

I told Snow about my predicament later and he said it was a great idea because of how close you two were. From the beginning, I thought it was unwise, yet I went along with it anyway. I really didn't mean to hurt her or you for that matter, it just happened, you know." He says with his elbows resting upon his knees and his head in his hands. Duncan lets out a sigh and lays back against the bed. "I wanted to tell you about this ages ago, but again Snow didn't think it was wise." Even after all he has said fire still flares beneath my skin. *How could they be so stupid? Did they really not think about the consequences?*

"So, you're telling me that Flick was only a pawn in your game to get to me. You used her and, in the end, we were the ones who got burnt. Thanks for that." Arrayed I stand, grabbing my clothes off of the floor and turn to storm out the room. Duncan rushes past me and blocks my path towards the door. I'm so pissed and right now I want to be anywhere else but near him. Uncontrollably my tears begin to rain down my cheeks as I can't contain my hurt any longer.

"Kyra, please understand, we never meant for that to happen. I agreed to date Flick with the intention to end it all before anything were to happen with us, but then I met you. Remember that day near the entrance when you stuck your hand out to me. What was I supposed to do, say no? You have to understand babe, I've been dying to meet you my whole life." I snap my head up at that. *How dare he!*

"So that excuses you for the things you did? You could have rejected my hand, Duncan. Yes, it would have looked weird as hell but still, you could have said no. Because of your own wants and needs, you hurt her. I hurt her and we can never take that back." Suddenly everything becomes so overwhelming. Needing a moment to myself I push past him and begin to run to god knows where. I reach the dead end of a passageway and let out a blood-curdling scream as I fall to my knees. I'm crying not only for my friend but for all the fabrications I've been led to believe from the moment I was reborn. My whole life has been a lie and I can't comprehend what is real and what is not anymore.

I sit there for ages, wallowing in my own anguish and don't recall the moment Duncan came to find me. He took me back to his room and allowed me to sleep off my hurt. For a man who is supposed to be all dark and scary, he is more gentle than I could have ever imagined. Sometime later, he comes back in and I am once again staring at the wall of books. I feel his curiosity surrounding my obsession, but I don't avert my gaze.

"Do you want me to leave?" He asks from the doorway and I glance in his direction. He's fully dressed and is holding another bottle of water. I reach my hand out towards him in a silent demand and he walks over, handing me the bottle. Once I have the water in my grasp, I unscrew the lid and take a giant gulp. "I am sorry, you know, we never meant for that to happen." I just nod. *Part of me does believe him but I'm honestly just not ready to accept it.* "Is there anything else you want to know?" He asks while coming to sit beside me on the bed. He's back in his Zagorian form and no longer looks like the Dark Prince I met in my lounge room and yet I'm shinning like a damn light bulb.

"How are you able to hide your true form?" I put the cap back on the bottle and hand it back to him. I'm careful where I place my hands as I don't want to touch him right now. *Zagoria knows if I do I will never get the answers I seek.*

"Many millennia ago, Snow found an incredible book of spells. This spell book was not like the one that Willow stole, it's even more dangerous. Within its pages, Snow found a ritual that can hide our appearances from all of Zagoria. All we needed was ink, a gemstone and blood to be able to bind it to us." Duncan rolls up his sleeve on his right arm, exposing a tattoo on the inside of his wrist. It's a blue and purple swirl like the one from the Book of Old and at the very centre is a tiny blue sapphire. "I can turn my appearance on and off by casting my own personal ritual. Watch…"

He closes his eyes and drops his voice into a hushed whisper. "Darkness comes and darkness falls. Let the veil hide it all. For the light may come too late. To save this world from its terrible fate." Green smoke thickens around us and I watch on in amazement as his whole persona changes. His messy hair is gone, replaced by tidy and sleek, while his clothes have become as black as the night. He opens his eyes as his transformation ends and all I see is the true blackness that lies within. "This is me, your

Dark Prince. I was really worried in the beginning of what you would do if you knew who I was. Christ, the last time I showed you, even after we bonded, you still tried to kill me. Thankfully you stopped or we would have both been goners" He gives me a sexy smirk and I blush as a smile spreads out across my lips.

"Yeah, sorry about that... But did you agree to bind this spell to yourself because of me? Because you felt like you couldn't trust me." Feeling a tad vulnerable I turn back to the books. *I can completely understand if he did, I wouldn't have trusted me either, especially with what I was led to believe.*

"Yes and no. When Snow took me from the parlour all those years ago, he kept me hidden here. He taught me this spell and warned me how it would affect those around me. He said that they would not be able to identify my true form and may only be able to sense me from time to time.

At first, I thought it was great, being able to go out and do my own thing without being detected by Willow or the others, but it does have its consequences. For instance, under the veil, the dark minions only see me as a commoner and not as their leader. It was a choice I made and now I'm trying to rectify it."

"That was why they attacked you at my house, wasn't it? They don't know the Duncan side of you, only this." I gesture towards him as he nods. "Does Snow have the spell inked on him too?" I ask as he nods again. "Wouldn't Willow know who he is though? I mean, they've spoken together on the phone a few times when she called in sick for me." I think back to the last time she called in and a shiver runs down my spine. I quickly glance down at my right bicep and remember the pain as the Cerberus's teeth ripped through my flesh.

"Ah, I don't think so, he probably changed his voice or something like that because if she was onto him, he would know it." And now it's my turn to nod. *He's probably right.*

We sit there together in complete silence for a few minutes staring at the stacks. The only noise I can hear is the sound of our breathing. "Do you want to read one?" Breaking my thoughts I snap my head in his direction.

"What?" I ask in confusion.

"The books, you keep staring at them, did you want to read one?" He points at the stacks and I blush. *Of course, he noticed me staring.*

"No, I'm good, thank you. I'm just trying to work my head around everything I've learnt these past few days and if I'm being honest, I find your wall extremely fascinating. I have never seen so much knowledge in one place like this before. Have you read them all? Or did you just bring them in here to make a statement?" I ask as I try to read the names on the spines. Duncan chuckles beside me and starts to speak.

"I had a lot of free time for the first 11 years. Snow taught me a lot, but I got most of my training from the pages you see before you." He looks down at my hand that is positioned between us and then back up at my face. "I really am sorry for everything. I wish you'd found out the truth long before now. As a matter of fact, we have been searching for you for many years and every time we thought we had you, you were gone again. It was frustrating as fuck." *They were looking for me?* I turn my gaze to the man sitting beside me. Green smoke swirls around us as he's still in his true form and I'm momentarily stunned by the beauty of his darkness. I am as bright as the sun and he is as dark as the night but together we are complete.

I'm still not one hundred percent used to the feeling he instils in me, it's so foreign, yet not. The more I look at my other half, the more I want to hold him and never let go.

"That doesn't make any sense though, I was always looking for you. Every time Willow and the team believed you moved, so did we. They told me that we were chasing you, however now that I think about it, maybe it was the other way around." *Another lie, no shocker there.* He was chasing me and even if he was hidden from her, she may have sensed an anomaly getting close and moved us before it could find us. *That suddenly makes sense!* "Wait a second... Back in Snow's office, you said that Willow has already tried to kill me, what did you mean by that?" I turn my head towards him and grab an apple off the tray he brought in early. Duncan looks at me wide eyed for a moment before letting out a sign.

"Do you remember when I told you that my minions don't listen to me," He pauses, and I mouth the word 'yes'.

"Well, I wasn't lying. This lifetime it's been hard for me to gain their respect and loyalty because I have spent most of my time in hiding. Willow though, has spent centuries twisting them for her own personal gain. The Cerberus attack, the Crawlers, The Bubak and all the creatures showing up at your home, that was all her. I never had a hand in any of it.

I tried to disperse the Cerberus's before you guys got there, but they wouldn't budge. I helped you battle the Crawlers because if I'm being honest, the order would never have made it out of there alive without your boosted powers. We took down the Bubak together and I broke my facade to scare the beasts enough to leave your home. Not once in my lifetime have I sent them after you, that was all Willow.

For the life of us, Snow and I can't figure out why she hasn't come for you herself, but it's only a matter of time." Duncan reaches for my hand and as his fingers brush against mine, a whole new rush ignites. My body instantly craves that release that only Duncan can provide and I don't know who moves first. Suddenly, we are a tangled mess of limbs as we try to pry each other's clothes off. Our lips crash together, and we are lost in a downward spiral that is our soul. He pulls me on top of him as he rips my armour and moves his mouth south to connect with my breast. I let myself moan loudly while fireworks shoot through my veins as the sensation within me intensifies.

I quickly rock my hips against his growing length while Duncan nips my tender nub making me yelp. More moans escape me as Duncan growls beneath me and pulls his mouth away from my chest. He rolls us over and before I know it, our soul is lighting up the room once more.

Chapter 12

A loud snort wakes me up hours later and I turn my head to look at the perfect being lying next to me. He has such flawless features and an amazing body. I can't believe he is all mine, but for how long. *How long do we have until it all must come to an end?* I can feel it even now, the pull towards my mate but also the pull towards something else, something broken. Its tugging is increasing and I don't know how long we will be able to avoid it.

I sit up slowly and slide out of bed while I look around for my clothes but I don't see them anywhere. I find Duncan's long black shirt and his briefs lying on the floor in the corner of the room and decide to put them on. *I'll have to find more clothes later.*

The stone floor is cold against my feet as I walk through the corridor and back into the main lobby of the library. I need to do anything I can to take my mind off of the naked man lying in bed. The pull towards him is so powerful now that we have consummated the bond and I'm finding it hard to stay away.

Light's streaming in from the windows high above and I rush to stand in its rays. Warmth invades my skin and I feel my power recharging. I throw my head back and bask in the glory of the light. I must have been down here in the darkness for far longer than I thought because I feel so refreshed after a mere few seconds. I gaze up at my old friend and feel her power surge but somethings different. *What's happening out there?*

"I was wondering when you would both emerge." I jump and turn towards the noise. Snow is lounging in an armchair to the right of the staircase with a book resting upon his lap. I must have been so distracted by the light that I didn't even notice him sitting there.

"Shit, you scared me," I exclaim placing my hand over my erratically beating heart.

"My apologies, I didn't mean to do that. I thought you saw me when you came in. My mistake." He utters as he closes the book in front of him and stands up. Snow walks over to the closest rack and places the book back carefully on the shelf. I glance around at the stacks next to me and notice there are so many gaps within the hoards. *I wonder...* I think as I flick my eyes back down the hallway towards Duncan's room. "To answer your question, yes, they are all in there."

"Pardon? I didn't say anything." I cross my arms over my chest feeling a little exposed. *How did he know I was going to ask that?*

"Sorry I didn't mean to pry." Snow declares as he taps the side of his temple. He racks his eyes over the stack in front of him before turning around and leaning back against it. He doesn't raise his eyes to mine but seems to just stare at the floor. *Why is he acting so strange?*

"You said before that you were wondering when we would come out, does that mean you've been waiting for us?" I glance down at my attire feeling a little underdressed and begin to lower my hands covering the front of my legs. *I should have grabbed a pair of pants too.*

"Yes, there are some things we must discuss. Especially now that you have fully bonded." He raises his eyes this time and I blush. *Oh, this is embarrassing.*

"Alrighty then, should I go back and wake Duncan up?" I ask as I start backing up towards the hallway. Honestly, I just want to go and hide under a rock.

"No need, I'm already up." Duncan's deep drawl resonates from behind me as he strolls into the room. He walks straight past me and right up to the chair Snow vacated early. I may have thought that I was underdressed, however he is so much more. All Duncan's wearing is a pair of pants and I have a feeling that he doesn't have anything on underneath which makes me turn a deeper shade of red.

Duncan glances in my direction, giving me a devilish smile as he winks before turning his attention back to

Snow. "Spill it old man." He requests as he slouches back in the chair.

"Watch your tone. I may be old boy, but I could still whip you." My eyes go wide as I jerk my head back. *He wouldn't!* Sensing my horror Snow raises his hands and turns to me. "I'm sorry, it's an old joke between us." Duncan covers his mouth, unsuccessfully trying to hide his amusement. Snow gives him a sideways glance and raises his middle finger. He takes a few deep breaths before addressing me once more. "I may not know what is to come, because this is new to all of us. However, I know for certain that Willow will be on the hunt for you now more than ever."

I glance over at Duncan for a moment and see concern flooding his features while he stares at the floor deep in thought. Feeling my eyes upon him, he looks up and our soul connects. His face instantly relaxes back to reflect his no care attitude but I can see right through it. He's scared. He's frightened for our future and he is not the only one. I tear my gaze away and look back at Snow. "What's changed?"

"The moment you consummated the bond, all residing in Zagoria would have felt its effects. There was what I can only describe as an earthquake type of event, that lasted for about a minute. Willow and the rest of the elders will now know that something has changed and they will do everything they can to try and stop it." Snow says with more seriousness than I've ever seen in my life.

"An earthquake?" I ask in disbelief as my hand flies to my mouth. My head flicks between Duncan and Snow as I try to reel in my thoughts. *The whole damn realm knows that I just lost my virginity.* That thought alone makes me turn a bright shade of red. *This cannot be happening.* Shaking my head I put my head in my hands. *I want to disappear; I want the floor to open up and swallow me whole.*

"Fuck yeah. I thought the bed was just shaking because of me." I look up at him in surprise. *Is he seriously making a joke out of this situation?* Duncan's smiling from ear to ear as he looks at Snow who's giving him a disapproving look.

"No, not fuck yeah Duncan. This is serious business. Natural disasters like that don't happen here in our realm. You know this." Snow voices seriously towards Duncan and then turns his eyes back to me. "I know this idiot already told you about the ritual, so I'll let you know now that I have a spare sapphire if you wish to use it. It will not hide you from Willow as she already knows your human form, but it will hide you from the rest of Zagoria. They will be on the hunt for your glow and won't notice the blonde girl quickly walking past them." He says as a look of determination crosses his face. Even if it doesn't hide me from Willow, using the spell might be our only chance to get to where we need to go without being seen.

"Thanks, I really appreciate it." I glance between the two men before me and decide to settle on Snow. "So, when can we begin?" *The quicker we get this done, the quicker we can find out where the secondary pull is coming from.*

"Now if you like..." Snow moves away from the stack and starts walking in the direction of his office only to stop mid-step and turns around to face me. "... Maybe you'd like to have a shower first and perhaps a fresh change of clothes. I have some stored away for you, just a minute, I'll be right back." He quickly runs off down the hall and I turn my head to Duncan.

"Why does he have clothes for me?" I ask a little dumbfounded.

"He always hoped you would come here. We tried many times over the years to retrieve you and one time we were almost one hundred percent sure that we found you. I discovered your armour hanging up in a property Willow owned in Kenya. Snow wasn't with me at the time, so I took it off the rack and brought it back to our base to show him. It was the proof we needed to storm the place.

I had every intention of returning the armour, however the next day when we went back to Willow's, you were gone. It felt like you were always one step ahead. Every time we thought we'd found your house, it was vacant or even an empty lot by the time we got there. Like the house or compound was totally hidden from us or something. After some time though we realised that Willow was onto us and there was nothing we could do but follow you to your next destination." *Kenya? That was nearly two hundred years ago and what does he mean by my house was hidden?*

My beautiful flowers come to mind, and I'm stumped by the revelation. *My peonies.* I was told that they stop the beings from congregating around my property but maybe they were created for a whole different purpose. Before I have the chance to reply, Snow comes speeding back into the hall with my armour in his hands.

"Here you are, they should still fit you." He says and I graciously take them from him.

"Thank you," I turn to leave but realise I have no idea where I am going. "Third door on the right." Snow calls over my shoulder and I nod my thanks again as Duncan jumps to his feet.

"I'll join you." He declares and I glance over my shoulder to see his cocky grin has returned. I can't help but smile. *If he joins me though, I know for a fact that we will not be showering.*

"You will do no such thing, let the poor girl have some peace. Plus, you are in desperate need of a shower too, I can smell you from here. Why not take this chance to have a moment to yourself? Zagoria knows it may be your last." Snow says while he crosses his arms over his chest trying to stare Duncan down. Duncan raises his finger to Snow and chuckles while walking over to me.

I'm rooted in my spot, unable to decide if I should let Duncan join me or go ahead alone. We stare into each other eyes as he comes to a stop in front of me and leans down to kiss me on the forehead. All my muscles freeze as I'm momentarily suspended in time. The bond is pulling me forward and yet I'm doing everything I can to fight against its urges. "Don't even think about it." Snow demands as he stands off to the side. Duncan being stronger than I, moves his lips away from my skin. He looks down into my eyes again and smirks before glancing over at Snow.

"I already thought about it." He says as he reaches out for my hand and I take it gently as I let my mate lead us back towards his room. We make it about twenty feet down the hallway before he spins me around and slams my back up against the wall.

"OUCH! What was that for?" I cry breathlessly as the impact takes my breath away. As the last word leaves my lips Duncan smothers my mouth with his, greedily taking what I'm not ready to give. I try to push him away but can't. Feeling my unwillingness, he pushes his body harder against mine and crushes me against the stone wall. I try to tear my mouth away from his but it's fruitful. I push his face and pull his hair, gaining myself just enough time to scream the word "STOP!", but he doesn't listen. The second before Duncan forces his mouth back upon mine I catch a glimpse of his eyes. They are as black as the night even though he's still in his human form. *What the...*

His lips are fast and harsh as he raises my feet off the ground and begins groping me through my shirt. I try to kick him away but my legs are pinned, I feel powerless against his onslaught. White shadows creep into my line of vision while I scream as if my life depends on it. I cry down the bond begging him to listen but there is nothing, it feels as if my Duncan is no longer there.

Cold air hits my body at the same moment Duncan is ripped away from me. My feet land on the ground hard and I scream as pain shoots up my legs. After a quick moment to regain my balance, I look up to see what's happening. On the floor a few feet away Duncan and Snow are brawling, their arms and legs are flying everywhere. Duncan manages to get the upper hand and punches Snow in the side of the face. His head snaps to the left as blood shoots from his mouth and he falls hard against the stone pavers. I go to rush over but stop as I see Duncan lean forward and grab him again. "NO DUNCAN, STOP!" I scream while Snow thrusts out his palm, hitting Duncan in the middle of the forehead. The second my mate hits the ground unconscious I rush over to them.

"Are you ok?" I ask checking him out, he will have a nasty bruise on his face but otherwise, he looks like he will be alright.

"Me yes, but him..." he tosses a thumb in Duncan's direction. "... I saw a glimpse into his mind, there was no light present only darkness. Not once in Duncan's existence have I ever seen something like that. I'm afraid it may have something to do with the bond, but I can't be certain. Whatever it was though, it wasn't him." Snow declares while looking at the sleeping man beside me and I pray to Zagoria that he will be ok.

"What should we do?" I ask as I run my fingers through Duncan's hair. I feel our power surging and hope that it will be enough to bring him back to me.

"Nothing at the moment, I think it would be wise if you go have your shower and let me figure it out." Snow utters as he moves himself into a sitting position next to me and stares down at Duncan, deep in thought.

"Are you sure?" I flick my eyes between the two of them, not really ready to leave them yet. If this is something to do with the bond it could eventually happen to me too. A shiver runs down my spine at the thought.

"Yes, we need you ready to go as soon as possible. Things are beginning to change and I am afraid of what that change may bring." Snow moves his hands and places them on either side of Duncan's head. I should have left and had my shower. I could've looked away and let him concentrate on his job, but I didn't. And that's when I witnessed Snow's eyes turn black as he focused on the body in front of him.

Chapter 13

Staring at my reflection in the foggy mirror I notice the flames upon my head have all but gone out. Bruises are beginning to show on my hips from the pressure Duncan used to keep me pinned to the wall and my eyes are all sunken in. I look like I haven't had nourishment in weeks. *What's going on? Isn't Duncan's touch supposed to make me feel more alive? So why do I look like death warmed up?* I peer down to my left and gaze upon the armour sitting on the chair that Snow retrieved for me earlier.

Duncan said he stole it from Willow's place in Kenya, but I don't recall Willow ever coming to Africa. *Everything is so confusing.* Especially Duncan, one minute he is my enemy and then the next, my lover. He's sweet and caring but he also has this darker side to him. Snow said when he gazed into his mind that the Duncan we know was gone, only his darkness remained. *I wonder what that means.*

Shaking my head, I look back at myself in the mirror and bring forth images of the woman I love more than life itself. *Can she really be trying to kill me?* Above all the things I've learnt, this is the one I'm finding the hardest to believe, even though I saw the writings in the Book of Old myself. Willow killed so many of us just to keep this world alive because she believed the original prophecy and wanted to stop us from ever achieving our destiny. I understand that she doesn't want to die however, she was created to lead us onto the path to find one another, not tear us apart.

I huff out a sigh as I rest my hands on either side of the sink and hang my head. I have so many confusing emotions within me that I feel like I'm going to explode. I have the weight of the realms resting upon my shoulders and there is nothing I can do to stop my unease. However, it's not just my weight to bear, it's Duncan's too. We are the only ones in existence who can restore the balance in both realms, bringing peace to all of humanity. With that thought in mind, I raise my eyes and look at myself in the mirror once more. *I can do this! I am Kyra, The Princess of Light and no one is more powerful than me.*

I emerge from the bathroom sometime later to see Snow leaning against the opposite wall staring down the hallway towards Duncan's room. Following his gaze, I see nothing but the darkness.

"How is he?" I ask as I cautiously step out of the bathroom and shut the door behind me. Tentatively, I lean back against it as I cross one foot over the other and fold my arms over my chest. I may look relaxed however I am anything but. What happened before with Duncan really scared me and I will not let it happen again.

"Honestly, I cannot say, I have never seen anything like that before. I hope he wakes to be his normal self but if he..." Anxiety floods his features and I force myself to look away. Snow cares for Duncan like he is his own son. Affection radiates off of him in waves when they are together and to see Duncan in that state would be heartbreaking for him. As he stands before me now with his arms crossed over his chest he may look relaxed, however he is anything but. Snow is ready to strike at any given moment if the danger were to present itself. Gone is the man I saw every day on the construction site, this man is an impeccable warrior that will stop at nothing to keep us safe.

"Were you guarding the room the entire time?" I ask quietly as I glance down the hallway once more and then back at Snow. He just nods his head not wanting to take his eyes off the passageway.

"If he is still not his normal self, I didn't want him to catch you off guard. It was hard enough witnessing what I saw before, and it scares me to think of what may have happened if I didn't hear you scream." He tears his gaze away from the corridor to look at me and this time it's my turn to nod. I feel conflicted about the whole situation, my body is being pulled in Duncan's direction and yet, after what just occurred, I don't want to go anywhere near him. Sensing Snow's eyes and the need to change the subject, I motion with my hand towards the grand library. *I need to put some distance between me and the man down the hall.*

"Thank you again for that by the way, I really appreciate it. Do you think while we wait that we can do the ritual for the appearance spell?" I ask although Snow doesn't reply. He just takes one final look down the hallway and then pushes off of the wall, following me into the library. Out of the corner of my eye, I see him peering over his shoulder multiple times as we make our way back into the main foyer. We pass the giant statue of myself and I am still amazed at how accurate it is. My flames are dancing high above my head and my armour seems to shine like the sun even though it's made of stone.

"No need to thank me Kyra," Snow pipes in after a while. "I would do it again in a heartbeat. Duncan is going to hate himself when he comes too, well that's if he recollects what happened and if he doesn't, he will hate himself even more because he almost hurt you and doesn't even remember it." Snow brushes past me and I follow him into his office. He walks over to his lavish desk in the centre of the room and stops in front of the chair closest to us. He pulls it out and waits for me to sit down before making his way over to the other side of the desk. "I will conduct the tattoo ritual first and then surgically implant the stone. I'm not going to lie, this is going to sting a little." From a drawer beside him, he pulls out a tattoo gun, a cloth and some pots for ink. "I would recommend the wrist but if you wish to get it somewhere else, tell me now." He doesn't even look up while he sets up. He grabs a new needle out of the drawer and carefully inserts it into the gun. He fills the four pots in front of him with white, blue, purple and black liquid. He then grabs a bottle of disinfectant and places it next to the clean cloth.

"The wrist is fine," I say as I stroke the bare skin on the inside of my right wrist. Soon it will have the same swirl that Duncan has on his.

Snow is in a flurry of movement as he gets everything ready and makes sure all the equipment is clean.

"Alright, you ready?" He asks and I nod my head. *Here we go.* "We need to do this quickly, but we also need to do it right. Once the ritual begins I cannot stop until the stone has been set, do you understand?" I whisper the word yes and place my right arm on the desk. Snow grabs a pair of black gloves from the drawer, puts them on and then wipes the skin clean on the inside of my wrist. Picking up the gun, he tests it and the sound of buzzing bees fills the room. Leaning forward Snow grabs my wrist as he glances up at me. "Let's begin." He declares as he sinks the needle into a pot of black ink. Raising the gun the bees come to life as he slowly lowers the needle onto my skin.

It feels like he's running a fine needle along an extremely bad sunburn. It's definitely not a pleasant experience and yet it's vital for my survival.

Two hours have passed and the swirl is now complete. "For this next part, I must make an incision in the centre of the swirl, at this point you may or may not feel it. I am only warning you, so you don't flinch." With my head rested against the table I move it up and down letting him know that I understand. I feel pressure against my wrist as the burning intensifies and I inhale sharply. "Do not move!" Snow barks sharply and I will my body into stillness. I feel him moving something back and forth within the middle of my wrist and I grind my teeth to stop myself from screaming. *Fuck!* I have dealt with a lot of pain throughout my life, but this is insane. *Ouch!* I have been bitten, sliced, stabbed and still, nothing comes close to the pain I am in right now.

Just when I think I cannot take it anymore; Snow lets go of my wrist and instantly the pain disappears. *What the...* "All done, the ritual is now complete, to activate it all you need to do is cast your own personal chant." He says as he turns around and immediately begins cleaning up as I stare down at my wrist. It's the beautiful blue and purple swirl of our existence. The reminder to keep fighting and make sure both realms stay at peace. In the middle is a tiny blue sapphire, the gemstone that binds the enchantment to me.

"Protect those who cannot fight, defend the light as it shines bright, the darkness cannot win this fight," I whisper softly and as the last word leaves my mouth, Snow whips his head around with a shocked expression on his face. Light as pure as the sun shines from within me and I feel the change occur. My hair becomes heavy upon my head and rolls down my back. My armour is replaced with my clothes from the human realm and my skin tone becomes a little darker as my face fills out.

"I didn't know your spell had changed." Snow says dumbfoundedly as he continues to stare at me.

"It hasn't," I state confused. *What is he talking about...?* I glance down to personally check out the changes and realise I'm in sweatpants and a tank top. *Great, well at least they won't recognise me now.*

"Oh, but it has." He grabs his chin and peers at the table as if he is deep in thought. "I remember it as 'Light comes and light goes, as the darkness always follows. Allow the veil to protect the flame. For when we are finally one, we will not become undone.' Within the pages I have found inside these walls, it always stated that the light finds the darkness first. You're the only one who can save him from his fate." Snow leans back in his chair and continues to watch me. *Ok... Well, that's new.* I think back to the moment when Duncan showed me his true form. *Darkness comes and darkness falls. Let the veil hide it all. For the light may come too late. To save the world from its terrible fate.*

"In Duncan's chant, what does it mean by the light may be too late? What fate am I to save him from? I didn't read anything about it in the Book of Old." I try to recall all that I learnt about the two of us and it didn't mention anything about his fate. It stated what will occur once we become whole, but nothing about what would happen if I never found him.

"What it means is, the dark minions are notorious for rebelling against their master. If they chose to do whatever they wanted, they could potentially wipe humanity off the face of the Earth. They would turn the whole world on its axis and Duncan is the only one who can stop them. He would unleash all his power to kill them all but it would mean sacrificing himself. He would do that to save us all. There are no teachings about what would happen if you guys take your own lives. We don't know if you would be reborn or not, but Duncan would do it regardless. He would save us all to protect you.

Now that you have bonded though, you have saved him from facing this threat alone. If both of you were able to restore the peace before they rebelled, you just might be able to save humanity too!"

"And how exactly do we do that? Restore the peace I mean?" I ask as I lean back in my seat.

"Do you remember when I told you about the Crawlers and how they got their leader out of the pool of the dead?" I nod as I cross my arms over my chest while being mindful of my new tattoo. "It caused substantial damage to the pit, many beings that we believed long gone have started coming back. The pit is draining out creatures daily and until you are both able to restore it; anarchy will unfold here and on earth." Snow proclaims while a shiver runs down my spine. *So I was right!*

"And how do we fix it?" As the words leave my mouth the prophecy comes to mind and I instantly shut my mouth. *They must sacrifice themselves and take the fall.* Before Snow has a chance to speak, I shoot upright "We have to jump, don't we? That's how we'll heal it." A look of sadness crosses his face before he nods his head. *Oh Zagoria, I didn't fully understand before but now I do.*

"You must choose to jump, to sacrifice yourselves into the pit. It's the only way you can save the humans from damnation. Heed my warning though, once the pit is completely drained, you will no longer be able to stop the apocalypse. The beasts will become uncontrollable and Earth will be in a world of pain. You must stop it before it gets to that point. You may have weeks or it could be only days, none of us really know. I do know this however, the first creatures to enter the pit were the Banshees, if they are free, we have lost." Snow sits up straighter in his chair while he finishes cleaning and a shiver runs down my spine.

I heard stories of the Banshees. I was told that they used to reside mainly in the human realm and how they used to maim and kill just for fun.

In the beginning of time, they tricked the Elders into allowing them to fade freely between our worlds. They claimed it was better for them if they were on Earth. Once the Elders found out what they were up to, it was already too late. The Elder counsel eventually ordered them to return and if they didn't, they were to be executed. It took the Princess of that time centuries to get rid of them and not a single one has ever come back.

Everything we have ever done is to ensure our realms remain in amity and what Willow's currently doing is going against all of that. The battle with the Crawlers comes to mind and I remember the newspaper I saw from 1929.

"I've been meaning to ask you something. A few days ago I came across a newspaper in an underground train station within our realm. At first, I was dumbfounded to see such a thing here but since then a few thoughts have been running through my mind. Could it be possible that was the location where the Crawlers cast the spell? I know that Damon was killed in Gage which isn't too far from Cossgrove, so I was thinking they may have moved him and cast the spell there instead. You told me that the spell caused damage to the pit but do you think it could have caused damage in other places too?" Snow rubs his chin deep in thought as he stares at the table before him. He moves his head from side to side obviously weighing something up.

"I cannot say no without actually seeing the site for myself and yet it is possible. Duncan told me about the station and how you battled the Crawlers there, correct?" He pauses and I nod, "If they were caught amassing there then it's possible that may have been the location for the ritual. We know the spell caused unfathomable damage to the pit which was created long before time, it's feasible that it marred other places too. Did you..." Snow stops as a loud crash filters in through the open door behind me and I shoot to my feet. Bracing myself for another attack I turn towards the noise. I see nothing but the bookshelves beyond the door. "SHIT!" Duncan's voice booms in the vast space outside and I instantly sprint in his direction. *He's ok.*

"Kyra wait, we don't know if...." Snow's voice trails off behind me. My heart skips a beat as I pass through the open door and head towards my mate. *Where are you?* The pull towards him is so great that it feels like I'm winding up a ball of yarn the closer I get. I come around the last bookshelf to see Duncan sitting on the bottom step holding his head in his hands. He looks beat up and distraught and my body instantly begins to move, wanting to do whatever it can to take his pain away. Snow's last words filter through my mind and I force myself to slow my pace. *I need to touch him so badly, but is it a good idea?* I think to myself as I cautiously walk up to him.

"What the fuck is wrong with me?" I hear him utter under his breath as he rubs his palms against his face before lifting his eyes to me. "Shit, Kyra..." Duncan says as he jumps to his feet and reaches his hand out towards me. Without even thinking I take a few steps back. I watch as his eyes fall to my hand and then dart back up to my face. *I will not let him touch me until I know for sure that this is my Duncan.* Confused by my reaction he drops his hand. "What the hell?" He asks almost angrily, and I feel the temperature around me rising. Duncan changes his stance and crosses his arms over his chest, peering down at me as if I'm a small child.

"I um..." Feeling a little intimidated by Duncan's glare, I glance back towards Snow's office. Hopefully he will come help me explain what's happened. "I..."

"What is it Kyra?" He demands and I begin to feel my own temperature rising. *I don't care who he is or what he's going through, I will not allow him to speak to me like this.* Deciding I need to stand my ground, I stare wildly into his eyes and witness the moment the blackness takes over once more. *Oh no! It hasn't left him yet.*

"Watch your mouth boy." Snow declares from behind me as he rounds the corner. I glance over my shoulder to see him looking more menacing than the man standing before me. Snow moves himself in between us and I really wish he hadn't done that. I cannot protect him in this position and even though he is strong, Duncan is by far the strongest in this form.

"Stay out of it." Duncan snaps taking a threatening step forward.

"I will do no such thing. You need to clear your mind son, banish the darkness from within you. It's..." Snow lifts his arms to try and calm Duncan which only angers him more. I stand there in suspended horror as I watch my mate's features turn into something wicked. He may be still in his Duncan form, however I don't miss the sickening smile that spreads out across his lips at Snow's words. They seem to be having a staring competition and I believe Snow is penetrating his mind to try and stop the Darkness from rising further. Duncan takes a deep breath and closes his eyes before opening them again to show off the full blackness within.

"Banish the darkness you say? I am fucking Darkness, you moron." Without even casting his ritual, Duncan switches into his true form and spreads his arms open wide. Green smoke erupts from his being and thickens around us making it hard to see. I take a hesitant step forward towards Snow, feeling the need to get him out of here. This will end in a fight and I do not want Snow in the middle of it. "... And I am going to show you just how dark I can be." As the last word leaves Duncan's mouth the entire conservatory goes black. I cast my ritual as quickly as I can and allow my true form to come forth. Light beams brightly from my being and I grab Snow's arm and rush him back towards his office. I thrust him inside and command him to stay put as I slam the door shut and begin to jog back to where I last saw Duncan. His smoke has thickened tenfold and I can barely see a metre in front of me.

Slowing my pace I yell, "You need to stop this!" as I turn in slow circles trying to see anything through the smoke. Lifting my arms I take small steps and feel around for anything that I can hold. My hand hits what feels like a shelf and I move along it until I find its end. Needing to move onto the next one, I let go of the stack and fling my arms out wide. I try to get a grasp on roughly where I am in this great library while I cautiously step forward. "Duncan please stop this," I whisper under my breath.

"You look so beautiful when you're scared." He breathes into my ear and a shiver runs down my spine. I toss my head from side to side trying to see him through the thick smoke however there's nothing, he's already gone.

"I'm not scared, you're just being ridiculous." I hear him chuckle in the distance and I begin to move in his direction.

"You're lying... I can taste your fear in the air. It's so erotic." He utters sexually as my fingers find another bookshelf. *Maybe if I read the names of the books then I'll be able to grasp where I am*. Reaching forward I grab the first book I can find and hold it up to my face. It's the book of maps I read on my first day here. *Success!* If I turn around and walk roughly two meters back, I would be standing at the base of Duncan's statue. With arms stretched open wide, I slowly move towards the monument. I sweep my foot out in front of me, feeling around with every step I take to ensure I don't trip over anything.

"BOO!" Duncan yells in my face as he instantly appears out of the smoke. I let out a startled shriek as my ass hits the ground with a thud and the impact causes a sharp bolt of pain to shoot up my spine. My heart is beating erratically in my chest and I cover it with my hand as I try to regain my equilibrium. Duncan gazes down at me and lets out a sinister laugh before opening his mouth to speak. "You should have seen your face... it was classic... my poor little damsel." He coos as he gives me his signature sexy smirk while he circles around me. Duncan's like a vulture ready to strike his prey, however little does he know this damsel can be a vulture too.

"Are you done playing your games?" I shout at him. His anger may be gone but this is the side of Duncan who loves to play and I have seen this side of him before. I know he won't back down until he has had his fun, so game on babe. *Protect those who cannot fight, defend the light....* Duncan stops directly in front of me and tilts his head to the side there is no blue present that I can see in his eyes and I need to get my Duncan back before he is fully consumed by the darkness rising in him.

"Not even close and you know how much I love to play... Especially with you." He moves into a crouch and as quick as lightning he springs up, grips my hair, pulling me closer. "Maybe we should go to the bedroom now, that way I can show you just how much I love to play." He turns my head and licks my cheek all the way up the side of my face. *Yuk!* A zap of electricity runs through me but the movement was too quick for the bond to take hold. I need to subdue him long enough to hopefully be able to penetrate the blackness within him. *I really need my Duncan back.*

While I continue to bring forth my power, I begin to take deep laboured breaths as the volcano starts to rise beneath my skin. I lift my hand ready to use the fire within but before I have a chance to do anything, Duncan stands with me in tow. He uses his might and flings me high into the air and shoots me halfway across the conservatory. My body crashes hard into a case of books before slamming to the floor. *Ouch!* I groan inwardly as I check my ribs to make sure that they're not broken and thank the stars I'm still in one piece. "Oh, I can't wait to do so many naughty things to you." He murmurs above me as he lifts me off the ground with his smoke. He holds me mid-air in front of him and stares at me with delight. "I'm really enjoying this game." He says with glee and tilts his head to the other side. *Enough of this!*

"Play with this asshole!" I growl as I shove my hand against his chest and release all the power built up within me. A fire like I've never felt before erupts out of my palm and Duncan tries to back away however, I grab ahold of his bicep keeping him still. We lock eyes and I watch my light fight the Darkness within him. *Come back to me.* A light as bright as the sun gushes from my hand illuminating the entire room around us. I close my eyes and reach down the bond begging my mate to come back to me. I feel his presence, his warm embrace and I hold firm. I open my eyes and notice the green smoke and darkness has vanished, only my mate and I remain. The last spurt of my power leaves my body and I slump to the ground with my mate in tow.

My senses are gone, I can't see, hear or smell anything. I am nothing but the vacant shell of a divine being. An empty vessel ready for the taking. Blackness from deep within the bond surrounds me and I happily invite it. I begin to blink uncontrollably as shadows appear in my line of vision. Muffled sounds enter my ears and I wish them away. *Just let me be.* I don't want to wake from this pleasant dream. My mind drifts off to my mate, my beautiful and handsome Duncan. He is the darkness to my light, the yin to my yang, my forever songbird. A massive burst of electricity ignites from within my chest and all my senses come rushing back at once. My body immediately shoots upright into a sitting position, headbutting Snow in the process.

"Ouch!" I exclaim as I raise my hand to my head and hold it as if that would miraculously take the pain away.

"Sorry Kyra, I wasn't expecting you to get up that quick." He says sheepishly in front of me as he too rubs the side of his head.

"Honestly neither did I, I have never bounced back from a huge use of power like that before. It was like a switch was flipped the moment I thought of Duncan." I'm about to say more when I'm instantly distracted by sobs coming from the man sitting on my left. Concern floods my soul and I peer back at Snow who mouths the words 'he will be okay.' I nod in uncertainty and turn my attention back to Duncan. His head is resting on his raised knees and I can distinctly hear his laboured breaths. My whole body wants to reach out and touch him but I should let him have this moment to himself.

We sit there in complete silence for a while and without raising his head, Duncan begins to speak. "I could see you... I could see and feel everything, but I couldn't stop it. It felt like I was trapped in a box within myself, and

I was unable to break free. I had no control over what my body was doing, it was like I was there but not there at the same time..." He lifts his eyes to mine and I notice his darkness is gone. His eyes are back to normal, although they are now rimmed red from his unshed tears. Not able to control myself any longer, I rush forward and throw caution to the wind. *I just need to hold him.*

Duncan moves as quickly as I do, dropping his legs and opens his arms to let me curl up on his lap. "I am so sorry Kyra..." He whispers into my hair while holding me tightly. "I am so sorry. Never in my wildest dreams did I ever imagine that I was capable of doing something like that to you." Duncan sniffles a little and I sigh heavily as the link between us begins to heal the bruises at my side. "When we were walking back to my room I felt this thing inside me building, this great old power deep within me. I believe it may have been feeding off my desire for you. I wanted you so badly in that moment and I wasn't entirely sure if we would make it back to my room in time. I remember thinking of taking you against the wall but dismissed the thought immediately, but then it was like a lever being pulled and I felt like I was shoved back, deep down within myself.

My dark half of the soul wanted the connection so badly it was willing to take it regardless of where we were. It was sick of sitting on the side lines and wanted a piece of the action for itself. I felt defenceless against its attack and I let it win." He whispers in my ear as tears flow steadily down his cheeks. His arms that are wrapped around me pull me in tighter and I don't resist. I swivel on his lap and position my hands on either side of his face, forcing him to look deep into my eyes.

"What happened was not your fault and I don't blame you for it. We already know our soul is drawn to one another and the pull has become greater since we made love last night. We will just have to make sure that what happened earlier, never happens again. If that was all caused by our desire, then we will have to try and resist temptation. We will need to be mindful of our touches and only connect when it's truly necessary. I was caught off guard this time and I will not allow that to happen again. Do you understand?" I whisper and he stares at me for a few moments before closing his eyes and nods his head. *Thankfully we are on the same page.* Leaning forward I rest my forehead against his and breathe deeply. "We will get through this... Together."

"Together..." He repeats as he pulls me closer and tilts my face up to meet his. I am lost in the feel of his lips against mine, they are so soft and tender. Eons of sadness passes between us and I try to ignore it.

This may be our last chance to throw caution to the wind and I want to savour every moment. Our soul grows stronger with every passing minute and we get weaker against its desires. The link that binds us is undeniable however, that's not all I'm feeling right now. There is a pulse below the earth that's beckoning us to it. I can sense it. It's begging us to free it from the horrible pain it's in and I don't know how much time we have left before it's too late.

Chapter 14

It's been two days since the incident in the grand library. Two days since the darkness within Duncan completely overcame him for its own personal gain. We have been searching this library from top to bottom to find out what's happening to us, but we keep coming up short. That doesn't surprise me though because we are the first ones to ever make it this far, so of course there is nothing documented about it. None of the others got to complete the bond as Willow never allowed it.

Just thinking her name makes my blood boil. How could she be so evil? So manipulative? She made me believe that she loved me, that she really cared for me. If she were here right now, I don't doubt that she would try to kill me again regardless of what is happening below the Earth. She believes the old prophecy and she wants to live so badly that she is willing to do just about anything to survive. Although I have to give her credit for one thing. She kept the power to destroy her close and made me believe that my true purpose in life was my enemy. It still shocks me to my core that she could even do such a thing but honestly, I haven't really known her that long. She is billions of years old, so she's had plenty of time to perfect her innocent persona.

"Enough of this, I cannot sit here looking for something that isn't there," I state slamming the book shut in front of me. Pushing my chair away from the desk in the middle of the library's study area, I pick up my book and return it to the stack I retrieved it from earlier. The smell of musty old books hits my nostrils and I inhale deeply. *I wish I knew about this place years ago. There is so much here I could have learnt.*

"There is no harm in trying Kyra." Snow declares, never taking his eyes off the pages in front of him. We have been sitting here for hours searching through history novels written by people long before my time. Duncan vanished earlier this morning when Snow suggested that we should turn to the books to see if we could find anything of use to us. Supposedly he was going to get us some food, but he never returned. *Lucky him.*

"Actually there is, every day that we sit here in hiding, more creatures escape the pit. Creatures that the despicable *bitch* can gain control over. We should be out there hunting her down, ending her life before she tries to do the same to us. You said she would be looking for us more now than ever and with this spell inked into my flesh, we have the upper hand. She would be on the hunt for my glow, not plain old Kyra." I declare as I feel my temperature rising. *This is so stupid; I don't even know why we are discussing this.* We need to take Willow down and find where this second pull that I'm sensing is coming from.

Every day we wait, it grows stronger and stronger and getting harder to ignore.

I lean against the bookcase behind me and cross my arms over my chest. I need him to see reason, he cannot keep us here forever and we will leave whether he likes it or not. *We have to.*

"Kyra, you have to understand. You may have the spell to change your appearance, but she has the ability to sense the future. It may be for only a few seconds, but she can still do it. While you are inside this library you are protected from her gifts. This conservatory was charmed many millennia ago so no one can find it. It will be driving her crazy at the moment because she cannot locate you but as soon as you step outside these walls, it will only be a matter of time until she does.

She is an excellent hunter and always finds her prey, I've seen her do it many times before. So you need to be fully prepared for everything before you leave here." Snow says sadly as he crosses his arms and leans back in his chair. His grey suit still looks freshly pressed even though he's been sitting in a chair all day hunched over a pile of books. He believes that the answers we seek are within the pages, but I beg to differ, they are out there in the real world.

"If it is so dangerous for us to leave this sanctuary, then why do you let Duncan?" As I say his name, I feel my heart yearning for my other half. We haven't touched since last night and it's beginning to weigh heavily on my body. I feel my energy draining with each passing moment, I'm sluggish and not motivated. I need him to return, I need his touch. We have been so careful these past few days, touching only when needed. Duncan is terrified of the Darkness taking him over again and he has every right to be.

Snow showed me some of the things he witnessed within Duncan's mind, and it was horrific. My Duncan may have come back to me but he will forever be traumatised by what his half of the soul did to him. *It scares me to think if his did that to him, what can mine do to me?*

"I don't let him Kyra, he has always disregarded my teachings and my warnings. He likes to do his own thing however, he can also do one thing that Willow can't. He can fly. Fang is one of a kind and is loyal to Duncan through and through. She has been with him since the rebirth. I gave her to him the day I brought him back here and they have been inseparable ever since. If you're worried that they won't return, don't be. He will come back when he is ready."

"I have no doubt about that, but it still doesn't change the fact that he goes outside. She may not be able to fly but she can still trace him back to the forest, don't you guys realise that?" I stomp away from the stack and fling my arms out to the side. Anger floods my being at the foolishness of this situation. He knows what Willow is capable of just as much as I and still, he puts us in this situation.

Bright light bursts from my being and Snow shields his face away from the glow. Without even realising, I transformed myself into my true form. Burning hot flames dance upon my skin as they travel up my arms from the palms of my hands. I'm a glowing beacon of light in the centre of this conservatory, every inch of the grand space is lit up by my being.

I hear footsteps approaching from the hallway behind me and turn to see my mate strolling into the room. He takes one look at me then whips his eyes towards Snow. They appear to be having another one of their telepathic conversations to which Duncan just shrugs before turning his attention back to me. He sweeps his gaze all over my heated skin with excitement twinkling in his eye.

"It looks like I returned at a bad time, maybe I should come back later when you have calmed down." Duncan smiles as he raises the cup in his hand and takes a sip out of the straw. He lets out an obnoxious 'ah' when he finishes his drink and turns to walk back the way he came. *Oh, I don't think so.*

"Don't fucking move!" I growl at him. *I'll be damned if I let him walk back out that door.*

"Ok then." He says happily as he turns back to face me with a cocky smile on his face. *Oh, that does it, I'm done playing games with him.* Fire bursts from my being heading straight for him. He dodges it at the last second, letting the ball oirisf fire wiz past him and smash into the brickwork. He looks at the smouldering circle on the wall behind him before whirling back around. "What did I do to piss you off?" He asks while cracking his neck to the side as his true form takes shape and starts walking down the steps towards me.

Darkness trails in his wake and I begin to think that this may not have been a wise idea. *Here we go again.* Duncan reaches the bottom landing and stops. He stands there like the true divine being he was born to be. I would swoon at his feet if I wasn't so mad at him.

"You went outside! You put us all in unnecessary danger and all for the sake of what? A drink?" I point towards the now empty cup in his hand. "There are plenty of drinks here in this hall and you know it!" Now it's his turn to look angry. He takes a few menacing steps forward and then throws his now empty cup in the bin beside the chair I was sitting in earlier. He stops roughly two feet away and I see him taking deep calming breaths. It looks like he's trying to maintain control over himself. The blackness within his eyes is strong and thankfully his blue irises are still present.

"For a matter-of-fact smart arse, I wasn't out there looking for food, I'm not that stupid! I was out there looking for the entrance to my domain, to the pit. I may rule over the damn thing but at this point, I have no fucking clue where it is!" He flays his arms out to the sides while screaming in my face. His actions make me want to back down however something he just said makes me reconsider.

"Are you fucking serious right now? Isn't it your job to know?" My flames grow brighter as my temperature rises. *How the hell are we supposed to end it all if we have no fucking clue where the damn thing is?*

"Of course, it is my job! And originally, I knew where it was but someone FUCKING MOVED IT!!" Duncan moves mere inches away from my face and I resist the urge to step back. I stare deep into his black eyes as I pull on the link that binds us and realise he's telling the truth. Someone moved the entrance to his domain, and he has spent most of this lifetime searching for it.

I reach for his hand as my temper falters but I stop myself just before our fingers connect. I look down at his hand, wanting nothing more than to take this man into my arms but I know I can't. *We can't. We have to resist temptation, otherwise who knows what will happen.* I lift my eyes back up to my mate and let out a sigh.

"How are we ever going to end this if we don't know where we are going? We have weeks maybe even days to stop the end from coming to pass and you have been searching for the entrance for centuries... I don't understand how someone can just move something that has been around since the beginning of time? It doesn't make sense." I utter as realisation hits me. I was relying on him this whole time to know where the entrance was. It never occurred to me that we would have to find it in order to save the world. We don't have enough time to do that now and also evade Willow. We need to come up with a better solution and fast.

"I can help you with that..." Snow pipes in and we both whip our heads in his direction. "Sorry, I was prying again." He pauses to tap the side of his temple. "I've recently discovered that an unbinding spell may have been used to move it. It is an unusual ritual to cast and can only be found in one particular book, the one Willow stole from this very library." Snow stands up and closes the book in front of him. He places it on top of the pile he's already finished, acting like nothing has changed. *Well, that was probably the most useful piece of information he's said all day.*

"Well that's just great, that means the entrance could be just about anywhere," I say as I lift my face towards the window pails high above. I need her warmth to tame my rising anger unfortunately, though dusk is upon us. There is nothing outside these walls but darkness mixed with the last glimmers of sunlight.

"Not entirely. It states in the forbidden book of spells, that if you are to unbind something from somewhere you then must bind it to yourself before you can set it free again. This means the entrance will be close to Willow. She won't be able to be very far away from it." Snow states as he looks at the floor while resting back against the desk. "She will have the portal within her sights, so when you find it, you must act fast."

"Why are you only telling me about this now old man? I have been wracking my brain for years looking for this thing and even if what you're saying is true, how is that going to help us find the pit?" Duncan asks as he moves away from me to go slouch in the armchair closest to snow. He rolls his head on his shoulders and allows his true form to fade away.

If we were not discussing our imminent future I would go sit on his lap, I'm desperately craving his touch. Duncan senses my eyes and glances in my direction. We stare at each other, desire and longing drifts between us and I have to force myself to look away. *This is really not the time.*

"I have never told you about this as you needed to be bonded to use it. You, Kyra, were never permitted to know that some Elders are very powerful beings and are able to cast spells that would take the both of you to wield. For instance, an enchantment tracker is a highly compelling ritual and, now that you both have consummated the bond, the spell is yours for the taking." Snow glances over at me and I feel my whole body turn a deep shade of red. *Why did he have to look at me when he said that?* "It is a spell I know like the back of my hand. I've used it many times before, especially when I couldn't find the entrance to the library. Until recently, when I was pretending to be Connor, I rarely left the confines of this reservation. But every time I did, I couldn't remember where I hid the damn thing." I smile although something bugs me.

"Wouldn't Willow know of that spell too?" I ask as I cross my arms and stand up a little straighter. *If she had a book of spells, surely she would know about this one too.*

"Not entirely, this one's not in her book, it's in mine. I compiled a book of useful spells many eons ago and destroyed the others to prevent them from falling into the wrong hands. The book Willow stole was an exception as I never even knew of its existence until the day she took it. I searched for years looking for more, but that was the only one I missed." Snow pushes away from the desk and begins walking towards his office on the far side of the room.

"Well that was a smart move old man but what if you lost your copy?" Duncan asks as he stands and follows him into the room. Not wanting to be left out, I follow suit. I stop on the threshold and lean against the doorframe crossing my arms over my chest. Duncan strides over to the day bed and lays down. He stretches his arms high above his head causing his shirt to ride up and I want to run my fingers down along his hard abs as I make my way towards the gloriousness below. *Oh, there are so many things I want to do to you.*

"Do you mind!?" Snow barks at me and I shake my head to stop myself from staring.

"Sorry," I say sheepishly as I straighten against the doorframe. I risk another glance at Duncan who in return is just staring at me with his signature smirk plastered on his face. *He's enjoying this.* I give him the finger and then recross my arms. He just chuckles before returning his attention back to Snow.

"And to answer your previous question Duncan, I would never let that happen. I have the whole book memorised." He places his hand flat upon the desk and whispers something under his breath. Entranced by the green glow that begins to rise out of the centre of the dark wood, I stride over to get a better look. A small thin compartment pops up from within the desk, revealing a very old leather-bound book. *It's exactly like the Book of Old.*

I feel a warm breeze on the back of my neck and know that someone is standing behind me. Duncan is on the couch and Snow is staring at his book. This is an intruder. Moving as quickly as I can I whirl around and knock the heavy object to the floor. Duncan stares up at me with a startled look on his face.

"Oh my gosh, I'm so sorry, I didn't realise it was you. I thought you were still on the couch. Here, let me help you up." I reach down to lend Duncan a hand and he takes it without question. My fire swirls within me the instant we reconnect. We haven't touched in almost a whole day, and I feel its effects immediately. Duncan jumps to his feet and takes me into his arms, cradling my head against his chest as I breathe him in. He smells like rain and sunshine and everything I long to feel on my skin. *I wish we could stay like this forever.*

"I've missed you, missed this. You have no idea just how badly I need you." He says as he sighs against me. Duncan pulls me just that tiny bit closer and I wrap my arms around his waist.

"Actually I do, I feel the same way." I push back so I can look up at his handsome face. I want to kiss him so badly but I'm afraid what that might ignite. "Do you feel the bond getting stronger?" I whisper as if what I'm saying is a sin to be heard. "Like the longer we hold off from touching the worse this seems to get?... I have a weird feeling. I feel like we are fading away and I fear we won't be able to hold out for much longer. The end is coming... We need to locate the pit soon before we lose our chance to save it." I say as I stare into his beautiful blue eyes.

"I agree..." He utters as he tears his eyes away from mine to look at Snow. "We need you old man. Are you ready to teach us something new?" He asks and I turn my head just in time to see Snow smile.

"I'll try my best." He says as he gives us one definite nod.

Chapter 15

We spent the next few hours learning every way possible to activate the ritual. We all agreed that the best way to cast it would be from the air, that way we would be able to see when the spell is activated. Snow's book stated that a beacon of light will shine into the sky, giving the spell caster the ability to see where an unbinding or binding spell was used. Another awesome feature about this spell is that only the caster will be able to see the beacon, so Willow and her minions will have no idea that we are looking for the entrance.

Snow leans back in his chair and yawns as he stretches his arms high above his head. His shoulders crack from the pressure and I smile. He may have the presence of a young man however, he is anything but. His hair looks like it hasn't been brushed in days, even though he's been running his fingers through it continuously for the past few hours. Duncan was frustrating the hell out of him earlier with never ending questions that seemed to be nonessential to the task at hand nonetheless, he kept his grace the entire time and answered all of them to the best of his ability. Snow finishes off another yawn and I look down at the book before us. The spell is simple and exact:

Close your eyes and feel your power flow, your heart must seek what you want to see and say the words on a gentle breeze.

To reveal what has been done,

The magic must not become undone,

Give us the power to see the way

So, we can live another day.

It's as if the spell was made for this particular moment.

Duncan reaches for my hand underneath the table, throwing caution to the wind I lace my fingers through his. I don't know how much time we have left but I fear it's not much and I'll be damned if we miss out on moments like this because of it. I'm not afraid to die, I just didn't believe it would be happening so soon. I glance at Duncan and notice he's already looking at me. His face shows so much sadness and his eyes are lined red from unshed tears. If a single tear falls down his cheek it will be my undoing, so I force myself to look away.

It kills me to think that we don't have more time together. That even though Willow had no idea this would happen, she may have taken him away from me for good. Giving the book to the stupid Crawlers not only damned us all but killed herself too. Not once in my entire existence did I ever imagine that my end would be like this. I always imagined that I would go out in a blaze of glory, fighting some dark creature until it took me down or to be killed by the man sitting beside me. It never crossed my mind that it would be by my own hand. That I must sacrifice myself to save those who mean so much to me. Yet that is what I was created to do. To form the bond with my mate, my other half and bring forth everlasting peace to all life on Earth.

Sighing heavily I look up at Snow who has his elbows rested on the table and his head in his hands. He roughly rubs his face and then looks up at us both. Exhaustion weighs heavily upon him, and I have to remind myself that he is thousands of years old.

"You both should go get some rest, you need to leave early in the morning. This may be your last night together because we have no idea what is waiting for you outside of these walls, so in all honesty... Make it count." Snow declares getting to his feet and walking out of the room leaving Duncan and I alone. Duncan stares in his wake for a moment confused before turning to face me.

"Did he just say what I think he did?" He asks cautiously as his eyes light up with delight. I just shake my head smiling. *Of course, that's where his mind wandered off too.*

"I don't think that's what he meant..." I say shyly as I tuck a strand of hair behind my ear. I suck in my bottom lip and bite down hard as the fire deep within the pit of my stomach does butterflies at the possibilities of what might happen next.

"Oh, I do." He says as he gives me a cheeky grin before swivelling in his chair. He puts his hand on my left knee under the table and moves me so I'm facing him. He pulls my legs forward and my butt now rests on the edge of the seat. Lifting my head I look at his face and see fire and ice lying within his beautiful irises. Needing to create some distance between us for a moment, I hear Duncan grunt as I stand up.

"Of course, you do," I state as I start walking towards the door. These past few days have been great but the yearning for each other has never left. With the bond becoming deeper, my desire to have him has only grown stronger. I walk towards the hallway that leads to his bedroom and I feel his eyes on my back. Glancing over my shoulder I see him roughly ten feet back, he's stalking me. Feeling a tad courageous I give him a little flirtatious smile as I blow him a kiss. His lingering smirk fades when he begins to pick up his pace and I squeal as I break into a run. I almost hit every corner as I run through the maze towards his bedroom.

I just place my hands upon the door frame at the same time big arms wrap themselves around my waist, lifting me off the ground.

"Got ya!" He declares happily and I let out a laugh. Duncan turns me around and lets my feet drop back down to the floor. He holds me in his arms as he slowly leads us into his room. I raise my hands to his face, bringing his lips down upon mine. Ecstasy and desire like nothing I've felt yet washes over me and we crash into everything in our path as we make our way towards his bed.

My back hits a wall as Duncan's hands move from my waist to my ass as he lifts me off the ground. I wrap my legs around his waist and he tears his lips away from my mouth. He begins a luscious assault on my neck and for a moment I forget where I am. I moan loudly when desire sweeps through me and I force myself to blink the passion away. Duncan's fully black eyes enter my line of sight and I slightly pull away.

"Duncan stop... Are you sure you're ok to do this?" I whisper hesitantly, Duncan's lips continue to trail south of my neck and he hoists me a little higher against the wall. We haven't made love since the night before the Darkness took him over and I am still a little worried that it may come back. Sensing my hesitation, he pries his mouth away from my chest to gaze up at me.

"I have never been more certain of anything in my life..." I stare down into his loving eyes and see nothing but the beautiful white and blue of my mate. "Believe me when I say this, I am ok, I won't hurt you. There is nothing more I would rather be doing tonight than making love to you." He looks solemnly into my eyes and I decide to lower my lips back to his, ending our conversation. *If this is our last night together, we are definitely going to make it count.*

Chapter 16

I'm startled awake by a knock at the door. Duncan's arm is draped over me like a heavy tree trunk, making it almost impossible for me to move. As gently as I can, trying not to wake him, I move his arm just enough so I can slide out of the bed. Grabbing his shirt off the floor, I quickly put it on and run to open the door. Unintentionally I swing the door wide open and Snow jumps back from the sudden movement. He glances behind me before quickly averting his gaze and I turn my head to see a naked Duncan lying flat on his back. *Shit, he must have rolled over.* I step into the hallway and close the door behind me.

"Sorry, I ah... I didn't mean for you to see that." I stutter as my whole body turns red from embarrassment. *Oh Zagoria kill me now!*

"No need for the apology, I should be the one apologizing to you. It was not my intention to wake you both but as it's midday, I thought you might want to get going." He says while crossing his arms over his chest and stares down the hallway leading towards the library. *I wouldn't want to look at me either knowing what went down last night.*

"Midday? Are you serious?" I ask shocked. *How can that be?*

"Afraid so." He nods, not taking his eyes off the hallway.

"Shit! Ok, give us about 30 minutes, we will meet you in the grand foyer when we're ready."

"Alright." He says chuckling before walking off and leaving me to get ready by myself. *What was that about?*

Have we really been asleep that long? In my defence I have no idea what time we actually went to bed but still, we slept almost the whole day.

I walk back into the room and accidentally slam the door shut behind me. *Oops.* Duncan grunts and rolls back onto his stomach. *Oh, I don't think so.*

"Duncan get up, we have to go," I state, picking up a pillow off of the floor and throwing it at him. He grunts again as the pillow connects with his head and after a few short seconds he picks it back up and pegs it in my direction. It misses me by a long shot. "I am being serious, it's noon and we have to leave, now."

"Why? What's the rush?" He jokes while snuggling deeper into the mattress. *I wish this were a joke but unfortunately, it's not. Time is of the essence and we have wasted too much already.*

"You know why, the longer we wait the worse this shit gets! Now get up!" *If he does not move within the next two seconds, I'll... I'll.* I gaze at the grand wall of books to my left and an idea pops into my head. *He will learn not to mess with me.*

I call down the bond to make him understand the urgency of this situation and feel his laughter response.

"Make me." He declares as he grabs the pillow lying next to him and covers his head. *That's it!* Feeling my frustration rise, I stomp over to the first stacks of books along the wall. I peer over my shoulder and see Duncan sneaking a peek at me from underneath his pillow. He has a cheeky grin plastered on his face and quickly covers his head once more. *You're in for it now.* I pick up the first book on the stack and test its weight in my hand. *It's pretty light, so it shouldn't hurt too much if it accidentally hits him.* Duncan sneaks another peek from underneath the pillow but this time he sits up staring at me wide eyed.

"What do you plan to do with that?" He asks as he tilts his head to the side trying to read the name on the spine of the book. "I'll have you know, that's a first edition." He says as he points to the book within my grasp. I look at the scripture displayed on the front cover and shrug my shoulders. Turning around I face him head on. *This is going to be fun.* I think to myself smiling as I position myself into a great throwing stance. Pulling my arm back, I aim just next to him and fling the book forward.

"Whoa! What the fuck Kyra?" He shouts moving to the right as the book connects with the headboard beside him. *Bullseye!* A great boom ricochets throughout the room and I wink at him before turning around to grab another book off the pile beside me.

"For every second you waste, *babe*, I will throw another book at you," I state as I hold up the next publication to emphasise my point. Rearing back my arm, I aim this time for the spot between his legs on the bed. Noticing my desired target Duncan glances down at his black sheets and then sits completely upright.

"Alright, alright stop! I get it, I'll get up." He stutters as he holds his arms awkwardly in the air while manoeuvring his body over to the edge of the bed. I chuckle slightly as I watch him and he gives me a vulgar gesture which only makes me laugh louder. Dropping his arms, he reaches down, grabbing his clothes off of the floor and proceeds to put them on.

"You ruin all my fun." I pout as I place the book back where I found it. Duncan glances around the room for a moment before settling his eyes on me. A wicked grin crosses his face before he leans back against the bedpost and stuffs his hands into his pockets.

"You know... I am going to need my shirt back if you want us to get out of here." He says smugly and I glance down.

"Oh," I completely forgot that I still had it on. Feeling a little bit brazen, I reach for the hem and lift it over my head, removing it from my completely naked body. His smile falters as fire ignites within his eyes and I throw the shirt in his face.

"Hey! That's not fair." He murmurs and moves away from the bed heading straight towards me.

"Life isn't fair," I whisper as I rush over to where my clothes are piled up on the floor. Quickly gathering them into my arms, I head into his bathroom to get myself ready. I feel his heat on my back before the door slams shut behind us. "You will make us late." I mutter as I look at his reflection in the mirror. Duncan comes to a stop right behind me. His breath is hot as it hits my back and a blast of warmth fills my being. *I want him so badly even though I know we mustn't.*

"Humanity has waited for us this long; it can wait another five minutes." Duncan breathes as he steps forward, tightly grabbing my hips and pulls me flush against him.

"You're insatiable you know that," I say as I tilt my head to the side, giving him access to tease me with his mouth. We lock eyes in the mirror, and I watch as he mouths the words 'I know' before his lips connect with my neck and we get lost in the feel of one another.

I'm standing at the top of the stairs gazing at the statue of myself. This may very well be the last time I get to see it so I want to commit it to memory. The way my body is angled and the absent breeze in my hair. *It's such a remarkable sculpture.* Tearing my eyes away from myself, I look around the grand conservatory beyond the staircase. I wish I could have seen it in its prime, it's so hard to imagine what it used to look like when the whole place is in ruins.

I hear whispers coming from the hallway behind me and turn around to see Duncan and Snow deep in conversation as they walk up to meet me.

"Watch your back out there, they are very old and crafty. So trust no one. Treat everybody as an enemy that wants to kill you. You need to find the entrance and find it fast. Willow has minions everywhere and I believe she will track you down quickly once you step outside these walls. Especially now because it's the two of you and not just one." Snow pauses as they come to a stop before me. "... I wish I could go with you but I should stay here. If you need anything, anything at all, you know where to find me." Snow expresses as sorrow fills his features.

"We should be alright old man. I was taught by the best." Duncan says solemnly as he rests his hand upon Snow's shoulder, giving him comfort. He stares at Duncan for a moment before nodding his head and turning his gaze towards the floor. I can feel his sadness and wish there was something I could do. Without saying a word, I step forward and envelope Snow in my arms. I embrace the man that has recently become more than a boss to me. Once Snow overcomes his initial shock he raises his arms and I rest my head on his shoulder as he wraps them around my back.

"Thank you for everything and I'm not talking about just the past few days but for the last few years. Well actually now that I think of it, maybe even my entire life. You have always been there protecting me, even when I didn't know it." I say into his shirt as a stray tear rolls down my cheek. For many centuries they've both been there following me from place to place, trying to get me away from the one woman who's been constantly deceiving me. I will be forever grateful for what he and Duncan endured to make sure that no harm was ever done to me.

"It has always been my pleasure Kyra," He whispers as he chokes back his own tears. Moving his head slightly back he kisses my forehead and then drops his arms. I step away from him and unconsciously step right into Duncan's embrace. His touch makes my whole body come alive but my heart aches for the man before me. Snow may not want to admit it, but he's losing his son today. The child he raised all on his own, cared for and looked after until the time came when he had a chance to end it all. Snow might be thinking it's a worthy sacrifice, however that doesn't stop the pain from coming.

I feel sorrow radiating from behind me and know that Duncan feels the same. Feeling saddened by the situation at hand, I decide to trail my fingers along Duncan's arm that's wrapped around my waist, letting him know that I'm here. "You better go." Snow states as he moves to the side, clearing a path towards the forest door. I feel Duncan nod behind me before dropping his arms, he then grabs my hand and begins leading us towards the exit.

"We will see you soon," I utter to Snow as we walk past him. For a few seconds, there is complete silence and then I hear him whisper "No you won't." and it really hits me then that he is right, we won't be seeing each other again. I turn my head back to see him one last time but it's too late, he's already gone. Dread fills my features as we reach the end of the hallway and I cannot stop the tears that begin to fall down my face. *I wish we had more time.*

Duncan places his hand on the doorknob and pulls the door wide open. The musty, humid air hits me and for a moment I feel as if I can't breathe. The weight of the world is crashing down upon me and I feel like there is no escape. *Oh My Zagoria! What if we never make it? What if we are killed before we get a chance to end it?* My breathing becomes heavy as I raise my hand to my chest. I hear murmurs to my left but nothing more. I am a whirlwind of emotions, and my senses tell me I'm falling. *What will happen if we never make it?* I feel pressure against my legs as my body hits the floor and my entire world goes black.

Warmth invades my head and I hear his words calling to me through the bond. Calm soothing notions that have the power to break through my subconscious, "Come back to me, my beautiful Light... Come back." With my eyes closed, I see my black knight fighting away all my demons. He makes his way through my barriers and sets my mind free from its panicked state. My eyes flutter open and I see my mate in his true form staring back at me. His beauty is truly a match to no one. Without warning, Duncan brings his lips down upon mine. Sweet, feather light kisses touch my skin and then all of a sudden they stop.

He turns he gaze towards the forest, stands up and holds his hand out for me to take. Reaching forward I grasp his fingers and allow him to help me up. "Time to go." He whispers into my ear and wraps his arm around my back, helping me cross over the magical threshold.

I am unexpectedly hit by a severe wave of nausea the moment we step foot into the forest. I push away from Duncan as I double over and heave up all the contents within my stomach. "What the fuck!" Duncan harshly whispers as he falls to his knees beside me. I retch one more time although nothing seems to come up. I wipe my mouth clean with the back of my hand and lift my head up to look at the man kneeling beside me.

"Something's wrong," I mutter as I sit up looking around. Everything has a purplish tinge so I know where we are, although I see nothing other than the tall trees and greenery that the forest provides. "My gut tells me something is here. One of yours, I just can't see it, can you?" Duncan stares deep into my eyes while his appearance changes into something a little more menacing. I shriek back as he moves away from me to stand tall and radiate his true malice at whatever it is.

Duncan rotates in slow circles as he prepares to strike. After a few minutes of nothing he stops. Deeming the coast to be clear, he extends his hand down for me and I take it eagerly. "Stay in this form ok, if there really is a creature here, they will not be able to recognise you like this." He says as he gestures towards my human form. I nod my head while I lift my hand and place it over the storm brewing in the pit of my abdomen. "Is it gone?" Duncan asks as he quickly glances in my direction.

"No. It's still here." I state as I swallow the bile rising in my throat. *I feel it, its presence is close but where?* It's as if it's blocked from view, like how the humans can't see them from Earth... The newspaper instantly comes to mind and my stomach drops with horror. "No!" I utter under my breath and whip my head towards Duncan to see him already staring at me.

"What?.. What is it?" He asks as he flicks his eyes between me and the forest around us.

"The crack! The crack in the realms, they could of..." I turn quickly in all directions as I trail off. The monster is here, however we are in the wrong realm. I don't know why we can't see it but I'm not waiting around to find out.

"What crack?... What's going on?" Duncan almost rages as he grabs my shoulders hard, forcing me to stop. My breathing is quick and I'm finding it hard to talk. If the creature is where I believe it is, the people on Earth are already in danger.

"I don't have time to fully explain what happened, but the Crawlers accidentally created a crack within the dimensions when they withdrew the soul of their leader out of the pit and put him in Damon. This creature that I'm feeling now though, I believe is on Earth, so we have to leave now!" I almost shout as I gather my power.

"On Earth? Bullshit. That's impossible and not to mention illegal." Duncan states in disbelief.

"Do you honestly think they care about the laws right now? And it's not impossible especially with Willow running the show. I bet she's granted them permission to go just about anywhere." Scepticism crosses his face, but he doesn't interject, he knows I'm right.

The nausea seems to be getting worse and I choose not to wait. Relaxing my body I zone out. The purplish tinge of Zagoria disappears as Earth's shine takes shape, though that's not all I see. The sky above is no longer blue and in its place is rolling green storm clouds. I search the skies for my old friend when Duncan suddenly grips me hard around the waist and he shoves me behind him.

I'm about to ask him why when I catch a glimpse of the beast only a few yards away. Standing as tall as the trees with arms as thick as the trunks, a beast I have only seen in my dreams huffs and puffs as it rakes its leg against the ground. The half man, half bull is not something I have ever witnessed in my lifetime and looking at the creature before us now, I really wish I hadn't.

"This is going to hurt." Duncan declares as the minotaur rears itself back and begins charging towards us.

Chapter 17

Duncan and I are sprinting through the forest as fast as we can, fleeing the raging beast behind us. No matter how fast we move, the minitour remains on our heels. We tried to scare the creature away by using force, throwing it almost a whole football field back and yet it continues to charge forward. Duncan ordered the beast to stand down hours ago, but it didn't listen. It heeds the command of only one master now and that is not Duncan.

"We have to get out of this damn forest!" Duncan growls beside me while he turns his head to look back at the creature. I see a clearing through the trees to our right and reach for Duncan's arm. I pull him with me as I change our trajectory and head for the break in the trees. Duncan hesitates for only a moment and then picks up the pace. "I need Fang." Duncan declares out of nowhere and fades out. *What the... He did not just leave me here to battle this thing on my own?*

I glance over my shoulder and see the bull's head roughly ten yards back. *I am so screwed! This thing is faster than I thought.*

Throwing caution to the wind, I summon my powers. My brightness is devastating against the darkness that surrounds us as I change myself into my true form.

I finally reach the line of trees and keep going, I do not stop. I have not battled a beast like this one before and honestly, I don't plan to. I remember reading about them in the Book of the Brutes, the book that contained all the beasts throughout our history. Well all the creatures that the Dark Prince controlled anyway. Every soldier within the order had to learn about them to know what we were up against, even if those creatures have long been extinct.

The Minitours for instance are huge half man, half bull like creatures. Legend states that they are strong like a battering ram but as stupid as a lamppost. They are the type of creature that will always do your bidding and never ask why. They are the second most powerful being known to the Zagorian's and might I add, they are also one of five creatures that have the power to kill me.

Sneaking a peek behind me, I see the beast coming out of the line of trees and my stomach drops at the sight of it. *This thing is huge!* I'm running as fast as I can, but I feel my agility beginning to wane. I will not be able to continue much longer without Duncan's touch. *Where is he?*

I reach the centre of the clearing and stop dead in my tracks, enough is enough. With my power coursing through my veins, I believe I might just be able to stop this thing long enough to find a way to make it out of this alive. Whirling around I face the creature head on and it tilts its head to the side as it continues charging forward. I forgo my old ritual and decide to use the one of old Snow taught me, the one of my ancestors, "Light comes and light goes, as the darkness always follows. Allow the vail to protect the flame, for when we are finally one, we will not become undone."

My power swirls around me like a beacon of hope in this never-ending darkness. I stand there bringing forth heat and flames from the sun high above, creating the divine link between the star that gives us life and myself. I disregard the beast heading towards me and look up. The storm clouds and smoke have been pushed aside to make way for the sun's rays. I spread my arms out wide as my old friend shines down upon me. Flames dance along my skin and I know it's time. *I am a blaze; I am warmth, I am... Her, the Sun.* Lowering my head I look at the beast who's two feet away and explode.

Rays of light as hot as lava erupt from my being, hitting the monster square in the chest. The minitour flies back to the line of trees behind it and hits a thick trunk with a great bang. A triumphant smile crosses my face as I watch the creature fall to the ground hard.

I wait a moment for it to return to its feet but it doesn't. The beast is down and I slowly begin to let go of my power. Looking around I try to see anything that might remind me as to where I am, on Earth. Trees and mountains surround me on all sides and the birds are chirping high above. There seems to be nothing here that looks oddly familiar. *How am I ever going to find my way out of this?*

I take a few steps and notice an unusual rock formation high up on the right-hand side. It kind of looks like three towers. *Hang on, I think I know this place.* Moving my eyes slightly to the left I see exactly what I was looking for, the viewing platform. *I am at the three sisters in the Blue Mountains, but where's Duncan?* Searching the skies above me I see nothing but the dark green storm clouds rolling back in. *Damn!*

I hear a grunt behind me and whirl around to see the beast's arms moving as it tries to get up. *SHIT!* Locking the remainder of my power within me, I sprint in the opposite direction. I have to put as much distance between us as I can before it gets to its feet. *If I let go of my power now, I am doomed! It will shut me down and Duncan is not around to save me.*

I hit the other line of trees and keep moving. Glancing behind me I see the beast getting to its feet and know I have mere seconds before it begins charging after me again. I can feel my strength depleting and yet I force myself to bring forth more power. *This is really going to hurt later.* I'm just hoping it will allow me to gain control over my agility once more and push me forward, up the hill towards the platform.

I feel the branches hit my cheeks and the bark scrapes against my hands as I move throughout the forest. I can hear the thumps of the beast's hooves hitting the ground behind me and glance back just in time to see it dodge a tree roughly a hundred metres back. *You will not catch me. I will not let you!*

With lava pulsing through my veins I make it to the top. People scream in terror as I jump over the railing onto the viewing platform. *There are so many bystanders here, how am I ever going to get them to leave?* Peering over the edge I see the disturbance in the treetops, caused by the minitour below. *I have roughly five minutes before it catches up with me.* Turning back towards the crowd I notice that everyone is running away in fear. *If only they knew what was coming.*

"Everyone needs to leave now!" I yell and they all shrink back further. I'm glad they are all listening, but they just need to move quicker, there isn't much time left. As I watch them flee I feel the need to do the same. Maybe I can draw the minitour away and still keep them safe, but I can only do that if I leave now.

Using my shine to my advantage I look around and see a carpark far in the distance. *Perfect! Maybe there's something there that I can use to get me out of here.* I spot a motorbike rider shedding his gear and dash over. "I need to borrow your bike," I say as I glance at the railing over my shoulder. I can hear the minitour's hooves galloping up the slope and turn back to the rider. "NOW!" I order and without waiting for a reply, I snatch the helmet from within his grasp. With quick fingers, I place it on my head and fasten the strap under my chin. I shove the rider out of the way and feel a little guilty for the attack, but he and everybody else will be better off when the minitour and I are out of the picture.

"HEY!... WHAT THE FUCK?... YOU CAN'T JUST TAKE MY BIKE!" He yells at me as more screams erupt from behind us. I peer behind me and witness the minitour jumping over the railing, it emits a loud thud as its hooves hit the ground. The creature lets out a tremendous roar before spotting me a short distance away. Turning to its side it rips away a chunk of metal from the railing and holds it high above its head, it rears back its arms and throws it forcefully in my direction. I see its trajectory and push the rider quickly out of the way. He falls back a few feet and out of the minitours lines of sight. The railing hits the ground with a clang and comes to a stop right beside my foot. I gaze down at the silver hardware and then back up at the beast. He is moving to the side to remove another chunk out of the railing. *I need to leave NOW!*

"SORRY!" I yell to the rider and then throw my leg over the heavy machine, getting myself ready to hall ass. Holding in the clutch, I rev the bike and drop it into first gear, taking off in a flash. I hear the metal hit the ground behind me but don't look back. Fire burns from within and I wonder how much longer I can hold on. I need to find cover, I can't leave myself out in the open.

I ride for almost an hour weaving in and out of the traffic as I make my way down the mountain. Creatures of the dark are everywhere and the humans are struggling to deal with all the chaos. People are driving on the wrong side of the road and amongst the chaos, some have even crashed into stationary objects in their attempts to flee. I pass multiple stores with their windows smashed in and witness total mayhem as the creature's loot and riot. There is so much pain. So much hatred and despair. These creatures are letting their powers run wild and the people of Earth are suffering for it.

I witness packs of Crawlers and Cerberus's on the hunt for their prey. Wendigos ripping apart shops and cars, practically anything that gets in their way. Even the bats are flying really low, swooping lower than normal as they attack people on the ground. It's complete and utter carnage. People are panicking all around me and until Duncan comes back, there is absolutely nothing I can do. My powers are draining and I'm finding it hard to stay awake.

I reach the streets near my home and I honestly have no idea why my soul led me here. There is nothing left for me here and, if Willow is on the hunt, this is the first place she'll look. Having rehidden my appearance long ago, I decide a quick drive by won't hurt.

I round the last few corners and make my way into my street, it's so dark and gloomy. Never in all the years I have lived here, have I ever seen it like this. I hear growls from monsters and beasts alike yet I still slow my pace. *I just need to see it one last time*. Shifting the bike into neutral, I roll to a stop on the pavement outside my home. *My beautiful old Victorian, the house I always dreamt of*. The red bricks and green trimmings, exactly what an old house should look like. Its beauty still takes my breath away.

Murmurs filter down from within the walls and I tune my ears to focus on the voices.

"Where is she?... We put our faith in you to end all of this and you promised us weeks ago that you wouldn't let it get this far!..." Someone bellows from the top floor of my house. The voice is so intimidating that even I quiver. I look up at the same time as the lights flick on and contemplate leaving but then I hear another voice begin to speak from within the room.

"Get your knickers out of your ass Kit, I told you I would handle it and I will... I don't see any of you willing to do the dirty work now do I?" My stomach drops at the sound of her voice. *Willow! She is in my house. I should...* I'm about to hop off the bike but change my mind at the last second. Now is not the time or place. I really need to get to a safe location so I can drop my power. *I'm like a volcano ready to erupt.* I don't have the strength anymore to do what needs to be done to end her. I'm only hanging on by a thread. *I should have dropped this ages ago.*

"Then explain to us why you let them live after they found each other? They are now even more dangerous than before. You really should have ended this instead of messing around with the Crawlers!" This time it was Elder Fox who spoke up. Have all the elders really been plotting my demise this entire time? *Well fuck you all!*

"SHUT... UP!" Willow yells and I shrink away from her wrath. I have only ever heard her use that tone a few times in my lifetime and it's not pretty to be on the end of it. "If I remember correctly, all of YOU had the chance to take them down too but you didn't! You were all with them way more than I and still, you did nothing. You're all a bunch of bloody cowards!" The fire within my veins stirs and I'm on the brink of eruption. *Enough of this.*

Grabbing the clutch I decide to do something extremely foolish and rev the bike as loudly as I can. The tail end swings from side to side as the rubber burns against the pavement. Releasing the clutch, I take off down the street leaving a grand burnout in my wake. I hear Willow scream my name and it kills me to think that she is behind all this. The sweet little woman who used to braid my hair before bed. The sweet little woman who used to tell me stories of the past and how we came to be. Now that I've seen the library and read the Books of Old, I see just how much I was manipulated.

I need a place to hide and fast. My childhood hideout comes to mind and I race off in its direction. It's the one place where I always knew I was safe no matter what. A place where no one, not even Willow could find me. *Maybe it's charmed like the library, I just don't know but it's my very own secret lair.*

I pull up at my riverside hideout and jump off the bike. Leaning the Harley up next to the old oak tree, I put my back against the trunk and take three giant steps towards the river. Crouching low I reach for the hidden latch hidden in the grass, swivelling my finger around I find the string and pull. There is a distinct click as the hatch door unlocks and I pull the lid up revealing a step ladder leading down into the bunker below.

I rush inside and quickly slam the door closed above me. I lock it up tight and with my feet resting on either side of the ladder, I slide down the rungs and rush over to the makeshift bed in the corner of the room. Laying down for the first time since leaving the library, I will myself to relax. I breathe in deeply and feel my power slowly leaving my body, the heaviness of it drops out of me to the point I feel almost weightless. Sighing peacefully, I close my eyes and let my mind wander off into the darkness.

Chapter 18

The sound of tapping on the metal hatch door wakes me up from my endless slumber. *Huh?* Groggily I sit up and rub my eyes. *How long was I out?* Stretching my arms high above my head I hear the tapping sound again and my stomach drops. *Oh no! They've found me! But how? Maybe they saw the bike. Damn!* I'm about to switch into my true form when I hear a familiar voice on the other side of the door. "Kyra, it's me, let me in." *Duncan.* Rushing forward I climb the steps two at a time and rest my hand over the latch. I almost unlock it when I notice something's missing. *That's odd.* Gazing down at my chest I freeze. *Where's the pull, the lifeforce that binds us together.* It should be stronger than ever, especially being this close.

Snapping my head up as bile rises in my throat, I begin to slowly make my way back down the stairs. *That's not Duncan above me, it's someone else, or should I say something else.* One particular beast comes to mind, and I almost throw up at the thought. *A Crocotta.*

It's half hyena, half dog, a beast I never wanted to cross paths with ever again. The creature has the ability to lure you by using the voices of your loved ones. They go in and cut off your air supply first by wrapping their jaw around your windpipe. Then they like to twist and turn until your neck breaks from the pressure. That way you will have a slow and nasty death and then they get to enjoy eating you while you're still nice and fresh. *Oh, and did I mention it's also another creature that has the power to send us back to the cradle.*

"Sweetheart, are you in there?" It speaks in Duncan's sweet drawl. *I need to get out of here.* Gazing around the confined space, other than the cot there isn't much in here. I could use the shovel in the corner of the room to dig my way to the river but which direction is that? *Think Kyra... Think...*

"MOVE!... NOW!" A voice growls outside in the distance and my back goes stiff. *Now that's Duncan!* Looking down at my chest again I can now feel the tickle that binds us together. *He's here! He's finally here!* I hear the beast moving around on top of the hatch door above me before it laughs like a hyena.

"And who are you to tell me what to do? *Prince!*" It spits out the words in a voice nothing like the one I heard before. This one is more like a snake with a forked tongue.

"Just try me furball and see where it gets you." Duncan's voice drops into a menacing level which makes all the hairs on my arms stand on edge. The beast just laughs.

"As you wish." It hisses before loud scrapes are heard against the hatch door and I listen carefully as it takes off to the right. Grunts and cackles alike are all I hear for the next few agonising minutes until there is a distance crack of a bone being broken. I inhale sharply and hold my breath, waiting for what feels like an eternity to know what's going on up above.

The thumps of human footsteps shake me out of my stupor and I rush to unlock the door. Pushing it wide open, I stick my head out just in time to see the Crocotta hit the ground hard. Swinging my eyes to Duncan, my mouth drops open at the sight of him. His shirt is torn in numerous spots exposing his masculine body beneath. Some of the cuts are so deep that I can even see the bones peeking through his skin. *Oh Zagoria, this is bad!* He is breathing heavily as he stares down at the now lifeless body before him. *How it must pain him to kill one of his own. I don't know what I would do if I was ever in the same situation.*

Turning his head he notices my stare and begins to walk over. He stops just shy of the trap door and leans forward extending his arm out to help me up.

"Finally!... I found you." He breathes as I take his hand and feel a zap the instant our hands connect. Yelping from the shock, Duncan yanks me out of the bunker and into his arms, cradling my head against his chest. *It feels so good to be in his arms again.* I take a deep breath and feel him swallow before he opens his mouth to speak. "You have no idea how terrified I've been while looking for you. When I came back to this realm, I felt the pull and followed it but about an hour ago while I was passing the great lake, it felt like someone took a knife to the link and severed it. For a moment I thought the worst but then remembered, if that was the case then I wouldn't be here either, so I kept looking.

I was flying high above when I saw a Crocotta acting weird and speaking to the ground. At first, I thought it was odd and then I remembered something Snow said. Years ago he found a hidden underground bunker and used it to hide from Willow and her followers. Thankfully, you know not to open the door for strangers." Duncan turns his head to look at something over his shoulder and I follow his stare. In a tangled mess of limbs is the dead Crocotta, green blood sticks to its fur and I count for ten seconds and wait, but nothing happens.

Scrunching up my face, I look at Duncan and see that he is oblivious of the situation as he pulls me in closer. He leans forward and brushes a kiss upon my forehead at the same time I push a little away from him.

"That's odd," I mutter under my breath as I stare at the beast willing it to evaporate. *What is going on?* Isn't the beast's soul supposed to go back to the pit? *But what if it's drained? No, it shouldn't be, not yet anyway.* Snow said that we would know if it was gone. That the world would be destroying itself because if the pool of the dead was no more, then the balance between the realms would be demolished too.

"What is it?" He asks as he looks down. Following my gaze, he looks back towards the creature and frowns.

"The Crocotta, it's still here," I say in astonishment as Duncan lets me go and moves to inspect the beast lying on the ground. He crouches down and with feather light touches he checks the creatures' tender spots, obviously checking its vitals.

"Well it's definitely dead, so what do you think this means?" He asks as he flicks his eyes towards me for a second.

"I don't know and to be honest, I don't really want to wait around to find out. We have a job to do and by the look of it, we need to do it fast." I cross my arms over my chest and lean back against the grand oak tree. It's warm against my back and I snuggle up to it a little more. It's only now that I realise there is a slight chill in the air, that's very abnormal for this time of year. I hear a piercing screech coming from my right and whip my head around to see Fang on the neighbouring oval stretching out her mighty wings and stomping the ground rather impatiently too.

Duncan lifts his head and smiles as he glances at his mighty creature. The adoration in his eyes is unmistakable and I have to force myself to look away. That is going to be another, inevitable, painful goodbye. This is all so unfair.

The water flowing downriver is calm as it drifts through the reeds, swishing this way and that. It seems so peaceful when the world around us is anything but.

Feeling warmth to my left, I lift my eyes to my mate. Duncan wraps his arms around my waist and pulls me away from the tree. He rests his hand on the back of my head, guiding me towards his shoulder so I can nestle in closer. He lowers his mouth and whispers, "I found it." into my ear before placing a gentle kiss at the base of my neck.

"What?..." I utter a little confused and then our mission comes to mind. "You did? Where?..." Duncan doesn't reply, just continues to trail sweet little kisses up and down the side of my neck. Desire begins to build in the base of my abdomen and uncontrollably I pull him closer. I need him to extinguish the fire deep within. Feeling my yearning, he moves his hands to my ass, lifts me off the ground and backs us up against the tree. Freeing his left hand he slides it underneath my shirt and cups my breast through the fabric of my bra. He squeezes it until the point of pain and I throw my head back in pleasure. "We don't have time for this," I silently declare, even though this is all I want to do right now.

"I'm pretty sure we do." He growls as his lips travel further down to the base of my collarbone. White lights begin to dance in my line of sight and although I try, I can't seem to blink them away. *What is that?* Duncan hooks his fingers underneath the strap of my bra and pulls hard, ripping the material from my body. His lips become almost desperate against my skin as he hoists me higher against the tree. *What is going on?*

Taking his face within my grasp, I force him to look at me. Through the stars in my vision I witness the whites of Duncan's eyes turn to black as the true darkness takes over. *Oh no! It's back.* Removing his hand from my breast he lifts it up and grips me hard around the neck. The lights behind my eyes become unbearable as Duncan yanks me forward, forcing my face down to meet his. "D...uncan..." I manage to get out in-between kisses, while trying to push him away. *He needs to stop. We need to stop!*

I am pushing at him to stop when all of a sudden it feels like lightning zapping my body and my consciousness gets shoved back within myself. I am confined to a small black box, while I watch my body move on its own accord. I am helpless as my hands dip into his hair, ripping his lips from mine and forcing his face to meet my chest. I feel the climax building deep within and dread what comes next. My apex grinds against him while his tongue does wondrous things to my tender nub.

Duncan growls against my skin as he pulls me closer and starts moving his hips in time with mine. My right hand reaches down and pushes his pants just low enough to spring him free. Grabbing his thick length with my long fingers I play with his smooth skin all the way down to the base. This is so wrong and I begin to scream hoping this will end, for anything really that will take me away from here.

Don't get me wrong, I love this man with all my heart, but I can't sit here and watch this thing within me make love to him.

My head leans forward to gaze down between us so I can witness all of his god like glory. I feel my body lick its lips as it raises its eyes back to our mate. "I think I may need a little help," I coo in this ultra-sexy voice, one very much not like my own. His eyes seem to sparkle as he glances down. He obviously sees my dilemma and a panty dropping grin breaks out across his face. Duncan reaches down and grips the left side of my pants. With one quick pull, his muscles flex and tears the fabric. Without saying a word he switches hands below my ass and moves to tear the other side as well. The remaining material falls to the floor exposing my naked flesh to the cool afternoon breeze. *Oh Zagoria I can't watch this!*

A sensual shiver runs through my body and I force my consciousness to cover its eyes. I feel his lips move against mine again and although I try to ignore it, I can't, I feel everything. Every touch, every sensation. It's completely torturous but insanely pleasurable. Duncan swiftly enters my body and begins pounding me up to the heavens. My body is thrashing against his as it tries to keep up and we both begin to make noises that are no longer human. We are scratching and biting each other as we fight to get closer while our power builds stronger than ever before. I feel the fire within my veins getting ready to explode and my consciousness screams out as loud as I can.

It feels like eons have passed by the time our bodies finally release and explode around each other. Breathing heavily they both relax back against the tree. Our soul just connected like it never has before. It was erotic and empowering but the lack of control was scary as hell and I fear something has irreversibly changed.

Chapter 19

My eyes flutter open as a cool breeze hits my skin. *Where am I?* I look up and see the bright green leaves on the branches of the grand oak tree. *I'm still at the river?* Lifting my head slightly, I notice that I'm on the ground with my back against the trunk while bats fly low overhead. As quick as lightning I push myself further back against the tree, trying to hide from sight. Thankfully I'm back in my human form, otherwise they would have ratted me out already. The sky is now dark as night and the trees around us seem to have lost their sway. The grass doesn't even look as green as it should be for this time of year either.

I hear snoring coming from my right and I push myself up to take a better look. Duncan is fast asleep beside me with his back also against the tree. He looks so calm and content as I watch his chest rise and fall with every breath he takes. His shirt is long gone and so are the claw marks from the battle with the Crocotta. His skin looks radiant with no imperfections to be seen. The bite I received from the Cerberus comes to mind and I look down at my bicep. *Shit, I'm NAKED!*

Quickly I cover my body with my hands and look around for my clothes. Examining my surroundings, I see the scraps of material that were once my pants lying on the floor not too far from where I'm sitting. Well, I'm not going to be able to put those back on. Without a second thought, I jump to my feet and run for the hatch door, I pull it open and dive inside. Making quick work of the stairs, I walk over to a chest that holds a spare set of my armour. Even in the human realm, it is here. It's the one thing that always transcends both realms.

Once I'm dressed, I go to the mirror on the far wall and stop dead in my tracks. *What in the world?* Holding my arm up to the light, I move it around trying to see any remnants of the bite I received not so long ago. The skin is smooth as I run my finger down my arm trying to picture what it used to look like.

Even after Duncan helped with the healing process, the scar still remained. A thought comes to mind and I begin to search the rest of my body for my other blemishes, yet I come up short. *All my scars, the visible memories, gone! Maybe it has something to do with whatever the hell that was that I just experienced. I've never felt us create that much power before.* Another cool breeze brushes over me and I shiver. Even here, down in the Earth, I'm still not sheltered from the world above.

Grabbing a bottle of water from my supplies I take the stairs two at a time, needing to get back to the surface above. Reaching the top, I look for my mate and see him resting against the tree with his arms crossed over his body. He's staring at the riverbed beside him. Quickly, I climb out of my hideout and close the lid, setting the lock behind me. *You never know when we may need to come back here.* Startled by the sudden movement, Duncan whips his head around and looks at me. I see sadness in his eyes and wish I could take it away as I make my way over to him.

"There you are, I was wondering if you left me here to fend for myself or not?" He jokes as he tilts his head up as I come to a stop before him. He eyes the bottle of water in my hand, and I toss it to him without question. He catches it with one hand and quickly unscrews the cap, taking huge gulps, almost finishing off the whole thing in a matter of seconds.

"Thirsty, are we?" I utter smiling as I watch a few water droplets escape the side of his mouth.

"Very... thanks." He puts the lid back on and hands me back the near empty bottle. I take it and then cross my arms, trying to act like what just happened between us didn't affect me. *What am I supposed to say to him now? This is so awkward.* I felt everything. Everything that he was doing to me. Everything we were doing. I couldn't stop it. It wasn't him, it wasn't me. *It was our soul, not us. I'm so confused.*

I glance at Duncan and look away the instant our eyes connect. I turn my gaze towards the calming river and sigh. *This is going to be harder than I thought.* "Do you um...." He pauses as he glances at me before following my stare. I hear him take a deep breath before he continues. "Do you want to talk about what happened?" He asks as he stands and shoves his hands into his pockets. The movement makes the muscles in his forearms flex and I have a hard time looking away. His abs are also on full display and I tear my eyes away the second the image of him pounding me up against the tree comes to mind.

I quickly peek in his direction, wanting to talk about what happened before I can't. *I need to put some distance between us for a minute.* Eyeing Fang over on the field, I uncontrollably head towards her. She is asleep with her wings spread out wide. *I have no idea how that is comfortable.* Without saying a word, he moves away from the tree and follows me towards his beautiful monster.

"Actually, I don't want to talk about it. I did but now I don't. This is already awkward enough and honestly, I don't want to relive what happened. So please, let's just drop it and move on. You said earlier that you knew where the entrance was, so let's go." I say with a manner of authority, and I feel him relax behind me. Suddenly there is so much tension between us but now is not the time to try and sort through it. *Let's just finish what we started and hopefully, the world will be ok in the end.*

Duncan picks up his pace and strides past me on his way to Fang. With slow precise movements, he walks up to her face and runs his hand along her snout, gently waking her up from her slumber. She emits an awful screech as she retracts her wings and beats them a few times against the ground. Fang moves her beady eyes towards me and snarls in my direction. Having a strong desire to live, I slow my pace as I continue to approach her.

"We need to stop by my place first. I need to grab a few things before we get going" he declares as I stop less than five feet away from the creature. Duncan turns and waits for me to reply, so I just nod my head. I'm staring at his half naked body and realise he probably wants to go home so that he can grab some clothes. Hopefully he has some food there too, we need sustenance, especially if we plan on surviving the day. *That's if we survive the day.*

If I thought the breeze on the ground was cold, I was clearly mistaken. It's absolutely freezing this high up. Fang, with her wings spread wide, glides under the darkened clouds. I can feel Duncan's power all around us, like the chaos everywhere is making him stronger. I know it's only a matter of time before mayhem breaks out on the surface below. I can feel the people suffering already and I know it's only going to get worse.

I glance over the edge and notice that all the monsters seem to be travelling in the same direction. *They are heading east.* I hear roars and screams rising from below and dread what will happen if we don't make it in time. *We really need to find the pit and do it fast.*

Green clouds continue to roll in and it's only now that we are up so high that I am able to see the gigantic tear in the sky over the city. Even from this great distance, I can see beings coming to and from the centre of the rift. *That must be where they broke through the dimensions. Maybe it wasn't at the station after all.*

My arms are circling Duncan's waist and his warmth is seeping into my skin. We are so high that the houses below look like little squares, and I see that the traffic has come to a standstill.

Duncan emits a high-pitched whistle and Fang quickly changes direction. I look around to see if there is anything I recognise, anything at all that will remind me where we are. I notice a few ovals and a shopping centre to the left, but other than that there is nothing familiar.

I notice Fang tucking in her wings and hear Duncan yell "Hold on,". She changes direction once again and dives towards the ground. I let out a tremendous scream while I cling to my mate. Duncan's stomach jiggles beneath my arms as he laughs and I pinch his side out of annoyance. *Asshole!* He flinches a little while laughing even louder and I smile in return. *That was not funny... Well, maybe a little bit.* With a few hard beats of her mighty wings, Fang lands in front of a small apartment building on the outskirts of Sydney.

The people on the ground scream in terror as they try to put substantial distance between them and the giant bat. Fang hisses in their wake and my heart plummets from the sight. *Was that really necessary? They are already afraid of her.* "Stop that," Duncan orders as he pats Fang's hide before jumping down from the saddle. He does a quick perimeter check before coming back to help me. Duncan raises his arms and guides me down from the saddle. Raw electricity ignites from his touch and I tuck my hands under my pits the second we part. *I think that's enough touching for the time being.*

Duncan gives me this weird look before shaking it off and turns towards his beast. "Don't go anywhere alright, I'll be right back" he commands giving her a stern look and she shrieks her reply. Duncan turns to me and holds his hand out but I shake my head. I'm not ready to touch him just yet. He gives me another weird look before shrugging it off and strides over to the entrance of the building.

"Do you really live here?" I ask semi disgusted while I glance at all the marks on the walls as we make our way up to the second floor. The beige paint is crumbling which indicates that it's been painted over multiple times, making everything look so much worse. The carpet beneath my feet is also falling apart and I have to be careful not to trip on any loose threads. *This is not what I expected at all.*

"Hey, it may not be as grand as your place, but it was enough for me." He says a little offended.

"I'm sorry, I'm truly not trying to be judgy. I just thought with your attitude and growing up in the library, that you would have something a little nicer."

"That's just it, you see. It was because I grew up in the library that I wanted something a little bit more normal." Duncan mutters over his shoulder as he directs us to the last apartment on the left. He places his hand against the door frame, whispers his incantation and the door swings wide open.

"Do you guys ever use a key?" I ask rolling my eyes. *Show off!*

"I've never needed one." Duncan chuckles as he holds up his hand and then steps forward into his apartment. I begin to follow him but freeze halfway through the doorway. *Oh Zagoria! His apartment is the size of a damn shoe box.*

There is a tiny kitchenette along the right wall next to the door and to the far side of the room, it looks as if there may be a tiny room back there. If I was to guess, I bet it would be his bathroom. Lying on the floor against the left-hand sidewall is a mattress that rests beneath the tiniest window I have ever seen. He has a few items scattered here and there but other than that, there is nothing else. *This is definitely not what I expected at all.*

He stops in front of his bed and picks up a shirt off of the floor, he brings it to his nose and takes a whiff. *Eeww,*

Gross! Obviously deeming it to be ok, he slides it over his head before turning around. "Are you going to stand in the doorway the whole time or are you going to come in?" I blink away my astonishment and nod my head as I step forward, closing the door behind me. "I'm sorry the place is such a mess. I wasn't really expecting company." Duncan rubs the back of his neck as he peers around the room.

"It's alright, honestly. I'm just a little shocked, that's all. This apartment is about a quarter of the size of your room back at the library." I state as I take another hesitant step forward.

"I think that's why I love it so much." He smirks while shrugging his shoulders as if it's no big deal. I slowly nod my head again, crossing my arms over my chest and lean back against the door. I'm still a little uneasy around him and this seems to be the furthest away I can get.

Duncan stares at me for a moment before walking over to the tiny bar fridge in the corner of the room. He crouches low and opens the door, peering inside. He moves a few things around but obviously finds nothing edible because he closes the door and moves on to the cupboards above the sink. He rummages through whatever he has in there before pulling out two tiny tins. Duncan opens the drawer next to his waist and grabs out cutlery before walking over to me.

I back myself up against the hardwood as Duncan stops in front of me to show me what he found. "Sorry it's not much but it's all I have that's safe to eat." He places the items in my open palm and then turns around to go sit on the bed. I hold the small tin up to my face and read the label. Freshwater tuna. *Not bad*. I slide my back down the door and decide to sit right here to eat my food. I can feel Duncan's eyes on me the entire time however, I try not to notice. *He knows how it felt "trapped" in there and I am thankful he is giving me some space.*

We exit the building an hour later and see Fang rearing back in fright. Duncan immediately jogs over to her and tries multiple times to grab her face, but she keeps pulling away. She won't take her eyes off the end of the road and I decide to follow her gaze to see what the fuss is about. There is a horde of dark creatures a mile wide heading our way. *Shit!* They are a little too close for comfort and without thinking, I conjure up my sun sword as I switch into my true form.

Startled by the sudden brightness Duncan whips his head towards me. "WHAT ARE YOU DOING?" He roars and I point at the onslaught heading our way. A pack of over a thousand beasts snarl and growl as they make their way towards us.

Duncan spins back around and scrutinizes the distance between us and them. They're about two hundred feet away and closing in fast. "There's no time, we have to leave. NOW!" He yells while running to Fang's side. Duncan grabs the reins and pulls himself up onto the saddle. I glance back at the horde and decide I'm not going into this battle alone. I would need him if I wanted to walk out of it alive and it's clear as day that he's in no mood to fight. Without another thought, I jog over to Fang and allow Duncan to help me up.

"We could've taken them you know," I announce over his shoulder, even though I agree that leaving is the best decision right now. Duncan's wolf whistle is the only sound I hear before Fang spreads her massive wings and catapults us into the skies.

The air's cool against my skin and I cling on to Duncan. I feel our power flowing between us the closer we get to the clouds and it's only now that I notice that they aren't clouds at all. It's the green smoke of Duncan's gift.

As Fang begins to level out Duncan turns his head to speak, "Don't get me wrong, I knew we could've taken them, but the thing was, we didn't have to. I personally didn't want to waste any unnecessary power, especially when we have a job to do." His words make sense and I nod in agreement. There is no point wasting energy especially when we have no idea what is waiting for us below.

"That's very true, which reminds me. You said earlier that you found the entrance. Where is it?" I shout over the wind as we fly near the gigantic hole in the sky. Bats and butterflies glide all around us, swooping and diving like they are having a battle of their own.

"Don't you see it?" Duncan asks over his shoulder and then turns back towards the city. He lifts his arm and points to something far in the distance, yet I see nothing but skyscrapers. Snow's words come to mind and I remember that only the caster can see the beam of light. Because we weren't around when the first spell was drawn, we would need to conduct another one to see it too. I realise Duncan has already cast the ritual and found it.

"No, I need to voice the other ritual."

"Sorry, I forgot. Here, close your eyes and repeat after me…" Duncan says as he moves one hand behind his back and links his fingers with mine. "With hands joined as one, show us what cannot be undone."

"With hands joined as one, show us what cannot be undone." We say it one more time with our voices in sync and then I open my eyes. Not too far ahead I see a purple beam of light rising from the ground below. *Our beacon of hope amongst the chaos.*

I squint my eyes trying to get a better look and notice that it appears to be coming from a large clearing, maybe a park or some kind of oval. Either way, we will find out soon enough.

Chapter 20

Fang lands on the ground near the centre of the clearing. The outskirts of the oval are so far away that I can barely see the trees lingering there. *How odd that a block of land this size near the centre of Sydney has been left untouched by developers all these years. It would be worth a fortune and go for a hefty price if it ever went up for sale.* Before I jump down from the saddle, I take a good look around to make sure we weren't followed. I see a few creatures flying overhead but they don't seem to notice us all the way down here. The moment my feet hit the ground, I hear Duncan slide off behind me.

Glancing back, I watch as he walks around to Fangs face, grabbing it and holding it dearly while he whispers something that only she can hear. Feeling like I'm intruding on their conversation, I turn around and gaze at the beam of light. The huge ray seems to be coming out of a lone tree in the centre of this enormous field.

Startled by a weird noise behind me, I whirl around and see Duncan stepping away from Fang. He wipes away a lone tear that escapes the corner of his eye before he nods his head. Maybe he's telling her it's time to go.

Fang looks reluctant to leave as she glances between the two of us, she stomps her feet on the ground while turning her head towards all the noise, far off in the distance. *If I was in her shoe's I wouldn't want to leave my master here either.*

Saddened by her predicament, I fold my hands in front of me and slightly bow my head. Quietly giving her my thanks for all she has done for us and for what I know she will continue to do for us until the job is complete. I hear Duncan's wolf whistle and raise my head just in time to see her spread her mighty wings and take off into the skies. Duncan doesn't take his eyes off of her until she is nothing but a spec in the skies above us. I feel his anguish through the bond and walk over to stand by his side. I don't really know what I can do or say that could make him feel better.

"Do you want to talk about it?" I ask, realising he just said goodbye to his longest companion.

"Nope" he says evading my question while moving past me on his way to the tree. Sadness and sorrow radiate off of him and I know there is nothing in this world that could make him hurt any less right now, so I walk in the wake of my mate.

The tree before us is enormous. It has a likeness I've never seen before, not in this lifetime anyway, but I feel like I may have in the past. It's calling to me even though I feel as if I should flee from it. It has no leaves, no sign of life and yet it's pulsing like a heartbeat. Nature seems to run from it and I have a feeling I know why. Not only does it look as scary as anything you would see in a horror film, but it also has this pungent odour. It reeks of trash and death. *This is not a place that I would like to call home.*

Its branches reach for the sky, as high as a five-story building and they are as black as the night. It has an unusually large, twisted trunk with its roots prodding out of the ground in multiple directions. Just being this close to it sends shivers running down my spine.

"Willow couldn't have picked a more scarier sight," I state coming to a stop at the base of the tree. I would rather be running away from this thing instead of being here, but maybe that's the charm, designed to make you feel that way. The closer we get to the trunk the more the feeling grows. That might be why this field is still here, the enchantment turns developers and residents away. I turn my head to look back at the grand space beyond us. *This place would really be worth a fortune if the tree wasn't here.*

"It was probably a normal tree before the entrance was put here, the gateway has a knack for doing this... Destroying life I mean." Duncan crosses his arms over his chest and stares at the trunk deep in thought. His eyebrows crumble together the longer he glares, and I get the feeling I should be doing something else. Not wanting to distract him, I decide to take a walk.

The base of the tree is so large it takes me almost ten minutes to walk around it completely. I look for any possible clues that might identify where the entrance is, but I come up short. As I stroll around the last bend I notice Duncan hasn't moved an inch since I left. His facial features have taken on a darker aura and I feel like I should pull him out of whatever's going on in his head.

"So, how do we get in?" I ask as I clap my hands and rub them together. The cool air is starting to chill me and the dark clouds above us are doing nothing to ease my rising unrest. *I need sunlight.* Duncan blinks a few times before he drops his arms and takes a step back, shaking his head.

"That's the thing Kyra, I don't know." He looks at me with uncertainty plastered on his face and I get a sense of bewilderment as I glance between him and the tree.

"What do you mean you don't know, isn't it your job to know?" I ask a little more irritated than intended. He controls everything that resides within the darkness, including the realm below and he tells me now that he has no idea how to access it?

"Don't be so damn patronizing. I told you before that it was moved. Did it ever cross your mind that whoever moved it also changed the fucking passkey too!" Duncan shouts and takes a menacing step forward. I may not like his tone, but he has a point. If Willow was the one to move it here, then I have no doubt that she changed how to access it too. She wouldn't have gone to all of the trouble to move it and then leave it the same, that's for sure.

"You're right and I'm sorry, I didn't think about that but please don't shout. We don't need any unnecessary

attention right now, especially as we are out in the open..."
I say gazing between him and the creatures flying overhead. "How did you access it before?" I ask getting my own temper back under control. Crossing my arms over my chest, I take a deep calming breath in. He needs to know that he cannot treat me like one of his minions. *He may be pissed off too but that doesn't excuse him for the way he just spoke to me.* Duncan takes a few deep breaths of his own and glances back towards the tree.

"Snow told me years ago that to access it I had to voice my ritual while I concentrate on the gate, the pathway between the two realms. That's supposed to open up a crack within this world just big enough for me to step through. I saw sketches of it in the Books of Old back in the library. I just really wish I'd found the entrance long before now. It definitely would have saved us some time." Duncan huffs while turning back to me. A sense of defeat comes down the bond and I almost step forward, needing to remind him that we are in this together.

I close my eyes for a brief moment and I'm taken back to when my half of the soul took over. It's like a bucket of cold water gets dumped on my head and I drop my arms to my sides. Moving them behind my back, I link my fingers together and squeeze tight. *I cannot let her rise again, her power was so strong and I'm definitely not ready to meet her again anytime soon!*

I clear my throat and begin to speak, "Why didn't Snow show you how to use the enchantment tracker earlier? He could have saved you all this trouble." I say as I look anywhere else but at him. The feeling of longing grows stronger with each passing second and I have to fight myself to stay put.

"He told me after we studied the spell that he wanted to. Years ago when we realised that Willow had moved the entrance, he was afraid that she would learn about the current prophecy if we had tried to locate it sooner. You're probably thinking right about now, "but it's your domain" which it is, but it's not necessary for me to go down there unless there is actual trouble.

It was rare for my predecessors to visit the darkest part of our world. There is a lot of death and decay down there, not something you enjoy seeing on day-to-day basis. There are also a lot of souls willing to do whatever they can to get topside, and I'm not just talking about Zagorians. There are heaps of human souls down there too, plenty that the worlds are better off forgetting about.

It's another reason why it's vital we repair the pit. We need to protect both realms from the evil within it." I agree wholeheartedly as I look back towards the tree. Most of the time the humans are a nice bunch of people, but just sometimes you will come across someone who has a meaner streak than the man standing before me. Some are pure evil. We need to protect all those nicer people from the not so nice ones who died long ago. *We just need to find a way in, but how?... What could work?* The time we battled the Crawlers comes to mind and I spring to life.

"What does the bridge look like?" I blurt out before collecting myself. "Sorry, but I have a thought. If we were to join hands and both say your incantation at the same time, it might just be enough to amplify your powers to open the door." I say a tad rushed while he looks at me with amazement. I'm guessing those were the right words because Duncan extends his hand towards mine. *This might work!*

"You know that's actually a pretty smart idea..." He gives me a wicked smile before a thought crosses his mind and his face falls. "The bridge though... it's um... it's dark and made of..." He pulls his hand away and rubs the back of his neck. *Why is this so hard for him to tell me?* He turns his gaze towards the tree for a moment and takes a deep breath before continuing. "... it's made of bones. Bones of the lives that were sacrificed to the deep in the beginning of time..." he lets out a breath before turning his eyes back to mine.

"There are huge stone pillars on the other side that mark the real entrance to the underworld, and a river of green flows beneath the bone bridge leading to pit of the damned. I don't want to scare you by telling you more, so hopefully that will be enough for the spell to work." He mutters a sigh as he turns to face the tree once more.

"Alright," I murmur as I nod my head and step a little closer to him. Extending my hand out, I find that even now I'm still a little hesitant to touch him. I may have held on to him on Fang's back, but nothing beats holding his hand and feeling the power truly flow between us. He glances down at my extended arm and I see that he is obviously having the same thoughts as me. Duncan sighs heavily and places his hand in mine. Under my skin, my whole body comes to life the instant our hands connect. Without another word, Duncan pulls me to him and cradles my head against his chest.

"Before we begin, I need you to know that I'm sorry for what our soul did to you. It was torturous for me the first time it happened and I can only imagine what it was like for you. I understand why you've been avoiding me." He utters as he nestles his face into my hair and gives me a tender kiss upon my shoulder.

"I'm n..." My voice ends on a slight sob as I go to say I'm not, although I have been. I have been keeping my distance from him since the moment I woke up on the ground outside my hangout. I was completely naked and ashamed of what I had just done and endured.

"Shhh, it's ok." He strokes my hair for a moment longer before allowing me to step back. It wasn't until now that I realised just how badly I needed him to hold me after what we went through. To know that he isn't the Darkness within him, but to remember that he is the sweet and caring Duncan that I have grown to love.

"Thank you," I whisper as I step into his embrace once more. I stretch up on my tippy toes and give him a chaste kiss on the lips before moving back.

"Anytime..." he smiles as his eyes shift to the monstrosity behind me. "Now, are you ready for this?" He asks as he takes a deep breath and I whisper "yes."

"Good." He claps his hands once and I swivel around so we are standing side by side. "Just envision what I told you and repeat after me." Doing as he says, I close my eyes and imagine the bridge made of bones, the green river that flows beneath it and the huge pillars awaiting us on the other side. Duncan grabs my hand and begins to speak, "Darkness comes and darkness falls. Be the ones to stop it all. For the light may come too late. To save the world from its terrible fate."

Duncan repeats it again and I speak in time with him as I feel our power surge. Warmth invades my chest and I know I'm glowing as bright as the sun. The wind picks up around us, trying to stop us, but we don't stop, we don't give up. *We can do this*. We repeat it one more time and as the last word leaves our mouths a thunderous crack sounds before us and we open our eyes.

There is a deep green crevice in the lower half of the trunk, the expanse only wide enough for one person to slip through at a time.

"It worked," Duncan whispers awestruck beside me and takes a step forward. I tilt my head to the side trying to get a better look but it's hopeless, I see nothing but darkness and smoke.

Duncan examines the hole for quite some time and then turns to me. "Are you ready? It's now or never." He announces a little too excitedly while extending his hand towards me. I grasp it and inhale deeply while moving myself right next to the black hole. "I'll go first, ok?" he asks, and I don't dare take my eyes off the cavity while I nod. He lets go of my hand and I watch him slide feet first into a land unknown. *This is it.* I sigh as I glance at the world around me, taking in the sights one last time before shaking off my nerves and following my mate down into the darkness below.

Chapter 21

All light vanishes the moment I slip through the crack and hit the ground hard as I fall to my side. There is a sense of nothingness around me and I hear, see and smell nothing. It's completely black. I want to stand yet I'm hesitant. I'm sceptical of how high the ceiling is, of everything within this place as I'm in a region unknown. *Where is Duncan?* Slowly I rise onto all fours, reaching high above me I feel around for anything I might hit my head on as I make my way to stand. *Why does it have to be so dark?* Reciting my ritual I pull power into myself but instead of feeling it intensify, it appears to dim instead. *That's weird.*

"Duncan?" I whisper into the darkness and my voice seems to reverberate off the walls around me. I wait for a minute or two for a reply but there's nothing. "Duncan?" I call out a little louder this time and again my voice seems to just trail off. *Where is he?*

Flaying my arms out wide I move in slow circles while I take a few small steps here and there. I need to find a wall or something, anything that might be able to tell me roughly where I am. I don't like being out in the open like this, especially down here. Anyone could be near and without my glow, I won't see them coming.

It feels like hours have passed by the time I feel the coldness of a stone wall beneath my fingertips. My throat is dry from screaming Duncan's name repeatedly and I sigh as I swivel around and place my back up against the wall. *Where is he? Surely he wouldn't abandon me down here.* At least if anything is going to attack me now, it won't be coming from behind. I try to increase my glow and yet it dims even further. *Shit! What am I going to do now?* There is nothing but blackness around me and I am completely alone in a domain not of my own. *I'm so screwed.*

Taking a few deep calming breaths, I need to decide on which way to go. Swinging my head from left to right it's hard to decide because I see absolutely nothing. I glance down at my feet and notice that not even a single glimmer emits from my being. *How is this even possible?*

Shaking my head in disbelief, I believe I came from somewhere on the left, so I head right. Keeping my back against the wall, I feel around with my foot as I slowly slide along its cool surface.

This place feels never ending. I've kicked a few stones here and there and manoeuvred myself around multiple corners and there is still nothing. Grazes have opened up on my palms, but I don't let myself pay any notice. I need to find something, anything I can see or feel to get myself out of this continuous situation.

I'm starting to give up hope that I'll ever find Duncan when I suddenly notice a greenish glow begin to appear around the next corner. *Finally!* Quickening my pace, I slide towards the light. The glow grows brighter as I round the corner and I'm startled for a moment by what lies before me, the bridge of bones. *Oh, Zagoria! I've found it, I found the entrance.*

I push away from the wall and almost run towards the bridge. Skulls line the top half of the railings and the body appears to be made of millions and millions of human femurs. I lift my head slowly and discover that the bridge is almost a full football field in length. A cold shiver runs down my spine as I am instantly filled with sadness. *How many people were sacrificed to the deep to make this horrendous abomination?* A green glow underneath the bridge catches my eye and I move to the left to take a better look. Twinkling little stars weave in and out of the moving current as they whirl in multiple directions. *The river of souls.*

Turning away, I look to the other side of the bridge and see a set of steel gates as high as the ceiling. Huge stone pillars stand on either side marking the real entrance to the world beneath. Terror and fear bleed from it, urging me to turn back. *I'm not supposed to be here*. This is the territory my half of the soul was never meant to see. I was created for brilliance, for light, not this, this goes against everything that I am.

"DUNCAN!" I scream as I begin to back away from the horror that stands before me. *I shouldn't be here.* "WHERE ARE YOU?" I shout as I almost trip on a small rock as I try to back away.

"I'm right here" He whispers behind me. I scream out loud and whirl around bumping right into him.

"Where h...?" I begin but stop as I notice his darkness surrounds him in a new way. Green shadows emit from within him and his appearance has morphed into something nastier than the one I saw above. His attire looks relatively the same but... different. A crown of green smoke sits stately upon his head and a black and green cloak is draped over his shoulders. I seek out the blue within his eyes, yet see nothing but the blackness that lies within him, the menacing Dark Prince that he truly is. "Where were you?"

"I've been around." He says nonchalantly as he crosses his arms over his chest. Duncan steps around me and heads towards the bone bridge. I wait for him to hesitate before crossing but he doesn't. He steps surely, out onto the bones of the past.

"Excuse me, what did you say? You've been around? And what, it didn't cross your mind that I was down here too?" I chase after him, pausing only for a second as I follow him onto the bridge. My stomach drops with guilt as I step on the bones of people, real people. I mutter a quick apology to those below me while I catch up to my other half. I grab ahold of his cloak and pull him to a stop, forcing him to look at me. "Are you even going to answer me?" I ask angrily.

"No" he says bluntly as he grabs my wrist, pulls his cloak out of my grasp and then drops my hand. He gives me a blank expression as he turns and continues on his way as if what I said means absolutely nothing to him.

"What is wrong with you?" I yell at his back while swinging my arms out wide. I refuse to let him treat me this way. It's been hours since we were top side and the man who stands before me is nothing like the one who entered this domain. This is the true Dark Prince, the one Willow and the Elders always warned me about. The one full of malice and hatred, a man that can create all types of nightmares. Maybe human Duncan was the farce and this is who he really is. *Maybe he's been playing me this whole time?*

"With me?" He mockingly whirls around with a hand upon his chest. "Nothing is wrong with me, *babe*." He drops his hand and then raises it quickly back up. "You on the other hand. There is definitely something wrong with you. You surely have seen better days." Duncan sweeps his hand up and down gesturing towards my glow before turning back around to face the gates on the other side. I glance down and even though I'm in my armour, I feel almost human. I don't sense any power within me and that's dangerous, especially considering I have no idea what lies beyond those doors.

"Where are you going?" I shake off my building rage and decide to chase after him, I almost have to run to keep up with his long strides. *When did he start walking so fast?*

"Come and find out for yourself?" He reaches the other side and stops just in front of the huge metal gates. "Actually wait, there is something I need to do first." He says while holding a finger in the air and turns around on his heel. "I think you're going to get a kick out of this" he states while giving me a pantry dropping grin and I instinctively take a step closer. *Stupid bond, why do you make me act like a fool.*

"And what is that?" I utter sweetly while gazing up at him and almost bat my eyelashes. *Zagoria! What has gotten into me?* I quickly force myself out of my stupor and take a small step back while placing my hands on my hips. *I really wish my body didn't react to him like that.*

Duncan laughs a little at my performance as his smile grows wider.

"Watch." He whispers and with a snap of his fingers, the tail end of a long silver chain magically appears within his hand. The other end falls to the floor before miraculously coming to life and wraps itself around my neck. I'm caught off guard as it tightens itself around my jugular leaving almost no room for air. I raise my hands to my neck and try to remove the chain the moment Duncan tugs me towards him. "You're mine now." He coos in my face as I drop my arms back to my sides. *What in Zagoria has gotten into him?*

I raise my hand again, but this time I'm not going for the chain, I'm aiming for his cheek. I feel victory within reach as I swing my arm forward but just as my hand is about to connect with his face Duncan grabs ahold of my wrist. "Tsk, tsk, no need to be feisty. You should save all that energy for the bedroom later." He chuckles as he toys with his end of the restraint.

"In your dreams. If you think I'm going anywhere with you now, you are most certainly mistaken." I turn and begin to walk back over the bone bridge even though I know it's futile. I make it about a metre away when Duncan yanks me back towards him. He grabs my face in a firm grip and forces his mouth down upon mine. He licks the seam of my lips yet I refuse to open my mouth. I will not allow him the satisfaction he so clearly desires.

Duncan licks and bites the outside of my lips for a few minutes before finally moving my face away from his. His grip is so tight that it feels like my jaw may snap from being under so much pressure. We stare deeply into each other's eyes and I believe I saw a twinkle of blue but I can't be certain. It disappeared as quickly as it came.

"You will do what I want, when I want and if you don't, I will make you regret the decision you made to come down here" he commands, yet his eyes seem to be saying something different. *What is that about?*

"I didn't come down here because I wanted to remember, we came down here because we have a job to do! Now release me!" I half yell at him. *He doesn't have that kind of power to control me, just like I don't have that power over him.*

"Or so you were led to believe." He whispers just loud enough for me to hear and my heart stops. *What did he just say?* I gaze into his eyes and try to see any form of truth, of hope but I see nothing but darkness. *He has to be joking, right? Or was this really all an act, a ploy from the very beginning to get me down here.*

A million thoughts run through my mind and I can't help the lone tear that escapes down the side of my cheek. Quickly I turn my face away and stare at the flowing river of souls, I am ashamed that I let his words affect me so.

Moving my head just slightly to the right, I eye the bridge and a thought springs to life. *Why is it when he speaks that his eyes portray something different? Could it be this place, could it be changing him or is he still the same Duncan I have always known?*

This entire cavern reeks of cruelty and fear, it may very well be the reason behind his behaviour. Or could it be because he is the ruler of this dominion and that requires him to act a certain way? To conduct himself in such a manor like the one he did when his minions entered my home. To show the true authority of the Prince of Darkness, scaring his beasts just enough so they follow him.

I gaze up into his big, blackened eyes and decide to give him the benefit of the doubt. *I really hope this doesn't backfire.*

"What do you want?" I ask kindly as a good submissive would. Bowing my head, I link my fingers together in front of me, proving to him that I am his for the taking. Well for the time being that is.

"Now that's much better my pet. What I would really like to do is to take you somewhere private so we can be alone, but first, you will see my domain." He strokes the back of his index finger down the side of my cheek before moving away.

Duncan pulls on the chain and walks us over to the real entrance of the underworld. Glancing over his shoulder, he gives me a cocky grin before turning back and places his hand upon the large steel frame. I can't make out what he is whispering but I have a feeling I know what it is. A familiar green glow appears underneath his fingertips and the clear sound of the door unlocking bangs on the other side.

The metal begins to creak and crack as the doors swing open and Duncan yanks hard on his end of the chain. I stumble forward and into his arms. Zaps of electricity course through my veins yet I barely have time to register them as I witness the true horror of the realms before me.

With one arm around my waist, Duncan holds me against him as he moves his mouth next to my ear. His hot breath upon my shoulder sends shivers running down my spine.

"Welcome home" he whispers before taking my earlobe into his mouth. He sucks it hard and I almost collapse not from the pleasure but from fear. *I shouldn't be here.* Nausea rolls torturously around in the pit of my stomach and I fight the urge to throw up. Everywhere I look, there are bodies hung from the ceiling and green flames, as hot as the sun, burn as far as the eye can see. Screams of the dead flood my senses and I force myself to remain composed. *There is so much pain.* In front of us is a staircase leading down into a giant chasm, the pathway seems to go on forever.

Duncan releases my ear as he turns me around, pulls me closer and nuzzles his face into the crook of my neck. "Your fear is driving me crazy. We might need to be alone sooner than I thought, unless you want everyone else to watch? Because that can be arranged." He chuckles knowing that's exactly the last thing I want.

Duncan lifts my feet slightly off the ground and moves us a few steps forward. I gaze over his shoulder and witness the gates closing behind us, locking us in. My fear spikes only for a moment as it now dawns on me that I am locked inside the abyss. *No!*

Duncan lifts his head, grabs a hold of my chin, and forces me to look at him. He searches my eyes for something before smiling as he recollects himself, "there is no escaping me now." He breathes as he leans forward and places his lips down upon mine. He draws me in closer with his arms wrapped around my back, I feel his erection digging into me and I wish I knew if this was real or is he playing a game.

Duncan removes his mouth from mine and trails kisses along my cheek towards my ear, "maybe I should just take you here. I bet my minions would get a kick out of it." He chuckles as his hands roam all over my body, stopping on my chest to grope my breasts through my armour. *Enough of this!* I scream down the bond. With my remaining strength, I lift my arms up between us and begin to push him away.

"Let... me... go." I manage to scream out in between kisses as Duncan settles his mouth down upon mine once more. He lowers his arm that is wrapped around my waist and grabs a hold of my ass, forcing my abdomen closer to his hard erection. I get the feeling that thrashing against him only seems to excite him more.

"Your mine, so there is no point fighting the inevitable," Duncan states, although I don't give up. I feel his grip loosen on my ass and decide to use it to my advantage. Grabbing a hold of his shoulder I force him down towards me as I bring my knee up, hitting him in the groin. He falls to the ground as an enraged roar leaves his lips. *Shit, where do I go?*

I eye the large double doors behind us and make a break for it. I'm almost there when my body launches forward and I slam into the steel gates. Duncan pins my body up against the cool steel frame while reaching around and grabs hold of my neck. "You're going to fucking pay for that" he seethes in my ear before swinging me around and throws me down the staircase behind him. Screams of pain leave my mouth as agony shoots throughout my entire body. Every bone on my left-hand side feels like it's broken.

Duncan's footsteps thump on the stone steps behind me as he makes his way towards me. *I need to get up, I have to fight back.* I just manage to get up onto my elbows when Duncan grips my hair and yanks me to my feet, shoving his face in mine. "Where the fuck do you think you're going huh?" he growls.

"Please stop, just stop," I whisper as I lift my hands to my hair and try to relieve some of the tension. *I shouldn't have done that.* Shame overcomes my being as another tear escapes down the side of my face. I try to turn away but I can't as Duncan tightens his grip.

"Stop what?" he spits in my face and then sucker punches me in the stomach, causing all air to leave my body. I choke and gasp as I riffle within his grasp. *This isn't my Duncan anymore, this is his Darker side, the version of him I never wanted to encounter again.*

"This." I cough out as I reach up and grab a hold of my flames. "I'm sorry, I won't fight you again I promise... I'll do whatever you ask, just please let me go," I say on the verge of tears and regret that I'm letting myself show so much defeat. I need to be stronger than this, but without my powers, I feel useless.

Duncan contemplates what I said for a moment as his eyes flutter. After a second or two they stop moving and a look of sorrow flashes across his face before he slightly moves his head away. He tilts his head to the side and rakes his eyes up and down my body. *I feel like a prize horse at an auction.*

"You'll do anything I ask?" He queries as he breaks out into a sly, cheeky grin and I feel like I just made the biggest mistake of my life. Knowing it's the only way he'll let go, I nod my head the best I can. "Oh, this is going to be fun." Duncan drops his hold on my hair and I sigh in relief. I barely have time to collect myself though as Duncan begins walking down the stairs, pulling me along with him. I stumble down the first few steps, but quickly right myself and begin walking in the wake of my master like the good submissive I am.

Chapter 22

The chasm goes on for miles and I'm beginning to wonder if it will ever end. High stone walls surround us and there is only dirt beneath my feet. Creatures of the dark have come and gone, all trying to get a good look at what the master has captured. Many of them cheered when they realised it was me, some of them even had the nerve to try and attack me. Duncan only growled and sent them on their merry way.

We have been walking for hours and I become fatigued as the last of my powers drain away. I look at the wall to my right and see the cool lines of time etched into the framework. Claw marks line the gap from the numerous beings that have passed through this horrid place. *Maybe I should leave my mark here too, I could dig in my heels or something. It may even alert Duncan to the fact that I'm still back here. It's been hours and he hasn't said a single word to me.*

Closing my eyes, I try to regain some of the strength I've lost. I feel "her" power beneath my feet and even though I reach for it, nothing happens. It's as if there is a barrier between us. Sighing heavily, I decide to give up.

However, I do need to come up with something because I can't continue on like this.

Lifting my head, I'm about to open my eyes when I stumble on a rock and crash right into Duncan's back. He comes to a halt and gazes over his shoulder before turning away to look at the rift in the chasm wall. A large cavern lies before us, inside is a huge black stone castle that stands far off in the distance. Its keeps are as high as the murky ceiling above which can only be accessed by another bone bridge that has been erected over a moat, filled with the souls of the dead. *Oh, Zagoria!* I think while raising my hands to cover my mouth as bile rises in my throat. *Just how many souls were sacrificed to make this horrible place?*

To the right of the castle, a large mound opens up to what I can only assume is the pit of the damned. Green lights flicker from within as noticeable droplets leak down the sides of the structure. The monstrosity is surrounded by creatures, all waiting for something or someone new to appear.

At the sight before me, my body begins to move on its own accord. It's being pulled to restore the peace within our lands, it wants to fix what's been broken.

I go to step around Duncan but he grabs my bicep in a firm grip. He looks down on me with horror and then moves his eyes towards his minions. His gaze flicks frantically around before landing upon the castle far in the distance. Duncan turns his eyes back to me for only a moment before shaking his head and begins moving us towards the stone structure.

We make it just inside the walls when Duncan loses his composure. "What the fuck, Kyra?" He yells a little frantically, while I stare at him. He stares down at me like I'm a little lost fawn before letting go of my arm and slamming the door shut behind us. He lingers there for a moment and he takes a few deep breaths. I watch his green smoke disperse a little as Duncan gains control over whatever is going on in his head.

All of a sudden he lets out an enraged growl, making me jump and begins prowling towards me. I back up a step and feel the coolness of the stone wall behind me. Duncan raises his hands and places them on either side of my head, caging me in. "Fuck Kyra, you can't go walking towards the pit like that. Have you ever heard of playing it cool? If the creatures realised what we were up to, they would turn on us in an instant. You do realise that don't you?" He ends his words solemnly as he stares down deep into my eyes. He may look angry however his eyes tell me a different story. I feel his breath on my cheek and know he is trying to keep his darker self at bay.

"Excuse me?" I ask a little baffled as I tilt my head to the side, trying to get a better look at the man standing before me. *Now that his creatures are out of earshot, maybe it's time to test just "who" is standing before me?*

"Don't play dumb, you heard me" he rages. *Well, there goes his composure.*

"Are we not going to discuss what you have been doing to me for the last five hours or am I supposed to just forget about that?" As the last word leaves my mouth, Duncan takes another step forward pressing his body flush against mine. I have half a mind to shove him away.

"If you want this to end badly, keep talking. I'm barely able to keep my darkness at bay but with the way you're acting, there is only so much I can do." He whispers angrily as he presses his growth into my abdomen. The light inside me quivers in anticipation however, I want nothing of the sort. Well, at least not now anyway. Duncan moves his face into the crook of my neck and takes a whiff of my scent. He sighs heavily as he lets out another breath.

"Is that supposed to be a threat?" I whisper as I push him back a little with a hand upon his chest. "I thought he took you over ages ago. Why else would you have been acting like such an ass?" I look deep into his eyes and see nothing but the blackness within.

"He practically did," Duncan utters on a sigh as he lowers his forehead to mine. "My darker powers are much stronger down here than I ever thought possible and its desire to be free is almost unbearable. There is this tingling burning sensation that runs through my veins the longer I try to keep him contained..." he takes a deep breath in and sighs again, "... I'm sorry Kyra, for what I did to you earlier, I didn't want to lay my hands on you, but you called my hand in front of them again. I have warned you before about what I have to do when that happens in front of them. How I have no choice but to show that I am punishing you for your behaviour. But please believe me when I say that it pained me beyond measure.

As for the chain, I couldn't let you walk around freely, especially down here. All of my minions want you dead. They have been twisted by Willow's ways for far too long, and they no longer know anything different." I stare at him and watch as a twinkle of blue shines in his irises before disappearing once more. *He really is still my Duncan.*

"I get that and I really should apologise to, for kneeing you in the balls I mean," I smirk as I shrug my shoulders trying to lighten the mood. *I do kind of feel bad about that.* He chuckles and I continue, "Also, I didn't mean to walk towards the pit before. My body was doing that all on its own. I felt the pull and before I knew it, I was moving.

The light inside me doesn't seem to work down here and I have all these other strange pulls and desires. My body wants them, almost needs them, and I'm struggling to control it." Duncan's scent fills my nostrils and I physically force myself back against the wall. *That is the last thing we need to be doing right now!*

"I get it, but you need to remember that when we are out there, you really have to try and control yourself. The beings down here are not like the ones on Earth. These ones are nastier and more deadly, honestly, there is no telling what they're capable of." Duncan states as he breathes me in. An unusual expression crosses his face before he pushes himself further against me. *Oh no!* White lights begin to dance in my line of sight and I inhale sharply. *Not again!*

"We have to stop," I whisper as I try to blink away the sudden surge of power within me. The lights are dominating my vision and I feel my body drawing into his. Closing my eyes, I quickly fight against my inner soul, I will not allow her to surface. I will not give up my control to her again.

"Oh, I don't think so." Duncan practically growls as he removes his right hand from the wall and runs it down the length of my body. He moves with a pace as slow as a snail as he glides his hand over my breast, moving lower to my waist until his hand hovers barely over the apex of my thighs. My eyes spring open and I gaze at the man in front of me. Duncan licks his lips as he removes his other hand and captures my chin, tilting my face up so we are eye to eye. His darkness is all I see but then suddenly, my soul shoves me back within myself.

I'm standing at the edge of a gilded cage, thrashing my arms against the steel bars as I watch Duncan lean forward and claim my mouth. I feel his lips move against mine and his hands roaming all over my body. With the hand over my sweet spot, he grips the fabric hard and pulls, tearing it clean away. There is nothing standing in the way of what our soul truly desires. Duncan gazes down between us as a cocky grin spreads out across his face.

I scream out at the top of my lungs for what's about to happen. *I can't go through this again.* A strange look crosses his face the second before he whirls me around and pushes my front up against the cold wall. Duncan reaches forward, grabs my leg and holds it up next to me while letting out a primal growl. He positions himself below my opening and in one swift move, he enters. My hand falls to his grip on my leg and our breathing becomes heavy as Duncan continuously thrusts himself deep into my vulvar. He reaches around with his spare hand and grabs my throat in a tight grip. This sets my inner soul aflame and I know her climax is close.

I feel the sensation building deep, while my body begins to shake from the inside out. I force myself to close my eyes. My soul physically screams out in ecstasy at the same time Duncan roars behind me. He pushes my body harder against the stone wall as we climax around each other. My body feels new, I feel her light burning and I want to claim her power as my own, but it feels just out of reach.

"Oh, this is going to be fun," Duncan says through laboured breaths as he withdraws himself and moves us away from the wall. My face turns to him and I feel her excitement grow over what's to come. My whole body is tingling with desire, and I cover my eyes not wanting to witness anymore. I feel a hand on my back and believe Duncan is leading us down a long corridor away from the castle's main entrance. He sweeps my hair over my shoulder and pulls me into another embrace. "My chambers are too far away, I must have you now." He declares and then I feel his lips massaging mine. *Oh, Zagoria! This is going to be a long night.*

Chapter 23

I'm delirious as I awake on a bed of black silk sheets. A soft pillow lies beneath my head and a warm throw blanket covers my body. I hear someone snoring soundly beside me and know it's my mate, my chest is fluttering with all kinds of emotions. It was not long after we entered this grand room that my consciousness passed out. Totally overcome with it all. The last time my soul took over I awoke on the ground next to the old oak tree. *At least this time it's a little more stylish.*

Lifting my head, I see huge double glass doors overlooking the cavern we walked through earlier. Not wanting to wake Duncan, I slowly slide out of bed and realise I am naked from head to toe. *Great!* Gazing around I see a soft black bathrobe hanging up on the far wall and run over to it. Throwing it over my shoulders, I quickly shove my arms through the sleeves and tie the sash around my waist.

Stalking over to the balcony, I stare down upon the large green pit just outside Duncan's bedroom window. It's as high as a small mountain and about double that in width. Once upon a time, I'm sure it would have even been filled to the rim however, right now only dregs remain. Waterfalls of green light flow from all around, letting unspeakable creatures back into the world. I watch as a twinkling light falls out of the pit, growing brighter and brighter as it travels its way down to the ground. The moment it connects with the soil below it bursts into a startling bright light. Its shine is too bright for even me to handle, so I shield my face away. I watch the lights around me fade back to normal and whip my head around to witness the newly formed Bubak standing in its wake.

Thousands upon thousands of creatures flock around the base of the mound, waiting to see who will emerge next. Will it be their kind or will it be another, either way, they will continue to re-emerge the longer Duncan and I remain cooped up in here.

"We have to stop this," I whisper under my breath as I cross my arms over my chest. I hug myself tightly as I ponder over what needs to happen next. *I know what we must do, and honestly, I think I'm ok with it.* I look over at Duncan who is still fast asleep and a sad smile breaks out across my face while I allow a single tear to fall. *I just wish we'd had time.* Shaking off my inner turmoil, I turn myself away and peer out towards the pit once more.

So many creatures have reappeared within such a short amount of time. I stare down at them and imagine what it would be like if I were to bring the order down here. The ones that I could trust that is! At first, I think the possibilities would be endless, but then I recall a major flaw in my plan. Thinking about what I have witnessed in the last thirty minutes, I believe for every creature my soldiers could takedown, four new ones would reemerge. The order would be completely overrun, and I'd be condemning them to death, with no possible chance of survival. Especially as I would be of no use to them without my powers.

"How long have you been awake?" Duncan's smooth drawl sounds directly behind me. Startled I almost whirl around, but he's quicker. He wraps his arms around my waist and pulls me back against him. I feel my heart beating erratically within my chest while he rests his chin upon my shoulder.

"You scared the shit out of me." I almost shout as I try to calm the storm inside me. "And to answer your question, I'm not really sure. I've been standing here watching them the entire time." I say as I point out the window. Duncan seems fascinated as he stares down at the minions far below the towering castle walls.

"What do you think is going on down there?" He whispers in my ear as he stares at the beasts milling around the base of the pit.

"They're eagerly waiting for their comrades to return. Some of them even celebrate when their kind reappears. Watch." A shiver runs down my spine as I hear the Crawlers cheering for the ten billionth time. So many of their kind have reemerged and I'm terrified to find out just how many there are down there. From this height, I can only make out the ones closest to me, and it's well beyond two hundred.

Shaking away the sickening feeling in the base of my stomach, I swivel around in Duncan's arms. I need to think about anything else for a moment, and Duncan is always the perfect distraction. "Did you eventually blackout too?" I ask nonchalantly and watch Duncan's face fall. He moves back a little while removing one of his hands from around my waist and rubs the back of his neck.

"Honestly, I don't know. I was... we were..." He tilts his head from side to side as he tries to recall what happened. "... anyway, the next thing I knew, I was waking up on the softest bed I've ever slept on with this beautiful angel sound asleep beside me" he says with a smile, changing the subject.

"But I woke up before you did..." I state a little confused. *Maybe he wasn't asleep after all.*

Duncan leans forward, "I went back to sleep" he whispers just before his lips connect with my forehead. *Of course, he did.* I don't know why but his words make me giggle.

Duncan lingers there longer than necessary and then moves away, peering down at me with sad eyes, "I'm sorry you had to go through that again."

"It's alright, I kind of knew what to expect this time. I'm not going to lie though; it still feels weird. Not being able to control your body like that, but you feel everything that's happening to you." My whole body shakes from the memories.

"I know exactly what you mean." He looks down at my attire and a sly smirk plays on his lips. It's only now that I notice he is fully dressed. *Where did he get the clothes from?* I push slightly against his chest and look around to see if there are any clothes I could wear. I see my corset draped over the couch but that's it. "I still have to get you some." Duncan utters with guilt lingering in his voice. Is he upset that his darker half tore my undergarments?

"What?" I ask trying to show that I'm unaffected.

"Clothes. I found these ones in the closet over there but for something that may fit you, I might know a place." Duncan drops his arms and steps away. Half turning back, he grabs my hand and leads us towards the open door.

We walk through a very long hallway until we reach a spiral staircase at the end. We begin to slowly ascend the stairs when Duncan begins to speak, "In the books of the past, my predecessors used to bring courtesans down here from time to time. Even though they were being drawn to their other half, apparently it never stopped them from having a little fun once in a while. Well, that's if you want to believe everything you read." We reach the top and see another short passageway leading to a small wooden door.

Duncan drops my hand and steps forward. He gives the knob a little jiggle, realising it's locked, he places his hand upon the door frame and whispers his incantation. From within the room, we hear a click and Duncan steps away, returning to my side. "I must warn you. I have no idea what lies beyond that door. Honestly, I don't think anyone does except those who have been here before." He turns his head to look at me and I nod. I understand what he's saying. He's asking me not to judge him for something he's had no part in. This room was made by his predecessors, not him.

Out of my peripheral vision, I see him move his head up and down obviously trying to psyche himself up while we step towards the door. Duncan places his hand on the knob once more and pushes the door wide open. I suck in a breath as I almost snort aloud in laughter. *Oh my Zagoria!*

When he said that they brought courtesans down here he wasn't kidding. *This room is like something out of a sexual fantasy.* Orange silk curtains hang from the ceiling high above, and the walls are covered in pink padding. There are huge piles of material in the corner of the room next to an overly stuffed wardrobe. Lace and frills fly out of every nook and cranny, and I dread the items that we may uncover. There are countless pink and orange throw cushions against the left-hand wall and in the middle of the room, there is an excessively large heart shaped bed. *What have we just walked into?*

I feel Duncan's eyes on me and I'm doing my very best not to laugh. Everything outside of this room screams Duncan's darkness, but in here, this was definitely a women's influence. The whole thing is just way too feminine.

"It looks a little cheesy if you ask me. Especially the bed." I state chuckling as I gaze up at the man standing beside me. He too looks like he is trying to contain his laughter while I watch his chest rapidly rise and fall. Seeing him looking so confused brings a smile to my lips. Duncan turns a little and clears his throat before strolling over to the bed in the middle of the room. He leans forward and runs his hand along the smooth surface.

"Honestly, this is not what I pictured at all. The books in the library depicted that this was some sort of torture chamber, and those who came down here never wanted to return." He utters the word torture chamber while using air quotations. "If those women believed that this was torture..." he says smiling while shaking his head, clearly dropping the subject. *I get what he means. This does seem torturous, but in a messed-up fairy floss kind of way*. I find myself laughing and smiling at the absurdity of what we are looking at. Polar opposite of what either of us was expecting.

Eyeing the cupboard off to the side, Duncan stalks over. Without a word, he begins rummaging through the frocks contained within. I'm momentarily stunned as Duncan pulls out a hot pink mini skirt with a see-through lace top to match. He turns around and holds it up for me to see, but I quickly shake my head. *Absolutely not*.

"No," I say crossing my arms over my chest feeling a tad exposed.

"Why not, you'd look hot as fuck..." he smirks while shaking the skimpy number in front of him. *He cannot be serious*.

"Not happening," I say while raising my face to the ceiling asking Zagoria to give me strength. Whatever Duncan's going to choose is going to be a disaster. *Maybe that's why they call this a torture chamber. Having to endure the men picking your clothes for you.*

"Suit yourself..." He shrugs and drops the ensemble on the floor before digging through the closet once more. "Oh yes, this is the one." He pulls out a sexy little nurse's outfit and I groan inwardly. *Not in this lifetime buddy.*

"Are there any pants?" I ask but he's not listening as he gazes between me and the outfit. A thought obviously crosses his mind because he breaks into a wicked grin.

"Would you at least try it on?"

"Ah, no. I'm pretty sure you would see what I had for breakfast in that one." His smile falters as a perplexed look crosses his face and I get the impression that I will need to clarify what I just said. "My ass would hang out the bottom." His eyes completely bug out while his face lights up once more and I just shake my head. *Men!*

"Prove it." He says throwing the outfit, hitting me in the head. I saw the mischievous look on his face the moment before my eyes got covered in material. *I know he's imagining what I'd look like with this on.*

"I'm all right, thanks." I swipe the material off my face and throw it on top of the other outfit he discarded earlier. *There is nothing he can do or say that will ever get me to wear that.*

"You're no fun" he says pouting before turning back to the cupboard. "And to answer your question, no, there are no pants. I don't even think there are shorts in here... In fact, I haven't even come across a pair of underwear for you yet." He throws me a wink over his shoulder and then crouches low to see what's piled up on the floor.

"That's ok. I'll just steal a pair of yours, I bet you have plenty downstairs." I say casually wanting all of this to be over.

"Probably... Hey, what about this one? It may not be as comfortable as a pair of pants, but it does have a huge slit up the side which would make it easier to move around in." Duncan stands holding a long black silk dress. It twinkles like the night sky as the lights within the room catch its silky folds. Intrigued by its beauty I move closer, tentatively taking the dress out of his hands.

"So, you don't have bad taste after all," I say admiringly as I hold the dress up by its spaghetti straps. *This could work.*

"You ever doubted me?" he asks, taking in the sights around us.

"For a minute there, yeah I did," I turn around, take off the bathrobe and slide the dress over my body. *It fits perfectly, like it was made for me.* The bodice is quite snug but I'm still able to move pretty freely. The neckline drops into a seriously low vee making my girls look pretty big, as for the split, it starts at my hip bone and continues all the way down to the floor.

I feel a cool breeze hit my sweet spot and I quickly pull the fabric together over my leg. *I may not even have to fight the buggers outside, but seriously, I need some underwear.* Duncan clears his throat behind me, and I whirl around to face him.

"You look stunning, it's such a shame that we have a job to do," he utters while crossing his arms and he leans back against the cupboard door, letting his eyes roam all over my body.

"Why is it a shame?" I ask as I look down and run my free hand over my stomach. The fabric is smooth against my fingertips.

"Because... with the way you look right now, I would like nothing more than to lock us up in this hideous room and never leave. Zagoria knows how hard it might be for us out there, and to make it worse, you will be going out there looking like that." He gestures towards me and desire ignites within.

"Maybe that's a good thing," I state as I raise my eyes to his.

"Why do you say that?"

"Maybe then you'll stand by my side and protect me. Not wanting to leave me alone even for a single second." I utter while he looks at me confused. "I'm weak down here Duncan, my powers are practically non-existent and there are countless beings out there that can take our heads off. So, if you want to end this thing, we need to stick together." I mirror his stance and rest my back against the nearest wall, hoping he realises just how serious this situation is.

"Trust me babe, I'm not going anywhere. Besides, you will probably be chained to me again anyway." A sly smirk crosses his face, and I suddenly have the urge to slap him.

"What! Why?" Suddenly outraged I accidentally let go of my dress and flash Duncan. He bites his lower lip as he glances at my sweet spot and I scrabble to close the split once more. *I really need underwear.* Duncan quickly rights himself and raises his heated stare.

"Because outside of these walls, my creatures need to see me as their leader, their Master. If you are not in chains or some sort of bindings, they will believe I see you as an equal, and to them, that is a threat. Anything that goes against Willow's wishes is dangerous. If we want to set foot anywhere near the pit, we will need them to think that I am still showing you my domain. It is the only way they will clear a path... But I need you to understand that if you defy me at any moment outside of these walls, you will force my hand and I will be forced to punish you in front of them." His words are stern as he stares down at me.

"What do you mean by punish?" I ask as I tip my head to the side. His arms look bigger and he seems taller, however, I can still picture the man I met all those weeks ago at the construction site. His carefree persona, his beautiful smile, and the way he looked at me in those first few minutes. All those initial emotions suddenly come flooding back, and I push them aside. We can't lose ourselves again, who knows how much longer the pit has left.

"It means that I will do anything necessary to make my people believe that you are beneath me. That you are truly my slave." He glances at me for a second before hanging his head and looks at the floor in front of him. "Even if it kills me to do it." The last of his words end in a whisper. *Does he seriously believe that this is the only way to get his minions to fall in line? By physically hurting me?*

"Then why do it if it pains you, you are their master. You do not need to show rank by hurting others." I say angrily, disgusted with what he's proclaiming.

"But I do Kyra. You have no idea how bad it will be if they turn on us. It's like you said, there are creatures out there that can, and *will* kill us if they see through our facade. If we die, it's over and the world will turn to shit.

The pit will not survive another eleven years waiting for us to come of age. Zagoria! I bet it won't even last until the end of the day. We need to end this now and the only way to do that is by getting as close to the drop as possible," Duncan declares as he pushes away from the closet and closes the gap between us. Peeling my body away from the wall, he cradles me in his arms, rests his forehead against my shoulder and breathes me in.

"I'm scared Duncan... frightened for our future, afraid that even if we take the fall that it still won't be enough. I'm just clinging to the hope that, as long as we make it to the edge, everything will work out fine."

"I'm scared too," he whispers as I move my body back, holding his face as I lift my mouth up to meet his. Our lips connect and we get lost within the fullness of our soul, the fire and ice that binds us.

Duncan pulls away after a short while and rests his forehead against mine. "Are you ready to do this?" he asks, while staring deep into my eyes. I believe he was asking himself that question as much as he was me.

"I was born ready, although I really think I need some underwear first." Duncan chuckles and nods before turning away. He reaches back, takes my hand in his and I let him lead me back down into the castle below.

Chapter 24

"I'm really sorry I have to do this," Duncan utters while we walk back down to the foyer.

"It's ok, I understand." We stop a few steps shy of the front door and Duncan ties the magical rope around my neck once more. Its coolness sends shivers running down my spine and I cross my arms over my chest as I feel my nipples perk up. I glance between Duncan and the huge wooden doors to my left, mentally preparing myself for what we are about to encounter.

Beyond those doors are the unspeakable horrors of the underworld. The world we must walk through to fulfil our true destiny. To finish what has been started by the selfish souls within our world. If only Willow and the others let our soul join many millennia ago, the realms would not be in this mess. Peace would have come to pass, but they were scared and selfish. They believed the old prophecy and wouldn't acknowledge that it had changed.

The Elders want to live long and happy lives, I get that. But they didn't care about the cost to procure it. Even now, with both worlds in peril, they're still determined to annihilate us.

Out of the corner of my eye, I see Duncan biting his bottom lip while he stares at me. "What?" I ask, as he tilts his head to the side and peeks up at me from underneath his beautiful long lashes. He's like a hunter watching his prey. His eyes roam over me and I have the urge to step back. He is giving me this weird vibe and I don't know whether to flee or get ready to fight. Shaking his head, Duncan stands up straight and raises his eyes to mine.

"Sorry, I can't help it. That dress looks amazing on you and it's hard not to stare at you. Maybe we should have looked harder for a pair of pants." I quickly raise my hand to my mouth and cover my grin as my body turns a deep shade of red. Pins and needles spread through my veins and I have to bite my lip to stop myself from moving. Duncan's words are stoking the eternal flame deep within me and I must not allow it to continue. We have work to do.

"Maybe we should have, but it's too late for that now," I say looking down at the boxer briefs I found in Duncan's drawer earlier. They may not be as good as underwear, but they'll still do the job regardless.

"Are you sure?" Duncan slyly takes a step forward, circling an arm around my waist pulling me closer. I crane my head back and look up into his big black eyes. *Man, I wish we didn't have to go outside.*

"Very." I lift my hand to his chest and push him back. "You need to control yourself. If you give in to your desire for me now, your darkness will come forth and we will never make it out of this castle." I look into his eyes and know he sees reason. *We cannot do this again, not this time.* Duncan gives me the saddest puppy dog face I've ever seen but agrees.

"Ok," he sulks. "But can I still kiss you?" he asks while moving his free hand to cup the back of my head, knowing full well what my answer will be. Pressing my body flush against his, I reach up on my tippy toes, moving my lips mere centimetres away from his.

"You may," I whisper tentatively, just before our mouths connect. Raising my arms, I wrap them around his neck pulling his face down closer to mine. I need to feel all that I can as this may very well be the last kiss we ever share. Our lips are slow and warm as they press against each other. We are savouring the taste we create. He licks my lips and I graciously part my mouth, allowing him to go deeper. His hands become greedy as they roam over my body, grabbing and pulling any bit of flesh that he can get a hold of. I stumble a little as I move my body closer, and Duncan tightens his grip around my waist as he hoists me up and backs us against the door. "We can't." I breathe through parted lips.

"I know, sorry. I just didn't want us to fall," he mutters as he places my feet back upon the ground. His lips are feather light as he trails kisses from my mouth along my cheek and up to my forehead. He lingers there for just a moment before moving himself away and places his hands on the sides of my face. "I need you to know something," he whispers as he gazes at me solemnly.

"What is it?" I utter while trying to catch my breath.

"No matter what happens from here on out, I am grateful for every day that I got to share with you. It may not have been as long as I hoped for, but it was still something. My life was so dark without you, and each day with you in it, it's only been getting brighter. You are my other half, the light to my darkness and I need you to know that I will love you even after my dying breath." I stare up at him in disbelief as tears begin to stream down my face.

I knew how he felt about me, it's just crazy to hear him say it. Not once in my entire existence did I ever imagine that I could find a love like the ones you see in the movies, one with a happy ending. Where both parties are so in love that you know nothing will stand in their way of achieving their ultimate goal. But that's the kicker, we don't have a happy ending, not really. We don't know what lies beyond the fall. Will we still be us when the deed is done, or will we become the star once again? Who really knows, it just kills me to think that we don't have more time. Time to explore what this world has to offer, what we really could have been together.

Without saying anything, I reach up and claim his mouth, pouring out all my emotions into our last goodbye kiss.

Duncan holds me tight, allowing me the time to feel all that I need to before he finally steps away. He grabs the end of the magical chain hanging from around my neck and wraps it tightly around his fist. "I won't let go," he whispers and I nod. *Even if I don't fully agree with what he's doing, it's vital for our survival.* "It's going to be ok out there, trust me," he says while worry floods my senses.

"I do."

"Good, now let's go." Duncan steps around me and places his hands on the grand wooden door. *There's one thing I need to do first.* Turning around quickly, I reach out and grab his bicep pulling him back.

"Wait..." I utter while he gazes down at me. "... Before we go out there, I need you to know that I love you too. I have since the very beginning, I just didn't know how to say it until now. You've told me a few times since we met that you love me and I never once said it back. I'm so sorry it took me this long." Duncan places his hands on either side of my face and lowers his mouth to mine. His lips are sweet and tender, so soft as they push against mine. This would have to be the nicest kiss we have ever shared.

"It's ok, you may not have said it, but I knew. I felt it every time we were together. You've shown me more love and affection than I ever could have hoped for... My sweet Kyra, please don't apologize for something that I already knew." Duncan leans forward and gifts me one more long tender kiss before turning away. He places his hands back upon the mighty doors, gives them a great big shove and we watch as they swing wide open.

I bow my head and fold my hands together in front of me, trying to look as compliant as I can. "Fuck." Duncan whispers angrily and I spring to attention. Moving slightly, I look beyond the stone entrance and on the other side of the bone bridge, stand all the people I thought I knew.

"Finally! It's about time you two stopped canoodling and came out to join us," Willow states wickedly as an evil grin spreads out across her lips. Her glasses are long gone, and so is her frail persona. She's knotted her hair above her head, and her back is as straight as a needle. She's wearing blacked out armour that seems to glow from the greenish lights within the cavern, and there is a yin yang looking image that lies solely on her chest. One half is dark, the other light. The two halves of one soul. *Our soul.* All the other elders seem to be wearing the same type of armour too, they are all geared up for a fight. *If that's what they want, that's what they'll get.*

"I was wondering when you were going to show up." Duncan spits in their direction as he crosses his arms, acting like their presence doesn't affect him at all. Anger, like lava begins to brew within my being and I have to physically force myself to stay put. *Now is not the time for heroics.*

"It was only a matter of time." Willow shrugs her shoulders as the elders around her begin to raise their swords, triggering all the monsters within the vicinity to roar and cheer. Everyone seems eager to fight.

I swing my gaze from left to right, trying to note all the people ready to charge when the order is given. Elder Fox, Kit, Nurse Lexi, and even a few of the soldiers from the order are here. Almost one hundred Zagorians have come to stop us from concluding our final mission. They have been brainwashed into believing that killing us is the only way to save themselves, but they are wrong.

If we die and the pit collapses, there will be nothing stopping the darkest creatures of the underworld from rising. They will overthrow Willow and her band of misguided misfits, killing anything and everyone in their path. Creatures like the Banshees will be everywhere, and they are not the kind of creature to mess with. You need an unfathomable amount of strength to take them down. Strength that Willow and the others do not have.

"True, I was just hoping you would show up a little bit later," Duncans says smugly.

"And why is that boy?" Willow raises her eyebrows as she stares at Duncan. She flicks her gaze towards me, only for a second but I see sorrow lingering there before animosity takes over once again.

"Because now we will have to kill you," he states as a matter of fact.

"Many of you have tried," Willow replies, while slowly repositioning her body. She is ready to charge when the time is right, and I feel I should do the same.

Moving my left leg back and my arms up around my chest, I watch as Duncan relaxes his arms to his sides and slightly turns towards me. A sly smirk crosses his face as he lifts his hand and with a quick flick of his fingers, the chain around my neck disappears. I break out in a smile knowing that I will finally be able to avenge all of those who these elders have wronged. *Payback's a bitch, Bitches!* I only wish I had more power.

"Yes, but none of them had the power of the sun to help them." Reaching back, Duncan grabs my hand and pulls me forward as we rush those before us. Magic instantly ignites from our conjoined hands and I am able to grasp just enough of my power to conjure up my immortal blade. We bound over the bone bridge and I watch as all the elders begin to charge forward. *This is it.* Lifting his free hand, Duncan shoots thick green smoke out towards the line of bodies before us, throwing them at least fifty feet back. We reach the other side and I pull on our conjoined hands, forcing Duncan to look at me.

"What is it?" Something in his peripheral vision grabs his attention and he lifts his free hand, shooting off another blast of smoke towards the soldiers heading our way.

"Don't let go, no matter what happens, ok?" To emphasise my point, I lift our hands up between us. "I am drained down here and holding you is the only way I can access my power. If we part for any moment, we may not make it out of this alive. Do you understand?"

"Yes." He nods his head vigorously and then turns back to face the Elders heading our way. Countless creatures have joined their ranks and are now all charging our way at a grand pace. I honestly have no idea how we are going to survive this. *But what's that old saying? Where there's a will, there's a way!*

Chapter 25

Swords clash in a dance around the base of the pit. Many soldiers and creatures are dying by my hands, and it pains me to think of how many more will perish because they believe they are fighting for the chance at a longer life. Little do they know it will be a life filled with pain and misery the moment the pit collapses. They have all been so blinded by Willow and their fear of dying that they no longer see the bigger picture. Many of them probably haven't even heard about the prophecy. They might not even know about our true reason for being and are here only because of the troubles they've seen arising on Earth. I hate fighting them. Even worse, I hate that I'm killing them but creatures that are both deadly to Zagorians and humans are coming back and if the pit isn't repaired soon, there will be no stopping the unspeakable horrors that will emerge if we don't make it.

A blade stops mere millimetres away from my face and I have to blink a few times to register what is happening in front of me. Elder Fox collapses to the ground with a gaping hole in his chest. Duncan's gift evaporates from within its centre and begins to circle us once more. Thick green smoke twists and turns, smashing through any being that gets in its way. Flames shoot out from my fingertips as I try to help Duncan as best I can, but my powers are depleting. If only I could access what lies beneath my feet, that power I felt tingling earlier. It's so close yet held back by an invisible barrier I cannot penetrate. Thankfully I still have Duncan's touch. Without it, I would be instantly powerless against those around us.

With a powerful tug of his arm, Duncan pulls me forward. He spins me around while I aim my sword out wide and slice through any creature within my reach. Body parts fall to the floor as we slowly make our way towards the pit's edge.

It's clear to see that many of the creatures no longer see Duncan as their master and have instead joined ranks with the evil witch at the centre of all this madness. Willow remains at the base of the pit, biding her time while she watches us battle our way over. With her head held high and her arms crossed over her chest, she looks like the menacing leader I have recently learnt her to be. She is staring at us, waiting for just the right moment to attack. Our eyes connect and an evil smile spreads out across her lips, making that angry lava within my veins ignite into a new raging inferno.

"AAHHH…" I scream out as a beast drags its claws down my back. Duncan pulls on our conjoined hands tugging me into his arms, hoping the healing powers will kick in. "We need to end this Duncan; we can't continue like this for much longer." I breathe heavily as I inhale through the pain shooting up my back. Hundreds of beings begin to swarm, and I feel like a mouse caught in a trap with no possible chance of escape. Duncan raises his left arm, rotating it in slow circles above our heads as a wave of thick smoke forms around us.

"Don't you think I know that!?" he spits out frustratedly as he drops his arm, forcing the wave to come crashing down upon those in its wake. It smashes, and pushes the creatures within its reach back to the outer walls of the cavern. I swivel in his arms and see that he has bought us a few seconds of peace.

"What can we do?" I ask while glancing up at him, but his eyes are focused on all the chaos happening around us. Malice and hatred radiate off of him and he looks like the frightening tyrant I was led to believe he was.

"There is only one thing I can think of," he states as he turns his gaze towards Willow, giving her one mighty death stare. *If only looks could kill.*

"And what is that?" I peer to my right, watching as the hordes of beings reassemble their lines.

"Let the power take over," he states as a matter of fact.

"What? No!" I say on a hushed whisper as I stare up at him in disbelief. *He cannot be serious.*

"Come on Kyra, I don't know about you, but I have felt my darkness surging the moment we stepped foot outside of the castle. Zagoria! I felt it even long before then." Glancing down at my chest I feel her there, the lava, the sun. She wants to be free but I just don't know if I can. I'm scared.

"There has to be another way." I raise my hands to my neck knowing that no matter what I say, he's right. I have to let her rise and it terrifies me to my core. *She's stronger here, I might not come back this time.*

"Well then, you think of something because my powers won't protect us for much longer." A massive boom ricochets throughout the cavern and everyone stops dead in their tracks. "Oh no! That can't be good," Duncan mutters and turns his gaze towards the pit, as a cracking echoes all around us. I look up just in time to see the side of the pit wall crumbling in on itself.

"We have to get up there! We need to stop this," I yell not caring about those around us. I barge past Duncan and drag him behind me while I make my way up to the side of the pit. *We have to end this, NOW!* My fire ignites anew and I feel as empowered as the day I was created. Red hot flames begin to swarm around us as we pass masses of beings, all too busy staring at the chaos to notice us walking by. We make it at least fifty feet from the edge when Willow comes into view. "GET OUT OF MY WAY," I seethe to the monster standing before me.

"Not a chance sweetheart. I know about the prophecy and there is no way in Zagoria I am letting you two anywhere near that pit," Willow declares as she stands her ground whilst staring us down.

"How do you know about that?" Duncan asks irritably over my shoulder as he tries to take a step forward. I quickly place a hand over his stomach keeping him in place. *You'll have your chance just not yet.*

"You're not the only ones who know about the hidden library now, are you?" Shock overcomes me as Willow begins to smile. *Oh no! Snow.* Shifting my gaze towards Duncan, I witness the lightbulb moment when he realises what she just said. As quick as lightning I move to the side and physically force my mate to stay put. This is exactly what she wants, and I will not let him fall victim to her game.

"WHAT DID YOU DO TO HIM?" Duncan bellows. Smoke thicker than I've ever seen gathers around him, and I shudder at the sight of it.

"Nothing that I haven't done to the others who turned against us," Willow declares proudly as she lifts her chin a little higher. *She killed him? Sorrow floods my being although I don't give in. This is exactly what she wants.*

"How did you find him?" Duncan spits towards her. *She really is a monster.*

"That doesn't matter now does it." She winks in my direction and I'm overcome with guilt, I feel like I'm going to throw up. *She followed me... of course she did, but if she was there why didn't she come for us?* Before I have a chance to speak, Duncan takes another step forward and I almost lose my balance trying to keep him back. *Why am*

I doing this? I should just let him attack her after all she has done.

"WHY?" His temperature's rising the more they continue, and I'm afraid Duncan's monster will show his face sooner than planned.

"I couldn't have him running around ruining all my plans now, could I? He stole you once before and I will not let him do it again," Willow barks as if the matter actually pained her. However, thinking about it now maybe it did. Perhaps her not knowing where the Prince was this whole time actually frightened her. Because if we were to figure out the truth, we would finally be her undoing. For millennia she has fought black and blue to survive, laying waste to the notion of peace just so she can gain a few more years on this planet. *That's all about to change because we do know the truth and we will not sit by and let her continue.*

"There isn't going to be a next time," Duncan and I seethe in unison as we turn towards each other.

"We'll see about that," Willow utters while Duncan lowers his head staring deep into my eyes, deep within me. He is asking the silent question we both know the answer to. I know he's drained and there isn't enough time for us to gain enough power to end this. There is only one way we are going to win this battle and whether we like it or not, we know what we must do.

Nodding my head slowly, I let go of the wall I have built up between me and my "darker" light within. Power like

I've never felt before begins to surge within my veins and I know it's almost time. Reaching up on my tippy toes, I grab ahold of Duncan's face and pull his lips down upon mine, giving him one final kiss. I quickly move my face back and whisper the last words I know that will truly be mine, "I love you."

Resting my forehead against his chin, I hear him repeat the words back to me as he takes me into his arms. He holds me tight as a ring of smoke and flames erupts from deep down inside, travelling around us like a tidal wave growing stronger and stronger with every passing second.

"What are you doing?" Willow asks angrily as she takes a few steps forward. Turning my head, I glance over at the woman I once regarded as family. Astonishment and hatred for what we are radiates off of her, and I am glad that I will not be in control for what is bound to happen next. Even with everything she has done, I know it within my heart that I would not be able to hurt her.

"We are doing what is right," Duncan whispers at the exact moment I am pushed back within myself. The cage walls close around me and I feel the power beneath my feet break free from its invisible barrier. Our bodies back away from each other, holding hands as they turn towards Willow.

"It can't be," Willow mutters under her breath while she stares horrified at the two halves of the reconnected star. "GET THEM!" she screams at anyone within earshot.

"THEY CAN NOT MAKE IT TO THE PIT OR WE ARE ALL DONE FOR!" Everyone stops what they are doing and charge towards us, but we don't move. Our bodies never take their eyes off of Willow.

"Willow, high elder of sight, you have gone against the true nature of Zagoria and for that, you will be punished. You were given the ability of foresight in exchange for helping the star to reconnect, but you used it against us for your own personal gain. For many millennia you have fought to survive, and turned loyal Zagorians against us.

All of those who you selfishly murdered in your pursuit for a longer life will be given another chance of survival on Earth. Those who didn't know the true meaning of Zagoria will also be given another chance. However, the individuals who chose not to follow the true nature of things will perish when this world collapses. You have destroyed the peace within the realms with no regard for your consequences, however all of that is about to change," Duncan and I say in unison as the smoky flames create a tornado around us.

Creatures and Zagorians alike try to break through the barrier, only to be incinerated the moment the flames touch their skin. The powerful wind sweeps all of those closest to it off their feet, throwing them to the outer reaches of the cavern.

"STOP THEM, YOU IDIOTS!" Willow shouts at those standing around her, but to her disgust everyone has started backing away from the ever-growing tornado. The ones who still want a fight begin to do whatever they can to try and stop what's coming. Archers shoot their arrows while soldiers throw their swords, though nothing breaks through.

Sensing their imminent demise creatures begin to flee, believing they will be able to outrun what is coming.

"ZAGORIA HAS SPOKEN!" we shout as we raise our hands to the ceiling, lifting the wave high into the air above us.

"NO!" Willow screams as she comes charging down the pathway. She barely makes it fifty feet before we bring our arms crashing back down towards the ground. The ring of smoky flames lashes out like a sonic boom, killing anything and everyone within its path. Screams of pain and distress fill my ears, and I all but turn away from the massacre happening before me. Burnt flesh hits my nostrils and I cringe inwardly, wanting so badly to curl into a ball and cry for all of those who will never see the light of day again. But then, I remind myself that they brought this upon themselves.

They knowingly killed our predecessors in the quest for a longer life and even made us believe that we were enemies. They fed us lies to keep us apart just so they could survive.

My head turns to the left and I watch as Duncan's dark eyes focus on me while he opens his mouth to speak. "Peace will be restored," he whispers and I feel my head nod as my consciousness gradually slides back into my body. I sense her inside me, swirling deep within my chest as she moves lower into the pit of my stomach. *I can feel you and I finally understand. You kept me safe, now it's my turn.* I think while I strum my fingers directly over her presence.

"Kyra?" My head snaps up as my name leaves his lips and I jump forward. Wrapping my arms around his neck I pull his face down to meet mine. Feeling excitement and triumph, knowing that I let her out, yet I am me again. Tearing my face away, I feel the pull towards the pit once more. "How is this possible?" Duncan asks as he looks at the mayhem surrounding us. Burnt bodies lie all around and I notice a glint of silver hair in my peripheral vision and force myself not to look. I don't want to see what remains of the woman I used to love.

"They let us return so we could say a proper goodbye," I utter thoughtfully as I take his hand and bring it to my lips, placing a gentle kiss on his knuckles.

"Why?... Why not just end it themselves?" he asks, a little confused as he glances over his shoulder at the pit behind him.

"Because it is our lives to give, not theirs... Come on." I say as I lower his hand away from my face, turn and begin walking towards the pathway leading up to the pit's edge. "The prophecy stated that the two of us must be bold and sacrifice ourselves to the fall. If the star were to do that for us, it would be taking our choice away and therefore, the prophecy would not be fully fulfilled. We have to willingly enter the pit for everything to be restored." So many emotions are rummaging through my mind and I can't decide whether I want to laugh or cry.

I'm glad we get to spend these last few moments together, but I still wish we had more time. Although I feel it within my bones that this isn't the end for us, not by a long shot. More like the beginning of something new. Duncan and I will be together again, I just know it.

"And you're ok with this?" he asks sceptically as we climb up the steepest part of the mountain.

"You're not?" I question him in disbelief as I look over at him. *He can't be having second thoughts, especially not now that we are so close.*

"Of course, I am. You just seem a little too happy about it." His breathing becomes heavy as we near the edge of the pit. I can feel the heat rising from within and almost want to step back.

"Well duh, of course I'm happy. Harmony will finally come to pass and our star will be complete once more. We will live another life, for that I'm almost certain. This isn't the end for us, you have to be able to feel that too?" We reach the top and I look over the edge, down into the base of the pit where only dregs of the river remain. The last of the most dreaded souls lay within, swirling down there and, Zagoria forbid, I will not let them see the light of day ever again.

Peering out into the surrounding cavern, I see the magnificent black stone castle in the distance and images enter my mind of all the beautiful moments Duncan and I shared together. To the left, I see the chasm walls we entered through only hours ago and the charred bodies of the delusional souls sprawled out along the ground. *So many lives were lost today.*

Duncan steps forward and pulls me into his arms, he lifts my chin and I gaze into his blueish black eyes. He lowers his forehead down upon mine whilst circling his arms around my back.

"It's time," I mutter under my breath while closing my eyes and breathing in his scent. He smells of love and affection and I wish I could bathe in it forever.

"Are you scared?" he whispers as he tightens his hold.

"No."

"I am..." his hot breath hits my cheek and my eyes spring open. I feel his heart beating erratically against his ribcage and know I must do whatever I can to calm his nerves.

"It's going to be ok," I whisper as I raise my hand and run my thumb along the stubble that lines his jaw. *He is so beautiful.*

"I know." Duncan leans forward and places a long loving kiss upon my lips while a single tear slides down my cheek. *We need to end this now before I change my mind.* Moving slightly back, Duncan gazes down at me before lowering his forehead against mine once more. I watch him mouth the three words I've longed to hear since the moment the star set us free. "I love you."

"And I you... I understand that goodbyes are horrible, though this one isn't going to be forever. We will be together again soon," I whisper gently as tears begin to stream down my face. *Thankfully, I am not doing this alone.*

"I'll be with you always and forever," Duncan utters while taking a small step back. He lowers his hands from around my waist and links his fingers through mine, holding tight as he turns towards the deep plunge before us. "Together?" he asks whilst turning his face slightly towards me. I nod my head, knowing that this is not the end.

Duncan moves his feet closer to the edge and my heart skips a beat for what we are about to do. I feel the heat of the pit burning my skin but I don't turn away. "Always and forever," Duncan whispers again just as we both lean forward and surrender ourselves to the deep beyond. *We will be together always.*

Epilogue

One week later

"All right class if you will all follow me, please. Right, this way." Mrs Sail directs her class as they make their way into the grand observatory. Feet climb the staircase two by two as they all rush inside to get out of the unusually cool weather. Standing in the centre of the room waiting for them is the lead astronomer, Randle Flats, he will be the one leading the tour for the day.

"Good morning children and Mrs Sail, it's always a pleasure to see you," he says while extending his hand towards her.

"Likewise, Mr Flats," Mrs Sail says as she shakes his hand before turning back to her class. "All right children listen up. This is Mr Flats, he is the lead astronomer here at the Sydney observatory and he requires your full attention. So please be polite and no talking," she says giving her students a stern look, she doesn't want to hand out any detention slips today.

"Okay children let's hop to it, shall we. We have lots to see and I'm afraid we don't have much time. Especially if you would all like to look through our mighty telescope," Randle speaks over his shoulder as they make their way from the grand hall to the transit room.

Scattered everywhere there are countless historical artifacts. Hanging from the walls there are images of time and space, and even a huge sculpture of the solar system. "Every planet within our galaxy has been named and documented throughout history. Can anyone tell me why that is?" Randle asks the class and only one hand shoots to the skies. Little Rosy Memphis, Mrs Sail's brightest student. "Yes." Mr Flats encourages her with a nod of his head.

"We study the planets within our solar system so that we are able to learn about our planet but also other planets too," Rosy says proudly.

"You're absolutely correct. We study the planets surrounding us, so we are able to gain a better understanding of what is happening to our own. For instance, climate change and global warming." Mr Flats gazes out at the group of students in front of him and notices that they are not staring at him but the room beyond. "I have a feeling that you all want to move onto the next room, so let's jump to it," he says while clapping his hands together, and turns on his heel. "You are about to see something really cool," he smiles while he waits for a few students to walk past him before he begins to move.

The children all pipe up with excitement as they enter the equatorial room and begin to circle around the giant contraption in the centre of the room. Mr Flats has to almost push past them as he moves to stand next to the telescope. "This bad boy is named Fred. Well, that's what I call him anyway. He is known as a refractor telescope and was built in 1874. Can anyone tell me how old that makes Fred?" Randle asks as he gazes around the room. This time it's Matt Flemming who raises his hand, and Mr Flats nods his head in acknowledgment.

"One hundred and forty-six?" Matt replies, more as a question than a direct answer.

"You're close... He is one hundred and forty-seven years old. He is the oldest telescope to still be in commission here in Australia. But that's enough chit chat for now. Who would like the first look?" Mr Flats asks and all hands rise to the ceiling as the excitement in the room picks up. Mrs Sail encourages everyone to form a single line and allows Mr Flats to direct the children on how to use the telescope. Many of them have a quick glance and walk away, but not Rosy Memphis.

She spends a great deal of time examining the world beyond before stepping away with a look of confusion on her face. She makes it to the outer rim of the class before Mrs Sail realises something's wrong.

"Are you alright Rosy?" Mrs Sail asks while stepping away from the other children to come to stand by her side.

"Yes... no... sorry," she utters while shaking her head. Rosy may only be ten years old but she is incredibly bright for her age. She is at the top of her class for almost every subject and it's not common for her to appear so bewildered.

"What is it?" Mrs Sail questions with concern lingering in her voice, but Rosy practically ignores Mrs Sail's question as she turns to face Mr Flats.

"Excuse me, Sir. Please correct me if I'm wrong but is there a new star within the Boötes void? I've been studying constellations and planets for a long time, but I've never seen that one," Rosy says as a matter of fact and appears to grab the attention of the entire class. They all turn their heads towards the lead astronomer in the centre of the room who takes a gander through the mighty telescope. He moves the scope a few times before pulling back with astonishment plastered on his face.

"Well my little friend, I believe you may have just discovered a new planet," he utters in wonderment as he places his eye back upon the scope. "I think I need to call NASA."

"Well done Rosy." Mrs Sail announces and the whole room erupts into a flurry of excitement.

"What are you going to call it Rosy?" One of her classmates calls out and everyone turns towards the little girl standing off to the side of the room.

"That's right child, you found it, so you get to name it," Mr Flats encourages as he walks over and picks up a pen and paper to jot down the coordinates of the newly found star.

"I think... I think I'm going to call it Zagoria."

THE END

Acknowledgements

Firstly, I would like to say a huge thank you to you for reading my book. I would not be here today if it wasn't for you, so thank you.

I would like to thank my husband and children next for allowing me the time to write. I had a lot of sleepless mornings trying to get this book finished however, I wouldn't change it for the world.

Thirdly I would like to thank my mother, Cindy for her continuous support and for editing yet another one of my books. You truly are amazing!

Alex, again, you did such an amazing job on the cover and I am truly grateful for your talent. You brought my ideas to life and created two wonderful covers that match my books perfectly. What a wonderful way to start a long life career.

And lastly to Gregg for conducting the final proofread. I cannot thank you enough.

I hope you enjoyed Kyra and Duncans story just as much as I did and I look forward to showing you all the wonderful stories I will create in the future. Until next time.

Always and Forever

Kristen

Follow Me

I would love to hear from you!

You would seriously make my day if you got in contact with me on my social media pages.

You can find me on Facebook – Author Kristen Dovnik. I'm on here quiet regularly.

I'm also on Instagram – @authorkristendovnik I'm frequently on here too.

And for those of you who do not have social media you can find me at my website. www.kristendovnik.com

I hope to hear from you soon

X

.